COPPER DIVIDE

BETH KIRSCHNER

Relax. Read. Repeat.

COPPER DIVIDE
By Beth Kirschner
Published by TouchPoint Press
Brookland, AR 72417
www.touchpointpress.com

Copyright © 2021 Beth Kirschner
All rights reserved.

ISBN-13: 978-1-952816-40-6

Editor: Jenn Haskin
Cover Design: Colbie Myles
Cover images:
Children's Parade, Calumet Copper Miners Strike, RPPC by Calumet New Studio, Calumet, Michigan, 1913 (Wystan / Flickr), https://www.flickr.com/photos/70251312@N00/8425164400/, License CC by 4.0; Adove Stock, Mine Shaft. Mine shaft with winding trail through the interior. Keewenaw National Historic Park. Calumet, Michigan by ehrlif'; Map, Michigan Technological University Archives and Historical Collections:, https://www.mtu.edu/library/archives/

Internal map images:
Michigan Technological University Archives and Historical Collections, https://www.mtu.edu/library/archives/; Upper Peninsula Regional Digitization Center, http://updigit.uproc.lib.mi.us/cdm/.

"1913 Massacre" Words and Music by Woody Guthrie
© Copyright Woody Guthrie Publications, Inc. Used with permission (License on file).

Connect with the author at https://beth-kirschner.com/

First Edition

Printed in the United States of America.

For hope.

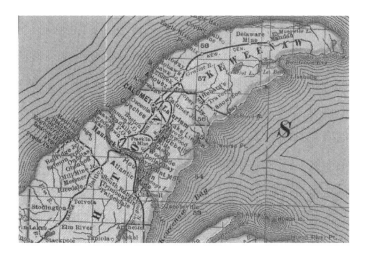

Take a trip with me in 1913,
To Calumet, Michigan, in the copper country.
I will take you to a place called Italian Hall,
Where the miners are having their big Christmas ball.

I will take you in a door and up high stairs,
Singing and dancing is heard everywhere,
I will let you shake hands with the people you see,
And watch the kids dance around the big Christmas tree.

You ask about work and you ask about pay,
They'll tell you they make less than a dollar a day,
Working the copper claims, risking their lives,
So it's fun to spend Christmas with children and wives.

There's talking and laughing and songs in the air,
And the spirit of Christmas is there everywhere,
Before you know it you're friends with us all,
And you're dancing around and around in the hall.

Well a little girl sits down by the Christmas tree lights,
To play the piano so you gotta keep quiet,
To hear all this fun you would not realize,
That the copper boss' thug men are milling outside.

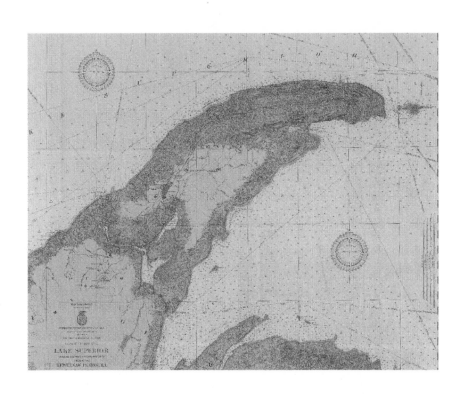

AUGUST 15, 1913

HANNAH WEINSTEIN SAT ON THE cashier's stool at her father's department store, watched the clocks on the wall and thought about the blood. Business was slow and there was no one to interrupt her thoughts, or worse, ask what they might be. She wondered who would have to clean up all that blood. Two men killed and several others fired upon must have made quite a mess.

It would likely be the landlady and Hannah felt sorry for her. She could imagine the woman scrubbing on her hands and knees. There would be stains no doubt, and damage to the walls and furniture. Her skirts would be soiled and perhaps need to be burned, depriving her of what might have been a favorite outfit. The deaths were as real to Hannah as her brother's pulp fiction novels. She imagined herself as the landlady, cursing the dead union men under her breath, dead but guilty and leaving their mess to the living. Hannah had to get out of this city. This wasn't the future she wanted. She thought of her friend Nelma, who could probably speak to what happened last night, but there was no chance of seeing her anytime soon. It was all too disturbing to dwell on.

Outside, Mrs. Simonson waved as she passed by the picture window, and left the imprint of her patent leather boots in the droppings of a stray dog. Her brother needed to clean the walk, but they had just argued and she was reluctant to seek him out. Mother had postponed her studies at the university due to the strike, and her brother taunted her about it. Too bad, he had said, too bad you can afford the tuition but you can't tell Mother how.

Hannah unbuttoned her shoes to scratch an itch and walked into the next room. The dining room tables, set with lace and china, had acquired a thin layer of dust. No one was shopping. She took a rag from inside a wardrobe and wiped them clean. Upstairs, Father had put away much of the work clothing, lunch pails and carbide sunshine lamps when the strike began three weeks ago. Instead there were shoes, dresses, petticoats and accessories for the women; boots, pants, shirts, and ties for the men.

Her brother, Sam, was likely in the back office having a smoke. Father would reproach her for leaving the front of the store unattended, but he would also disapprove of the dirty walk. He didn't so much worry about theft, as he feared a missed sales opportunity.

Hannah pushed open the heavy door, which always stuck a bit in the humid summer air. Her brother was pacing back and forth, cigarette smoldering between his fingers. His limp greasy hair, an indecisive hue between brown and blond, hung impertinently down on his forehead; his long lanky frame showed a swelling of his midsection, evidence of indulgence in his wife's home cooking.

"Mother doesn't like you smoking back here."

"The window's open," he said.

"It still stinks."

"Is that what you came to tell me?"

"You need to shovel the walk. There's dog droppings outside the clock-room window."

Sam nodded his head, blowing smoke rings at the ceiling, showing no inclination to work.

"When is Father getting back?" Hannah said. "I should visit Nelma this afternoon. I could be back before sundown."

"After what happened last night?" Sam stopped pacing. "I'd keep your distance."

"She's my friend. I'm sure she's not involved with those people."

"She's as Red as they come. Her husband was one of the first to join the union."

"When is Father getting back?"

"Early afternoon. He wouldn't be happy to see you gone."

2

"Fine," Hannah glared. "Did you at least get beer for tomorrow night? We're running low."

"Everything's set. I got it all yesterday."

Hannah went back to her stool and flipped through the *Jewish Ladies Home Journal*, without any desire to read. The grandfather clocks chimed at half-past the noon hour. Mrs. Valsuano bought some china for her daughter's wedding; Mrs. Parnall spent over an hour looking at dresses and left without making a purchase. Mother had promised sandwiches for lunch, but she was late. Hannah began thinking of food: warm challah with golden braids, smoked whitefish, corned beef, blueberries and cream. She had a fondness for blueberries and for berry hunting, especially with Nelma. Since they were grade school friends, Nelma always knew where the best blueberries could be found, plump and sweet. They would eat half of what they would pick before they came home.

The morning fog had burnt away. The dust on the street was dancing around in tiny whirls, like dozens of crazed spinning tops set loose by an energetic child. Two carriages were stopped up the hill, facing opposite directions, with the drivers sharing some news. Mother walked past them, draped in her black shawl, not pausing to look through the window before coming inside.

"These are fearful days, fearful days. I've brought lunch for you and Samson."

"What? What's happened?"

"Shush, let's get your brother."

Mother told of thousands protesting in South Range and Calumet since yesterday's shooting in the Seeberville boarding house. She suggested closing the store early, lest the unrest come to Hancock.

"This was just a matter of time," Sam said. "The strikers pushed things too far."

"There's too many guns on both sides," Mother said.

"I'm sure the guards acted in self-defense," Sam said. "It will be in the papers."

Hannah tried to imagine circumstances that might have provoked the shooting of two men. She wanted to keep an open mind, sympathetic with Nelma's cause, but could only conclude they had deserved their fate. She hoped the protest wouldn't affect tomorrow night's turnout, which had already been lagging since the strike began.

"What should we do?" Hannah said. "Have you heard anything from Father?"

"He telephoned with the news; he's coming straight back," Mother said. "Hannah, I need you home to help with the Sabbath dinner. Sam, you close the store at the first sign of trouble."

THAT EVENING, AFTER THE house had quieted, and everyone had gone to bed, Hannah lay in the dark of her room, listening to the night sounds outside. Crickets were singing in the garden below, and in the distance, someone was arguing. She couldn't make out their words, but could feel the anger, and it scared her. The whole county had been on edge since the strike began.

There had been walkouts in the past, but none had ever shut down the mines. The governor had sent over twenty-six hundred national guardsmen to stop the rioting and their pup tents spread out like an invading army. Hannah just wished the strike would end and she could get on with her life. The whole thing had occurred at the most inconvenient of times. If not for the strike, she would be downstate right now, sharing a house with other college women, perhaps dancing and dating men who had never even heard of copper mining. Instead, she was stuck working in her parent's store.

She stayed awake until the moon rose high, watching fireflies float past the window like airborne Chinese lanterns, and bat silhouettes swept past the stars in their nocturnal search for insects. The ore freighters sounded off, several an hour, as they made their way through the portage canal and back to Lake Superior. She thought about the protesters this afternoon and wondered if Nelma had been among them. They had thrown rotten fruit at storefronts thought to favor the mining companies, and at least one window had been broken. She wondered if Nelma would target their store and imagined looking through the window, as Nelma stood ready to throw an apple. Would she do it?

They had been friends since grade school, when Hannah had admired Nelma's easy banter with both girls and boys. Hannah had felt awkward by comparison. She would sometimes find herself jealous of Nelma's social skills and anxious that their friendship was imbalanced. These jealousies were childish, and long outgrown, but still she felt those old insecurities, even now.

Hannah woke to the sound of bottles jingling in their metal cages, as the milkman delivered his wares, with the valley still draped in the shadow of the South Range hills. She felt tired, as if she hadn't slept at all, with last night's worries still fresh in her head. She dressed, walked down the back stairwell and quietly left the house. This would be her only chance to remind the guardsmen about tonight. She climbed Quincy Hill, weaving through neighborhoods that housed people from almost every corner of the world: Finnish and Croatian, English and Austrian, Lithuanian and Italian, all digging for copper. She stopped in front of Nelma's old house and supposed her mother still lived there. Inside someone was cooking breakfast; the smell of dark Finnish coffee slipped out the windows.

Hannah continued up the hill toward the idled Quincy mine location, but stopped within several yards of the armed national guardsmen. Awake and alert, several young men leaned on their rifles while behind them others were emerging from the tents, like misplaced campers in search of the woods, long since cut down for timber in the mines. One of the men recognized her.

"Hannah!" He called out, casually swinging the rifle over his shoulder as he approached. "Is your party still on for tonight? I have friends with deep pockets who'd love to come."

"Every Saturday night, regular as the clocks in my father's store. Just knock on door like we showed you."

Hannah turned away and looked down at the too familiar view, wishing to find something new. Her house was obscured by the curvature of the ground, but she could make out Father's store, and to the east, the swing bridge over the portage. Farther down the shore on the other side was the Michigan College of Mines, and beyond that, the portage canal opened up into Portage Lake. Looking south, she could see the old growth forests of spruce and pine, too far from the mine locations to be cut. The sun was halfway up the hills now, casting a red-orange glow; an illusion of fire. She wondered what the sunrise looked like at the university downstate.

She took the footpath that cut behind the mine location and thought about all the gamblers who looked forward to her Saturday night parties. And it was she, Hannah Weinstein who bested them all. It was a good feeling. Mother would be up by now, firing up the samovar, perhaps cooking pancakes with thimbleberry jam for breakfast.

The birds were the first to sense what was to come and all flew off in a synchronized squawking; a rush of wings into the sky. Hannah's scalp tingled; her hair felt on edge. The earth began to move, first a subtle vibration, then a more violent shaking that threw her to the ground. A sharp booming noise vibrated her bones and bullied all other natural sounds into submission. When finally it stopped, she was afraid to move. After several minutes, she stood up and took a tentative step. Her ankles held her weight. She wasn't hurt, except for a sore hip that took the brunt of her fall. The miners blamed these "air blasts" on cave-ins and would always be nervous about re-entering the mines. She wondered what they felt like thousands of feet down, surrounded by darkness illuminated only by the light on one's headlamp. It had been months since engineers had proclaimed the problem solved and Hannah was spooked by their failure. The air blasts seemed ominous, leaving behind a litter of fear and distrust in their wake.

At home, Hannah touched her fingertips to the mezuzah and its parchment prayer, before going inside, something she hadn't done in years. Mother was in the kitchen, scrambling eggs and frying potatoes. Hannah was disappointed, she had hoped for pancakes. But the samovar was gurgling and boiling, and Hannah held her hands up to its warmth before pouring herself a cup of coffee.

"Where were you this morning?" Mother asked, without looking up.

"Just a walk up the hill, I woke early." Hannah wanted to steer the conversation elsewhere. "We had another air blast. Was there any damage?"

"Just rattled the china, nothing broke," Mother said. "Can you put this bread on the table before Sam gets here with his family?"

Saturday was usually their busiest day in the store, and the whole family would be working. They would always go to shul Friday night, but made certain compromises on Saturday, breaking the Sabbath for the demands of the store. Father insisted it was written somewhere in the Talmud that this was allowed. Hannah was often tempted to ask what these many books had to say about gambling, but never dared. Sam and Ida arrived a short time later, with their two-year-old son Daniel.

Ida talked of last week's outing to Electric Park, where there had been dancing and vaudeville. Hannah used to love riding the streetcar there, with its bumpy ride over the high wooden trestle; the deep valley far below. But since she took over her brother's Saturday game night, nothing else compared for excitement. She had turned Sam's neighborhood pinochle game into the undisputed happening of the city's nightlife. Every weekend in the basement of the family store, deputies would play against scofflaws, and miners against merchants. Nelma, with all her aspirations of a socialist society, would be impressed, though Hannah knew this was the one piece of her life that she could never share with her friend. Nelma loathed gambling as the low values of a failed society, even while her husband was a regular guest at Hannah's tables.

The hours lagged as Hannah worked throughout the morning and afternoon. With few customers, she helped Mother with an inventory of winter clothing, boots and long underwear at the store. The cold weather would be here soon and they couldn't afford to be unprepared. Finally, it was time to close the store, return home for dinner, and read under the lamp in the sitting room while her parents turned in for the night. When she was certain they were asleep, she slipped into her coat and re-opened the store for a different sort of business.

Three knocks at the door announced the first guests: Joseph, a shift captain, and several of her brother's friends. Sam arrived a short time later, as Hannah was collecting coins for the beer at their table.

"Sam!" Joseph called. "Come join us for a game."

"Maybe later," Sam said. "I promised a hand with your neighbor tonight."

"You owe me two bits," Joseph said.

"For what?"

"Remember that agreement we had? Calumet & Hecla re-opened the mines today. We got the first shift working again."

"You better not let Father find out you've been gambling," Hannah said, winking.

"I should have known I'd lose the bet," Sam said.

"So is this the end of the strike?" Hannah asked. "You've negotiated?"

Joseph laughed and shook his head. "We'd never come to the table with those people. They're not to be trusted."

"But what about the local miners? I've heard their complaints –"

"Trust me, Hannah. We're better guardians of the miner's interests than those outsiders with their socialist agenda."

Hannah was certain he was patronizing and flushed with anger. She thought of her friend Nelma, and decided to speak on her behalf.

"The argument against the one-man drill seems valid," she said. "Why shouldn't they work in teams? They say those machines are intolerably heavy and dangerous."

"Those were the old ones. We've got drills now that can easily be operated by one good man. We can't afford not to use them. We're losing market share and our profit margin is shrinking. If we don't start modernizing the mines, we'll all be out of business. Your family runs a store, you should understand this."

Hannah couldn't think of a suitable retort. Joseph made a good argument, but she didn't want to back down. She settled for "maybe," and made a note to play against him later, when he was drunker and more foolish with his money.

The tables began filling up, and Hannah made sure everyone had drinks and respected the house rules. Stakes were up to the players, though most bet no more than ten cents every one hundred points. But Hannah was firm on disallowing the tricks and cheats she herself had learned along the way. Cards were always provided by the house.

A couple new guests, guardsmen, were looking for a game, and Hannah offered to play them herself. It would be the best chance to check for a rifled stack, false cuts, bad deals or signaling. Hannah won the deal.

The bearded guardsman placed the opening bid, his friend passed, and Hannah raised him by ten. She had a good hand, an easy win, but decided to let the guardsmen win the bid. Trump was in her favor, and she set him by thirty points. The friend won the next hand and Hannah again won the third before bowing out. They were social players, relying on luck, she concluded. Not clever enough to cheat.

Hannah finished the night winning a two-dollar kitty from Joseph. She loved the feel of the cards, the bidding and the strategy. Every time she lost, she made a mental catalogue of the game and replayed it with different ploys. Every time she won, she would act surprised. The acting was critical and provided her an edge. Saturday night was her center; the one routine in her week that brought comfort.

Back home in the dark, Hannah lingered on the porch that skirted two sides of their house. Down at the railroad station, a train crept conspicuously to a stop. It was an unusual time for any train, let alone a passenger train, as this one appeared to be. Hannah was curious and thought a short walk might help put her to sleep.

The night train carried at least one hundred men, all young, all carrying a knapsack on their back and a cache of papers in their hands. Hannah felt her scalp tingle; her hair once again felt on edge. Each of the passenger cars was sandwiched between two cabooses, with cupola lookouts on each side. Every lookout had an armed guard who surveyed the station. The men looked bewildered, perhaps surprised as much by their new surroundings as their militant escorts.

Hannah watched from a distance as the men climbed into their waiting carriages, with drivers accompanied by another armed guard, until the station was empty and the night train disappeared. The scene left her disturbed. These men were scabs, miners brought in to break the strike and replace the union men. Hannah returned home and changed into her nightgown. She worried about Nelma's family. She worried they had picked a battle that was bigger than any of them could imagine. Outside her window, the night seemed darker.

AUGUST 18, 1913

NELMA JOKELA RETURNED FROM the funeral both mournful and enraged. She felt a deep camaraderie with all the men and women on the picket lines, as if they were family. As if two of her own had been lost. There had been a procession behind the hearse, a Croatian custom when a young man dies before marriage. Murdered without a chance for love. Ana Prka, dressed in her sister's wedding dress, led the somber promenade. Ten girlish bridesmaids in white dresses and veils had followed behind.

Nelma wiped her eyes with the back of her hand and went upstairs to change her clothes. They would have company today; she needed to clean the house. She chose a pair of Edward's old trousers, binding them to her waist with a women's belt. She scrubbed the kitchen linoleum, the front hall, and the children's bedroom where the union representative would be staying. She imagined this man, Mr. Berlusconi, was a young man, muscular as a trammer, handsome as a mine captain. It excited her that they had been chosen to be his host. She moved the last of the children's bedding into the master bedroom.

Next she turned her attention to the windows, where a dirty film colored the outside view in shades of brown. She remembered the dirt that had been shoveled on the coffins, the crying and the anger. The pall of injustice. Everyone was ready for a fight. Thousands had walked away from the funeral with a shared vision of better working conditions, better wages, a better life. Nelma was confident they would win.

She surveyed the house. The windows were still a bit sooty, but things were otherwise orderly and clean. Nelma noticed the quiet; the children were with the neighbors. She put a pot on the stove to boil water for coffee, and went to the bedroom to clean up at the washstand. She pulled up her pale blond hair with a backcomb, washed the sweat from her face and toweled herself dry. A carriage pulled up outside and she hastily pulled a skirt over the pants; there wasn't enough time to properly change.

As soon as Edward came inside, she knew he was drunk. Again. The door was pushed open just a little too hard and slammed into the wall of the anteroom. Edward shuffled and tripped on the threshold, catching himself a little off balance. Nelma was embarrassed. Mr. Berlusconi stood behind them, studying the room, perhaps pretending not to notice.

"Welcome to Calumet, Mr. Berlusconi." Nelma extended her hand, surprised that he was an older man, grey at the temples, no taller than she, a walking stick on his left.

"Call me Frank," he said, lightly taking her hand. "Let's not be so formal."

Nelma prepared some coffee while Edward brought Frank's belongings up to the bedroom. There was a large carpetbag covered with exotic geometric designs, bringing to mind western Indian nations or perhaps places even more remote. She wondered where it had been and what it carried. She was curious, though she had no desire to leave the Keweenaw herself. This was her home. She felt as married to the place as she did to her husband. Perhaps even more. Over lunch they discussed the morale of the men, the need for strike benefits, the reopening of the mines with imported labor.

"It's not just scabs working now," Nelma said. "It's the locals. Some of 'em are back to work."

"Bunch of fools," Edward said. "Forgetting the old ways; trusting their lives with the copper bosses' money pinching ways instead of a partner. Just a matter of time before they die alone with that one-man drill."

"People thought it'd be over by now," Nelma said. "They weren't prepared."

"They'll learn," Frank said. "They always do. I've walked more picket lines than I care to count, and I know what works. We'll see this through."

His optimism brought to mind Nelma's own Father, dead six years ago this fall. They said he never saw it coming, the boulder crushing him between the shoulder blades. They had to break apart the rock with nitro to free his body. Her mother held firm to their Lutheran faith, never doubting the Lord's motives or existence. She was thankful that she was allowed to remain in the company house, a widow with three children. Nelma wasn't so accommodating. She failed to find any proof of the divine in her life. She kept a running tally of the boarders in her mother's house over the years. Two died by fire, one by falling rock, and one was blinded in an explosion. She would do anything to assure that Edward did not share a similar fate. Ever since her father's death, Nelma cultivated a simmering anger, a wandering blame, in search of vengeance.

"We'll parade at dawn, when the mines open," Frank said. "The women and children should be in front."

"Why does it matter?" Edward said.

"It matters when they take pictures," Frank said. "The newspapers matter."

"What about the picket lines?" Nelma said.

"We'll make 'em more difficult to cross," Frank said. "Edward, tomorrow you can show me the Number Seven shaft – I've heard it's the worst one."

Nelma was up early the next morning. The damp air condensed water on the windowpanes, creating a feeling of isolation, a stronghold in their battle, a lonely outpost in a war. The men had already left for the picket lines, and the children were still sleeping. She took a pail of lime to throw in their Sears catalog outhouse, sprinkled it down the two holes, looked forward to when the cool autumn air would take away the smell. The privy was filling up; Edward would need to move the outhouse soon, before the ground froze. She left to fetch a long-handled shovel to measure the depth of the hole, and returned with a large bucket and an idea. She asked if her neighbor Ellen would look after the children, but Ellen was too excited by the plan, and instead left her teenage daughter to watch after Nelma's children. They enlisted two other neighborhood wives, Eunice and Fran, and carried the bucket on a stick between them to the streetcar stationhouse and waited.

The sun had broken above the horizon, a mourning dove was singing and butterflies flew haphazardly above the tracks. Two men came to sit on the outside bench, but upon seeing the women they elected to stand against the side of the building. She recognized the men from a Lithuanian boarding house down the street. One was clean-shaven; the other wore a tangled mass of beard. Nelma nodded at her friends and they walked over to the men, trapping them against the wall with a barricade of skirts.

The men held their lunch pails with two hands and averted their eyes; the carbide lamps on their heads angled toward the ground.

"You shouldn't be here," Nelma said. "You need to respect the picket lines."

"Ma'am, I'm sorry," the clean-shaven Lithuanian said, "but I need money to eat, to pay the rent. I'm just minding my own affairs."

"That's a problem for us," Nelma said and set down her load. "I don't like problems."

The men continued to stand uncomfortably, eyed the bucket of excrement, and looked uncertain as to the women's intent. The smell drifted between them in the still air. The clean-shaven man swatted at a gathering of flies that had been attracted to the stench. The bearded man was angered beyond the point of reason; she recognized the look. She had once seen it in Edward's eyes before he struck a man down. It was time to act.

Nelma dipped her broom into the bucket and scooped the sullied bristles high into the air, as if to paint a giant invisible canvas. She cast it over their heads and spread the muck over the men's faces. It dripped over their shoulders and down their chest.

"Son of a bitch!" the bearded man exclaimed. He tried to push her but Ellen caught her and the other women held their ground defiantly.

The other man brushed his face with his sleeve and scowled. "What the hell do you think you're doing? I'll have you arrested!"

"Arrested for what?" Nelma said. "Some women accidentally spilled some muck on a couple of no good scabs. I don't think that's a crime." Nelma kicked over the bucket, watching as the dark contents crept toward the men's boots.

Ellen recoated the broom and pointed it at the bearded man's chest. "You best be on your way home, boys," she said. "You're not wanted on the job today."

"You're crazy," he said. "You can't be doing this. It ain't right."

The bearded man glared for a long minute, but his friend gave his sleeve a tug and the two men turned to go, leaving a trail behind them as they walked.

Nelma let out a long sigh. She realized she had been holding her breath, and started to laugh. With the men gone, she noticed they were standing in front of a stationhouse window. Inside, Erik Tomlinson peered at them, disapproval in his eyes. He was a friend of her father's, a deeply religious man, and as he turned away she was ashamed. She felt outside herself, watching with disbelief at what had been done. But then her friends gave a friendly jab and returned her gay mood. She went to Ellen's house, to wash and pick up the children, before returning home.

Frank and Edward came back from the picket line an hour later.

"There's two less men in the mines today," Nelma said, regaling the morning events with excitement, gesturing with her hands, never pausing until she finished her tale.

Frank smiled slightly and rubbed the burnished wood on top of his walking stick. He let a truncated laugh slip out from his mouth, and then was silent again. Another small titter. Nelma couldn't recall him ever laughing before. He always presented a sober, controlled façade. Perhaps he was angry and trying to make light of the situation. But now he was laughing again, unrestrained and with an element of infectiousness. Nelma started to giggle, and found it difficult to stop. Her children, Lila and Toivo, came in from the next room and looked at their mother with curious faces. Finally, even Edward couldn't resist.

It had been years since she had seen Edward like this. She remembered when he had courted her with flowers at her mother's house, dumbstruck as to what to say after presenting her a bouquet of daisies. He would take her on long walks along Torch lake, holding her hand and smiling the whole way until Nelma began to worry he would catch bugs in his teeth. When she accepted his marriage proposal, he seemed surprised by her answer. He had started laughing, nervous at first, until she had joined him, and they had laughed until their ribs ached. Laughed just like today.

The next morning Nelma was up before dawn to start the coffee and rouse the children. Breakfast was a slice of rye bread and thimbleberry jam. She put her five-year-old daughter in her best Sunday dress, a white cotton and lace gift from her mother. Her one-year-old son had to make do with whichever set of short pants and shirt was clean. The sun was just above the horizon when she stepped outside, a warm orange glow full of promise. Nelma felt as if she owned the streets. They paraded downtown through the business district, past the National Guardsmen bivouacked at Agassiz Park, down to the mining locations and back.

The march was different today than it had been in the past. There was sympathy in the eyes of the people watching, in the storekeepers opening their shops and in the early risers out for a walk. There was a change in mood as discernable as the red leaves on the maple trees, already turning and preparing for winter in the late August heat. Nelma invited several neighbors to their house afterwards, and Frank purchased a pound of raw green coffee beans that Nelma roasted in her rännäli pan. She felt a bit like they were on holiday, with her women friends seated around the kitchen table drinking coffee, and the men out back playing cards.

"Did you hear what happened to Ellen's son?" a neighbor said in hushed tones. "He was in a fight and the sheriff just looked the other way while some of those goons took turns. Broke two ribs and then threw him in jail for disorderly conduct."

"That sheriff's bad news," Nelma said. "Frank says he's pocketing money from the copper bosses and we shouldn't trust him."

"Anyone can see he's not a man to be trusted," another said. "But it's our men I'm worried about."

"Edward's been staying out late after union meetings," Nelma said. "Drinking and going down to the Helltown neighborhood looking for a fight."

"They don't know what to do with themselves, without work for so long."

Nelma got up and threw a quarter split log into the stove. Thought about what they had accomplished after five weeks on strike. Some days they seemed to be winning the hearts of their neighbors; other days she found herself a pariah, as backs would turn and conversations would stop as she walked down the street. The papers were no help either. Frank brought home the dailies and left them on the table for her to read. The *Tyomies* was full of support and vigor, promising victory just around the corner. The *Mining Gazette* reported the struggles of the mining agents to protect their interests. Struggles, they called them. As if their moneyed portfolios were the real victims.

"Three dollars a week," her neighbor was saying. "We need strike benefits at least twice that. What's your union man have to offer us, Nelma? What's he have to say?"

"He's been working on it," Nelma said. "Says it takes a while to arrange."

"Sometimes the union sounds about as useless as them copper bosses," her neighbor responded. "One by malice, the other by empty promises."

Nelma considered defending Frank, but choked on the words. He'd only been here a few days, but she knew that sounded like yet another excuse. She would later tell him of her friend's frustration, and be impressed with his quick action.

Saturday afternoon, the hockey rink was reserved for a rally. Thousands of men, women and children packed the bench seats and the floor. The mood was festive; strike funds had been distributed earlier in the day. Nelma had never seen so many people in one place, the murmuring of thousands of conversations in dozens of languages mixing together into a modern Tower of Babel. Frank was speaking next, and she watched him tap his cane on each step as he climbed a small wooden stage.

His voice surprised her with its volume. He urged patience and persistence. Strike funds had been solicited from sympathetic unions and socialist societies across the country. Working people across the nation had pledged their support. He assured them that they had both the wiles and the resources to win.

Nelma started to think beyond the strike, beyond the eight-hour workday, three-dollar daily wages and two men on all machines. She imagined what life would be like after the battles had been won. Edward might work his way up to mine captain. She could live in a house like her friend Hannah, with a bath and a toilet inside.

The first time she had been in Hannah's home she felt she had walked into another world, with polished floors and Persian rugs. Hannah had a room all to herself with two dolls on her bed. The rooms were cool in the summer and warm in the winter. As a child, she couldn't conceive of ever living in a house like that. Now it seemed something to aspire to, something within reach. Nelma hadn't seen much of her childhood friend since the strike began. There seemed to be no time for recreation, no time for parlor talk. But now, she wondered if Hannah might be a useful friend to have, to stay in touch with the opinions of others, the merchants, and perhaps even the mine captains themselves.

A HARD FROST HIT the first weekend of September. Nelma felt it coming in the sharp chill of the evening air and brought in all the vegetables from her small garden the night before. She had two large pots boiling on the stove all day, canning the tomatoes and peas, pickling the string beans. Basil and oregano were strung up to dry above the kitchen window, filling the air with their fragrance.

Lila played outside, marching around the house with the other children in a mock parade, carrying flags and raising her fist in the same defiant manner her father used. Their noisy chatter woke Toivo, who had been napping amongst a pile of blankets in the next room. She picked him up, carried him into the kitchen, and gave him a wooden spoon to occupy himself. It had been a short nap, and she knew an evening of short tempers lay ahead.

Nelma turned her attention to dinner. Edward and some others had gone out to the pier to try their hand at fishing, though Nelma suspected he would sooner empty his flask than catch enough for tonight. They had eaten the last of the smoked whitefish weeks ago. It would be rice pasties again. Lila ran into the kitchen, barefoot and dirty, to see what her mother was preparing.

"Not again!" Lila protested. "Can't we have something else?"

"Go back outside," Nelma said, irritated. "You're tracking mud all over the floor."

She was tired of rice pasties too. Tired of hungry children, and frustrated with Edward's drinking and the way he brushed aside her concerns. She thought about the smug copper bosses, the hostile sheriff, and the stupid miners crossing the picket lines. Something had to change.

The next morning, her anger remained, strengthened by a night of turbulent dreams that left her disquieted but without any memory of why. At the start of the parade, she kicked up the dirt from the street, raised her fist and gave her children's wagon a tug. Lila and Toivo squealed in excitement.

When they marched past the guardsmen, she shouted at them, "Go home! You're on the wrong side of this fight, and you know it."

They ignored her. They ignored everyone. Everyday they would look right through them, talk amongst themselves, or lean on their rifles while drinking coffee from tin cups. She pulled her wagon to the side of the street, squeezing its handle hard.

"Look at me. Look at us," she shouted. "We're your mothers and fathers, your sisters and brothers. Leave us be."

She stood in front of a young guardsman, no older than her, close enough to see the stubble on his face, his unkempt hair falling out from beneath his hat, a sour smell filtering from the camp behind him. She raised her free hand to point at him, the same mannerism she used to scold her children. It surprised him and defensively focused his attention on his rifle. She was almost close enough to touch him when he raised his weapon, the bayonet stealthily cutting through the air, several extra inches that perhaps he had not accounted for. It raked across the back of her wrist, slicing the skin, shocking her with a pain before she even saw the wound. Her daughter screamed, scaring her son who started to cry.

"What have you done?" Nelma asked, confused more than angry, and then shouting, "Look what you've done!"

The other women yelled; the men heckled and belittled the guardsmen. Nelma felt a surge of fear and pulled her children away as the blood dripped down her arm. She ran away with them, away from the parade, back the way they had come, past Edward who picked a rock up from the side of the road and pelted it at a guardsman, narrowly missing him. Other men copied him, scooping up pebbles and small rocks to throw. Nelma turned onto a side street when she heard a series of sharp explosive noises, like a burst of firecrackers, echoing through the air, and then everyone was fleeing. Panicking. Screaming.

Nelma pressed forward, away from the shooting, away from the guardsmen. She ran with both hands grasped on the wagon handle behind her until she reached Fournier's hardware store and felt they were safe. Mr. Fournier was an older man in his fifties, with a neatly trimmed grey goatee. He bandaged Nelma's wrist and opinioned how lucky she was that the cut was shallow.

"It's criminal, what they did," Nelma fumed. "Criminal. But who do we report them to? Who polices the national guard?"

"Guns and boys is always a bad mix," he said.

Nelma sat on the front stoop with her son and daughter in her lap. Her friend Ellen rounded the corner followed closely behind by Edward and Otto with Ellen's daughter draped between them. She was only fourteen, but nearly as tall as her father already. A bloody trail tracked behind the girl, dripping down her hair.

20

"What happened?" Nelma asked.

"Shot," Edward said. His lips curled around the word.

"They shot my girl," Ellen said, choking as she spoke. "They shot my little girl in the head."

Mr. Fournier closed his shop and took Ellen and her daughter to the hospital in his carriage. He said he had served in Cuba during the war and had seen people pull through with worse injuries. It just grazed the side of her head, he promised. She'll be fine.

Nelma gathered her own children back into their wagon and took them home. Never had she felt so mortally at risk, and yet never had she been so determined.

SEPTEMBER 1, 1913

RUSSELL TOLL FELL ASLEEP SOON after leaving Chicago, with the sun still on his left and the Lake Michigan shoreline still on his right. The train drove north, through the Wisconsin Dells, into the densely wooded north country. Behind him was his family's crowded tenement, his fiancée, and her disapproving father. In front, he was sure, was a secure job, decent wages, and a house that he and Maria would share. His luck had turned. Recruiters had given him a free ticket on a private train, no experience required. He would work his way up from trammer, pushing carts loaded with copper, and pocket wages over two dollars a day.

A lean rat-faced man shook Russell awake. Having forgotten where he was, Russell's first instinct was to throw a punch at the man. It probably would have hit him too, if the man in the next seat didn't grab his arm.

"What the hell?" Russell shouted, looking between the two before he realized the train had stopped at a dark station, with the lights of a small town in the background.

"We're here," the man said. "Take your bags and listen for your name."

The outside air was sharp and cold, giving Russell the odd sensation that he had slept right through autumn into the onset of winter. Most of the other men had stumbled outside, taking in their new surroundings. Armed guards stood watch over the crowd, chewing and spitting tobacco. Russell worried who was being protected from whom. Looking back at the train, he studied how the passenger cars had been uniformly sandwiched between cabooses, where more armed guards leaned against the railing.

The cabooses hadn't seemed strange when he had boarded in Chicago, but their purpose hadn't been clear. Fear trickled through his veins. He wondered what the threat was, who the threat was, and why. He tried to imagine something that would prompt this many guns, but then reasoned they were simply being cautious given the late hour. His excitement returned; he was ready for whatever lay ahead.

The driver of a surrey called his name from a paper registry. He climbed in with several others, knapsack between his knees, and they were off, with the horse laboring up a steep incline.

He was let off at a small clapboard house, greeted by a tired looking woman with graying hair and a thick Finnish accent. Her speech had a rhythm to it, a soft singsong that welcomed, despite her stern, unsmiling composure. She introduced herself as Mrs. Huhta. "Your room is up the stairs, first door on the left. My children are asleep downstairs, so I'd appreciate your quietude. I'll knock on your door twenty minutes before breakfast. You'll need to catch the 6:30 train. The other boarders also work the Number Seven shaft, so they can show you around."

"Thank you, ma'am. Would there be somewhere I could grab a bite to eat? It's been a long trip. I haven't eaten since breakfast."

"There'd be nothing but beer and whiskey at any place open this hour. And I must warn ya, I run a respectable house here. I'll have no drunkenness and no guests. You can socialize at the local temperance hall, or take in a show at the theater if you're so inclined."

"Yes ma'am," Russel said, hoping to sound cooperative. Hoping she wouldn't let him go to bed hungry. "Of course. Would you have any bread in the house? I could make myself a sandwich, pay you back with my first week's wages."

"I won't have any men in my kitchen. I'll make you a sandwich, then you best be off to bed. Have you worked the mines before?"

"Tried my hand at lots of things, foundry work, farm work. I'll be starting in as a trammer, work my way up to a miner in no time."

Mrs. Huhta smiled for the first time, dimpling the right side of her face. She turned into the kitchen, leaving Russell alone in the narrow hall. Upstairs, he found his room furnished with a small wooden cot just inside the door, a writing desk with a lamp by the window, and a closet beyond the foot of the bed. The bare wooden floor was well worn but clean. The stuffy room smelled of damp wood, recently washed with an undertone of bleach. Russell cracked opened the window but in the darkness saw only the side of the neighboring house, built exactly like the one he was in. When he came back down, Mrs. Huhta had a thick sausage and cheese sandwich waiting, stuffed between two dark slices of rye. Russell consumed half the sandwich before he thought to make conversation again.

"Does your husband work the mines as well?"

"Did. Widowed six years ago this fall. You best keep one eye on your work and the other on the overhanging wall. If you see the other men leave an area, don't be left behind wondering where everyone went to."

"Yes, ma'am. Thank you."

Russell knew it was hard work, not meant for the average city boy. But he was built like a workhorse, took after his father and grandfather that way. With few expenses, he figured he'd save a lot of cash by end of the year. Send for Maria in the spring. Russell stretched his arms, tensing his muscles, breathing in confidence, exhaling hope, and went to sleep.

MRS. HUHTA HAD pancakes and fried eggs for breakfast, in endless supply, and Russell felt he could easily become accustomed to this menu every morning. He walked to the rail station with two other boarders, Thomas and Elias, who had been working the mines since the spring. They told him about the strike, warned him about the picket lines, and promised to show him the ropes. Again he recalled his arrival last night, the armed guards in the cabooses, and how easily he had brushed those signs away. Damn. He'd been bamboozled. He would make the best of it, but with eyes wide open from now on.

Russell found a seat on the train next to a window. As they moved, he saw a woman collecting wild apples from gnarly apple trees, and another tending cows grazing alongside shaft houses. They passed by a small settlement of homes where several small children sat at the feet of their grandmother, a long-stemmed pipe between her teeth. He wondered how Maria would fit in here. She'd never been outside Chicago. He hoped her sense of adventure wouldn't abandon her.

Thomas and Elias urged him off the train one stop early, away from the picket line, and took him round back of the rock house, where men were loading ingot copper into freight cars. They crossed the rail tracks to the dry house, and he learned how to pack his brass pocket container with the carbide crystals needed for his sunshine lamp. He could hear the angry shouts of the strikers, but he was behind them now, separated by a wall of armed security men.

He took a seat in the man-car, a giant contraption hanging precariously at the top of the shaft. It bore a closer resemblance to a staircase than a car, and the men were expected to sit on the steps, three across and ten deep. Russell tossed a pebble over the side and never heard it bottom out. Exactly what he had expected, he told himself. Nothing to be concerned about. The recruiters claimed the best engineers in the world had designed these mines. He hoped in this they hadn't lied. Thirty men climbed into the man-car, causing it to shudder as each sat down. The surface captain tallied the men as they settled in. A whistle blew and the entire man-car was sent plummeting down the shaft. Russell put the lunch pail Mrs. Huhta had given him around one arm and held onto his seat with his other hand. He understood he would be down under for ten hours, and hoped that his lunch was as hearty as the sandwich she had made him last night.

They passed dozens of dark levels before slowing down half an hour later; Russell lost count after the fiftieth level. This past summer, Maria's favorite book had been *A Journey to the Center of the Earth*. He was not an avid reader, lacking both the time and the patience. But she had described for him the fantastic world she found in those pages. He half expected to see it realized when he stepped out. Instead, a grey world devoid of color greeted him, along with a powerful stench of urine and damp rock.

"All right men," the mine captain barked. "Get to yer stations. Oscar, take the new guy to the end of the drift."

Oscar took Russell by the arm, showed him how to load up his lamp and watch it flame when the crystalline compound mixed with water and generated acetylene. He put the lamp back on his head. Oscar was a stout blond man. They looked to be about the same age. His right cheek was covered with a jagged pink scar, rendering his moustache short and uneven on that side of his face, giving him a constant comic expression.

The mine captain came over and slapped the back of Russell's head. "Come on ladies, get your Sunday bonnets on and get moving."

The two men walked the gravelly ground, past rock pillars and timber supports. Sometimes the roof of the drift was barely above his head, other times it opened into a large cavernous area where the copper had been removed. The stale air was hot, like an afternoon in August, and already Russell's bare arms were covered in black dust clinging to his perspiration. Russell tripped on the rail tracks and battered his head on the overhanging wall. A tingle of claustrophobia crawled up his spine.

"Okay, then," Oscar said. "This is it. They're still carving out the drift here. Haven't made it to the next shaft yet. That's why the air's so bad. We need to muck the rock into the tramcars, then push 'em back down the drift."

"All the way back?" Russell said, the intensity of the labor starting to take hold.

Oscar just grinned. They shoveled the gravel, stooped to pick up the moderate sized rocks, and rolled the larger ones up a wooden plank into the tramcar. When the rock was too big to hoist, they called in a block-holer, who drilled and blasted it apart. Sometimes the rock wouldn't fall down the stope, the large hollow areas where miners ripped open the copper-rich earth. Russell and Oscar had to climb up the incline and push the boulders along their way. Russell's whole body ached. Muscles in places he didn't know he had were sore. He kept his mind occupied with thoughts of Maria and the house they would share. It would have a sitting room and a proper kitchen. Every day after work she would serve him a sumptuous meal that even Mrs. Huhta would envy.

At lunch they sat down on the rough incline and unwrapped the food from their lunch pails. Russell had a thick meat pie, Oscar called it a pasty; he had one as well. It was still warm and ended his hunger with dense meat, potatoes, and rutabagas. Russell thought of the farm work he had done out west, picking apples under the glare of the unshadowed sun on the plains outside Spokane. He was never able to keep steady work, with both the employment sharks and the union organizers jockeying at his expense. He soon tired of their games. He was not an ambitious man, but simply wanted to work. Labor he could do without thinking too hard, that he could return to week after week, and cash his check in the bank.

He told Oscar of the union organizers out west. A bunch of charlatans at best. Making speeches in the parks, promising impossible rights for workers. They persuaded Russell for a while with their nonsense, until he realized they couldn't care less about his job. They had grand visions of society turned upside down.

The police would pick up the union workers every day, charge them with disorderly conduct and throw them in jail. Twenty-eight men to a twenty-by-eight-foot cell. The cops would turn on the steam until men would pass out against each other, nearly suffocating. Then they were placed in ice-cold cells until the judge would fine them, set them loose and they'd be at it again. You'd think they'd learn.

After weeks of this the mayor made a truce, allowing the union to freely meet, organize, and speak; called the employment agencies a bunch of crooks and slapped the backs of their hands. But in the end, Russell was still out of a job. Useless damn union.

Oscar finished his lunch and shared the crumbs with a mine rat. The rodent picked up its valuable treasure, stuffed its mouth and scurried into the darkness. Oscar had lived in the copper country his whole life. His daddy, and his granddaddy before him had worked the mines. He told Russell he'd never been anywhere else, and from what he'd heard, didn't care to leave. The mine companies were good to people here, deeding land to the churches, building houses, keeping the streets clean. There was plenty of game in the woods and reliable work. He'd come from a family of miners, and claimed he could feel the spirit of the rock, knew when and where it would break, smell a copper load before the engineers knew where to drill. Once they opened a second shift again, he'd been promised a shaft-sinkers job.

Russell felt a twinge of competitiveness, jealous of Oscar's confidence in getting the job that Russell craved. He knew that men like Oscar would be offered the choice positions before he'd be given a chance, but he liked Oscar, and let the feeling pass. A whistle blew and they were back to work again. They fell into a rhythm together, mucking the rock in a syncopated fashion, filling the tramcars and together putting their shoulders against it to move it down the tracks. Shards of native copper lay at their feet and Russell picked one up, bending it in a circle, fashioning a wedding band before he crumpled it in his fist and threw it back down. That would have to wait.

"You married, Oscar?" Russell asked. "Got a woman waiting when you get back to grass?"

"Not yet. I been seeing a lot of Miss Lisa Pohja, though. Daughter of a mine captain, but doesn't flaunt it. She's got a quick wit and a kind heart. I'll invite ya to one of her parties sometime. She's real social."

Russell considered this, wondering if Oscar's lady friend would be social with Maria. He wondered how she would manage up here, where women split wood, tilled land and gathered wild fruits for canning. It was a different world than Chicago.

"I've got a fiancée in Chicago," Russell said, relishing the word fiancée. "Her father owns a general store and tells me I'm not good enough for his girl. But she loves me, and we plan on marrying in the spring, with or without his blessing. I'm saving up for a nice wedding and honeymoon by Lake Michigan."

"Ah, that's a hard battle to fight," Oscar said. "She's worth it?"

"We've been friends since we was kids. Friends for years before I noticed the woman she'd become. She has dark red hair that makes your heart skip a beat when she lets it fall down her back."

The two men fell silent for a time, struggling with a large boulder as they rolled it up a plank and into the tramcar. This would likely be the last load of the day, and they turned to hoist another rock. It was too big and odd shaped to lift, and Russell suggested sending a drill-boy to fetch a block-holer, to blast it apart.

"Hold up, this one's solid mass copper, I can smell it," Oscar said. "Shine your light on it. See what I mean? It's got the right shape and the right feel to it."

Oscar chipped off a piece of the greenish rock and washed it with the hose used to dewater the mines. It shone like gold. Its bubbled texture reminded Russell of pictures he'd seen of volcanic rock. He was mesmerized by the immensity of the thing. It seemed a shame to break it apart, melt it down, tame it into man-made blocks.

"We'll get a bonus for this one—we'll need to get a flat car to get 'er out though."

At the end of the day they rode the man-car back up the shaft. It felt good to sit down again. The rocky ride seemed more comforting and familiar than it had that morning. When they reached the top, Russell's eyes burned against the bright sunlight. They went to the dry house to change their boots and clothes, drenched in sweat and caked in grime. Even his spittle was black as pine tar.

"Where you staying?" Oscar asked as they crossed back over the tracks, the strikers had gone for the day and with them the feeling of combativeness that had weighed the air down earlier that day.

"Huhta's boarding house up near the top of Quincy Hill. A widow runs the place."

"They've put you in a good house. But look out for that woman's daughter. She married one of them red Finns. Bunch of damn socialists. She's out marching in the strike parades, and her husband hasn't worked since July. When she comes for a visit, you best leave the house."

"That's a shame," Russell said. "Mrs. Huhta's a good woman. A good cook too."

"That she is, but I know a tavern that will serve you a damn good meal and a beer to chase it down. Got time for a drink? I'll buy the first round, in honor of your first day."

"Ya, sure. Maybe a quick bite to eat as well?"

"I got just the thing for ya."

Oscar's thing was a pickled egg, red and spicy from sharing a jar with beets and hot peppers. It went good with the first beer and even better with the second. Russell left for the boarding house whistling and feeling good. The drinks had loosened his knotted muscles and a pleasant fatigue settled in. It was already dark and Russell looked up at a sky littered with stars, like the night sky he had seen out west, undiluted by city lights. A carriage trotted by and the driver tipped his hat, offered Russell a ride. Friendly place, not like you'd see in Chicago. Russell waved the man on and picked up his pace a bit. Wondered if he'd gone too far down the road.

He knew his was the first left past the agent's house, but he'd forgotten to note anything on the other side of the street. The agent's house was a huge two-and-a-half story building with a side gable, central tower and Italianate detailing. The other men at the boarding house had pointed it out to him this morning, noting it as an easy landmark. But Russell wasn't sure whether he had passed it and wasn't willing to turn around just yet.

An angry voice broke the quiet, calling him a "scabby dog." Another called him a "no good son of a bitch." Russell looked around, but didn't see the source of the insults. He clenched his fist on his lunch pail, figured he could knock someone pretty hard with it if he had to. He looked up and down the road, but saw no sign of the agent's house. Nothing looked familiar. His heart raced. He knew he could put out a strong defense, but suspected the strikers wouldn't be the kind to fight fair.

The wind picked up and stirred the fallen leaves into a phantom striker on the side of the road. He imagined the darkness concealed a gathering of thugs at every corner. Years ago in Chicago, he and his brother had once been in a street fight with a gang of Irish boys. He felt the others had received the worst of the battle, but still carried a scar near his eye, which had been swollen closed for days. He saw himself as a reluctant fighter, someone who would never start a dispute, but was confident he would win. As much as he hoped to avoid a fight, part of him yearned to be tested.

He became convinced he had gone too far down the road, and wondered if it would be safer to double back or make his way along a side road. He chose the latter, and not hearing any further taunts, felt certain that the cowards had simply been shouting from their windows, afraid to face him. He relaxed a little, laughed to himself at the unseen accusers, and tried to lighten his mood.

"Hey, Russell!"

He turned right away, ashamed that he hadn't heard the approach from behind. Clenched both his fists, readied himself for a fight. When the man walked under the streetlight, Russell could see it was Thomas, one of Mrs. Huhta's boarders.

"Am I glad to see you," Russell said, "I got turned 'round a bit."

"You sure did," Thomas said. "You're on the wrong side of the hill. You gotta be careful walking here—they don't take too well to anyone working the mines. Bunch of strikers and troublemakers. Good thing I saw you going this way."

The two men walked back the way Russell had come. Many of the houses had already turned down their lights for the night, and when they reached their boarding house, just the outside light was on. Russell left his lunch pail in the hall, climbed the stairs to his room and sat heavily on his bed. He stripped down to his underwear, lay down and fell into a deep, dreamless sleep.

HANNAH OPENED HER WINDOW, breathed in the crisp morning air, and listened to the cricket sing in the garden below. Already there had been flurries, and she wondered how much longer it would survive. It had become a predictable harbinger of the morning and evening, and she found herself thinking of the cricket as her own. She had read that people in the orient kept crickets as pets, as omens of good luck. Charles Dickens wrote of a cricket that chirped merrily when things went well and was silent during times of trouble. She worried about Nelma, whom she hadn't seen since the strike began. She imagined her circumstances as both troubling and exciting, and hoped to visit her for lunch.

Down the stairs, coffee burbled in the samovar and biscuits baked in the oven, stirring her appetite with their aroma. After breakfast, she made gefilte fish for the winter months, mincing the whitefish and onions, separating egg whites, adding matzo meal and molding their shape before placing them in the pot to cook.

Mother covered the kitchen table with receipts and the store's accounting book, working the thin numbers. Several customers couldn't afford to pay off their purchases since the strike began, and Mother had relaxed the one-dollar payment schedule from weekly to monthly in order to bring in some cash.

"Do you think I'm needed in the shop today?" Hannah asked, "I might visit Nelma, perhaps a picnic at Freda Park with her children."

Mother continued adding the numbers without looking up, with implied disapproval, and Hannah tried to strengthen her case.

"Her daughter just had a birthday last week, and we haven't properly celebrated." Hannah said. "Perhaps I could bring a basket of food?"

Mother paused in her work, the pencil still poised on the accounts, and then nodded. "You can take the smoked whitefish we have left over from yesterday, and a few biscuits from the oven."

"Some candy from the store, for the children?"

"I suppose it would bring some cheer. I do wish they'd put an end to this strike. It isn't fair to the little ones."

Hannah chose not to debate the topic with Mother, thankful to have the day off. She didn't want to push her luck. She wasn't entirely sure where she stood on the subject herself. Oftentimes the strike seemed so futile; she wondered why they kept up what appeared to be a losing battle.

She caught the streetcar outside the store and rode it all the way to Calumet. The trees had already started wearing their fall colors, though they would still be green by the lake. She double-checked the contents of her basket, there was more than enough for the picnic, and she hoped to discretely leave the remainder in Nelma's kitchen. An act of charity, a mitzvah, that Nelma might not otherwise accept unless it appeared accidental.

It was a short walk from the station to Nelma's two-story clapboard house. Each house on the street was identical, the same wind-blown siding, the same anteroom entrance with a second door to insulate against the long winter cold. Each house leased from the same mining company that had caused so much bitterness in Nelma's home. When the strike had first begun, Hannah worried they might be evicted, but now reasoned there were too many strikers, too many homes, and that good will would prevail.

Hannah let herself in through the first door, as she always did, and knocked at the second, inside the anteroom. A man's voice welcomed her in, and she was surprised to see they had a visitor, seated at the kitchen table. He had jet black hair with flashes of grey in his sideburns and a dark intense look that Hannah found disquieting. Edward had brought him to play pinochle last Saturday night, though she hoped he had the good sense not to mention it.

"Hannah—what a surprise!" Nelma gave her a warm hug. "This is our guest, Mr. Berlusconi."

Frank stood with the help of his cane and winked his left eye. "So good to meet one of Nelma's friends, Miss…"

"Miss Weinstein. Pleased to meet you Mr. Berlusconi."

"The pleasure is all mine," Frank said, as he cast his eyes toward Hannah's basket. "What brings you here today?"

"It seemed like a nice day for a picnic," Hannah replied, irritated at how quick he assumed a position of authority in her friend's home. "Nelma, I brought some candy for Lila. I can just leave it here if this is a bad time."

"Not at all," Frank said. "You two should go on your picnic."

Hannah harbored a growing dislike of this man. He seemed well versed at subterfuge with his easy wink behind Nelma's back. Her own complicity in the lie made her uncomfortable. She avoided her friend's eyes.

"Well, let's go then, eh?" Nelma said. "I'll fetch my daughter, she's been asking 'bout you for weeks. Toivo can stay with the neighbors. I don't want to be changing diapers at the park."

Frank turned his attention back to Edward to continue what sounded like a lecture on economics. Hannah was thankful to leave the house. What had once seemed like a second home now felt estranged and formal. Her place in this household had been co-opted by the newcomer. His presence changed how Nelma talked with her, and she felt a slight resentment that she was unable to dispose.

Nelma called her daughter, Lila, from the dirt pile where she had been entertaining herself, digging small mine shafts and tunnels for the dolls that Nelma had fashioned out of sticks and fabric. When she turned to get up, the dry dirt collapsed on itself, burying the stick people without a trace. Pulling herself from her mother's grasp, she dug them back up with her fingers, then pushed them back down another hole, reserving them for later.

Lila made no complaints during the walk to the station, and Hannah thought she must be familiar with this walk through town, with the frequent parades, more familiar with the mechanics of protest at the age of five than Hannah would ever be.

The trolley made stops in the towns of Red Jacket and Swedetown, and then passed through Limerick and Hardscrabble, Sing-Sing and Frenchtown. At Houghton they switched trains and continued through South Range until they finally stopped at Freda Park. The woodland was situated up on a small rise of land overlooking Lake Superior. There were picnic tables, swings for the children, and a steep staircase down to the rocky beach, which is where Nelma's daughter immediately wanted to go. The two women sat on a large piece of driftwood, while Lila explored and filled her skirt up with rocks, tossing some into the icy lake water, saving others for a pile that she deemed superior for a reason apparent only to a five-year-old mind.

"You're still wearing that necklace," Hannah said. The Hebrew word for life or *chai* was inscribed on a small piece of silver dangling from her friend's neck. "I thought you had lost it."

"Oh, no," Nelma said. "I'd be devastated. This is the best gift I've ever gotten. I still can't believe you gave it to me."

Hannah smiled, pleased that it meant so much to her friend. "Who is this Mr. Berlusconi? He's staying with you?"

"He's a union organizer," Nelma said. "It's really an honor to have him stay with us. He has so much to teach."

"But isn't it a risk? The mine companies don't like these outsiders."

"They wouldn't touch him. He's famous," Nelma said. "He's been all over the country, from Colorado to Massachusetts. And he's a socialist, too!"

"What does that matter?" Hannah asked. "Its just politics."

"It's politics for us working people. Us that don't own any property," Nelma said. "You have a stake in your father's business, but we got no stake in the mines where our men and boys risk their lives for a bunch of Boston copper bosses."

"But you can work your way up, can't you? Isn't that how it works?"

"Maybe," Nelma said. "If you don't die first. We lose a man every week. Every week! And twice that are injured."

Hannah tried to remember the point at which Nelma had become so political, so focused. When did an individual miner's death cross over into a social movement? She wondered if there was something lacking in herself that made it difficult to believe in anything so strongly. The suffragettes pushed for women's right to vote, and last year had walked the same parade routes that the union now trod, but what difference would that really make in her daily life? At shul she could hold her own with any Talmudic discussions, yet the women were sequestered upstairs, in the cold women's section. Did she really want to sit beside her brother and father in synagogue, or was it the distance from the stove in the winter that bothered her? She felt incapable of committing to any issue of a serious nature and saw this as a flaw in her character, another secret she feared sharing with Nelma, lest her friend think less of her.

"You don't think of me as one of them do you?" Hannah asked. "Because of Father's store?"

Nelma shook her head, placed her hand atop Hannah's. "You'd tell me if you heard anything, wouldn't you? You know, any secret plans to undercut the union?"

"Don't be so suspicious; there's no secret plan."

"But you'd tell me? If y'heard anything?"

"You know I would."

Lila had tugged off her shoes and walked into the cold shallows of Lake Superior. The wind picked up and the waves started to get bigger and more violent, until Lila ran back up to the beach, unable to bring herself to move any farther. Nelma scooped her up and they went back up the stairs, back to the picnic table where Hannah had left the basket of food. Lila was still frightened and sniffling, until Hannah pulled out a piece of hard candy, quieting the girl.

Hannah unpacked the lunch, pulling out the whitefish and biscuits, mustard and pickles, apples and honey. There was a well and a small hand pump back by the station, and Nelma left to fill their tin cups. It was sometime after noon, and they were quite hungry, even Lila, who ate all that was put before her. Hannah was surprised, as she was usually such a fickle eater. Still, there was enough left over to bring back. Lila ran to a swing, which hung from a tree limb at least twenty feet in the air, and begged for someone to give her a push. The two women took turns for a time, before returning to the picnic table to talk.

"Your father still talking 'bout marriage?" Nelma asked. "He find any suitors?"

"Thankfully, no," Hannah said. "Mother promises that I'll go to college, though I think even she would like to see me engaged."

"You should wait, see the world and tell me what it's like."

"I don't want an arranged marriage. I want to choose," Hannah said. "What's it like being married? You know, in the bedroom?"

Nelma struck a pose of knowing maturity, sighed and waved her hand in the air, as if swatting a fly. "Oh it's nothing, really. It all happens fairly quickly."

"But is it romantic?"

"I try to think of something else when Edward has his needs. It's kind of funny, in a way. He pulls down his trousers, lifts up my skirts, and then usually goes out for a drink with the guys. It's really not too much of an inconvenience."

Hannah was disappointed. There were Jewish laws regarding happiness in marriage, and she thought there should be more to it than Nelma described. Why else would it be a topic in the Halakha if there wasn't something forbidden involved? She thought of the touching, the kissing, the pleasure that Ida had talked about when she had been courted in Detroit, before marrying Sam. But since she couldn't bring herself to ask Ida, she resigned herself to remain ignorant until she married. She had hoped to go away to college, become a more cosmopolitan woman of the world, but there were times when she had doubts that anything would work out according to plan.

Lila returned from the swing, tired of playing by herself, and begged for Hannah to tell her a story. Hannah liked to recount the wonder tales her mother used to tell her as a child, and tried to think of one she hadn't told before.

A long time ago, Hannah said, there lived a peddler who came to the Keweenaw to sell his wares, settle down and perhaps start a family. He was very poor and owned no horse or carriage. This was before they built the railroads, and he had to walk from Houghton all the way to Copper Harbor and back. It would take him months, and he became a familiar traveler, trusted and befriended by the townspeople he would meet. Over time, he acquired the reputation of a mystic and interpreter of dreams.

One day, a man approached the peddler and spoke of a dream he had of the legendary cave in Silver Mountain. The L'Anse Indians told of an enormous cave lined with silver that is protected by the great Indian spirit "Ketchi Menedoo." Now this man was a friend and good customer of the peddler, and did not seem a fool, so the peddler listened as the man described in his dream the location of the silver cave, and together they decided to have a look, deeming it a harmless venture at worst.

They hiked to the great upheaval of trap rock known as Silver Mountain, and as the man had described in his dream, there was a split boulder against a hill close to the Sturgeon River. The two men crawled through the small entrance that opened into a great cave glittering with pure silver. The peddler and his friend, dreaming of riches, started to fill their satchels with silver when the whole cave started to shake. Soon they were face to face with a giant shadowy beast, a manifestation of Ketchi Menedoo. When the beast asked why they had come, the friend betrayed the peddler, claiming he had been led there under false pretense, and laid all blame for their quest on the peddler. He then fled back the way he had come as the angry beast pounded the walls of the cave, shaking the whole mountain until it began to collapse in on itself.

Now this peddler was actually a very learned man. His father had been a great rabbi, and the peddler knew the five Books of Moses by heart, the Cabala and the secret name of names. Faced with this angry beast, the peddler had the presence of mind to fashion a golem out of wet clay on the floor of the cave. He then wrote the secret name of names on a scrap of paper and placed it into the golem's ear, transforming the clay into a living being. This magical being was bigger and stronger than the threatening beast and the peddler told the golem to ensure his safety as he fled. The entrance to the cave collapsed moments after he crawled back out. To this very day the golem battles the great spirit of the mountain, trying to protect the miners and keep the angry beast at bay. This is the source of the air blasts that sometimes shake the towns from the bowels of the earth.

Lila was playing with some acorns when Hannah finished the story and she wasn't certain if Lila had been listening. But Lila surprised her and asked what had become of the friend, the man who had betrayed the peddler.

"Ah, he was a false friend, wasn't he?" Hannah said. "A double-crosser. He made it home with a few pieces of silver still left in his satchel. But when the peddler told the townspeople what had happened, this man was shunned by all and died a sad and lonely man."

The two women then gathered the remains of the picnic into the basket and walked back to the station to catch the next train. Nelma wanted to make sure there was enough time to get home before dark. Hannah knew it would be too late to accompany them to Calumet and back, but found that Nelma was not too proud to accept the basket of food before Hannah got off at her stop in Hancock.

The house was already shrouded in shadows by the time she climbed the steps of the front porch. Inside, she could hear laughter, the hum of conversation, and a male voice she didn't recognize. Hannah ran up the stairs and checked herself in the bedroom mirror. She brushed back her windblown hair, washed her face, and adjusted her skirts. Back down the stairs, she found Father and the guest in the sitting room.

"Hannah," Father said. "I'd like you to meet Mr. Aaron Cohen, a journalist all the way from New York. He's been telling us how much things have changed back east."

Hannah curtseyed slightly and introduced herself. He was an attractive man, whose thin wiry body and spectacles gave him the look of an academic, a man of books and ideas. Hannah felt an immediate attraction, and was surprised at how much she wanted to impress this man. It was an unusual perspective; usually it was the men who were striving to impress her. "So tell me what stories have you been telling? I've never been east of Iron Mountain, though I will be traveling downstate to the university, perhaps next year." Hannah glanced at Father with this last comment, looking for any reaction that might confirm her plans to go to college there.

"So many automobiles now," Mr. Cohen said. "The streets are full of them, and the horses no longer startle when one drives by."

"We have a few here," Hannah said. "You can buy a Cadillac at Nikander's in Calumet. They're not very practical though, you'll not see any after the snow starts falling."

"I hope I'm here to see the famous copper country winter, though your father worries I might not have brought enough warm clothing."

"I'm sure we can lend you something to wear, some laced swampers and a mackinaw perhaps," Father said.

Hannah stole a glance at Aaron Cohen as Father spoke and caught him looking her way before he cast his eyes back to Father. He looked a little embarrassed and she wondered if Father had noticed. Mother came in to announce that dinner was ready and Father led the way into the dining room. Hannah tried not to look his way again during the meal, but it was difficult with just the four of them. Father opened a bottle of wine and they toasted to everyone's health, happiness, and a quick resolution to the strike. "*L'chaim*!"

Later, Mother excused herself to prepare a dessert in the kitchen, and Father excused himself to telephone a neighbor. Hannah recognized this as a planned moment, probably Mother's idea, but today she didn't mind. This man was different from the local boys they had invited over for dinner. His thin face wore a slight expression of sorrow when he wasn't talking, with brown eyes that seemed to open wider than anyone she had known, able to take in more of his surroundings in one look than others ever would.

"Which newspaper do you work for?" Hannah asked.

"The *Jewish Daily Forward*," he said. "You've heard of it?"

"No," Hannah said. "Is it an English paper?"

"It's a Yiddish newspaper. Very forward thinking, actually. Sympathetic to unions and socialism."

"My friend Nelma is quite the socialist. We had lunch today at the park. She thinks there will be a revolution, but I'm not so sure that there is cause for such change. What do you think, Mr. Cohen?"

"Depends what's in the cards. I hope the country will freely embrace change. But who knows what will happen. A lot rests on chance and circumstance."

"A bit of luck and a bit of skill, just like a pinochle game?"

"Perhaps," Aaron Cohen said, as Mother returned with a tray of small cakes. "Perhaps we can talk again sometime soon."

Aaron Cohen excused himself after dessert, with gracious compliments to Mother for the dinner, and a light touch to Hannah's hand as he left for the night. Hannah helped Mother clean up in the kitchen before retiring to her room, claiming to be exhausted. But upstairs she found herself reviewing the conversation in her head, looking for hidden meanings, and wondering when she would see him again.

SEPTEMBER 20, 1913

NELMA RETURNED FROM FREDA PARK to an empty house, with a note on the table in Edward's irregular scrawl stating that he and Frank had left to discuss union matters. They wouldn't be back for dinner. Sometimes they would go out to discuss legitimate grievances, provide an ear for those struggling to make ends meet during the strike. Other times she suspected they were out drinking at a tavern, putting down a beer or two, maybe even some whiskey. She found herself resentful. She attended the same rallies, heard the same speeches, and yet while they were sitting on their drunken bums, she would be patching old clothing, and cooking meager meals. Meals that she sometimes skipped so that her children wouldn't go hungry. She put away the leftovers from Hannah's picnic basket, which she imagined came from a well-stocked kitchen. She felt a touch of resentment at the thought of Hannah's more fortunate circumstances, but it didn't last long. She fingered her necklace, straightening the pendant on its chain.

She went to the neighbor's house to fetch her son Toivo, who sat in the lap of Ellen's daughter. The daughter still suffered terrible headaches from her injury at the strike parade and stayed home from school most days to help her mother. Ellen invited Nelma to stay for dinner, since they had a generous catch of lake trout, more than enough, she insisted. Nelma gratefully accepted and fetched some rye bread from her home. *Better than eating alone*, she thought. Ellen's husband pulled two more chairs up to the table, one for Lila, and one for Nelma. She fed Toivo from her lap.

"You shouldn't be treating him like a baby anymore," Ellen said. "He's over one year old. Big enough to feed himself."

"I know, I know," Nelma said. "But it's really no trouble tonight." She flaked the trout with her fork, creating a small pile of bite size pieces for her son, before feeding herself. It had been a day full of small charities from friends, though Nelma preferred to think of it as a pooling of resources, a sharing from each other according to one's ability, and to each other according to one's needs, as Frank had taught her.

Nelma left soon after dinner, with her son asleep in her arms, and her daughter bouncing alongside her, exhausted but giddy from the excitement of a day at Freda Park. The sky was obscured by clouds and a strong wind was rustling the leaves. All the night creatures were silent as if anticipating a storm. Her house was dark, except for the light she left on in the anteroom entrance. She hoped that Edward would be home soon.

By dawn, the night wind had increased to a howling autumn storm, raining down the colorful leaves, blowing a cold mist through the bedroom window. Edward slept beside her, smelling of whiskey and cigarettes. Nelma closed the window, wrapped herself in a cotton throw and started downstairs. Frank sat at the kitchen table, casting a long shadow from the one light he had turned on.

"Good morning," Frank said. "There was still coffee in the pot from yesterday, I put it back on the stove. Served myself. Would you like some?"

"You shouldn't have to do that," Nelma said. "Let me make a fresh pot. Any news from your meetings last night?"

"Nothing good, I'm afraid," Frank said.

The company had requested an injunction against all union gatherings, which the judge had obliged. Picket lines, protests and even parades had become illegal. Frank promised a strong legal battle. "It'll be just like the free speech battles we had out west. We'd always win."

"Shall we march anyway?"

"Not today. We need to win this battle in court."

Nelma refilled Frank's cup and sat down with coffee for herself. This was the first day they hadn't protested since Frank's arrival, and Nelma felt an absence of purpose, an uncomfortable stillness in her house. She tried to remember what she had done with her days before the strike began. Mornings she would take a Finnish pasty from the oven, slow cooked all night, packed with potatoes and fish, cabbage and garlic. She'd wrap it in thick paper and put it into Edward's lunch pail. He'd be off to work before the kids woke. She would stay in the kitchen all morning, feeding the children, preparing food for dinner. Afternoons she would shop, perhaps stopping at Ellen's house for coffee and a talk until Edward came home. The rhythm of her days had changed so much that the old routine no longer seemed satisfying and she felt a touch of disappointment at even a hint of its return.

Frank must have seen her concern, and he placed his hand atop hers. "It'll be okay. You'll see."

Nelma was surprised at his gesture; it seemed out of character somehow. Perhaps even affectionate, but she quickly dropped the thought as foolhardy. Yet he held her hand for a moment longer than she thought was appropriate, his warm dry palm weighing down on her smaller hand until she looked up and caught his eyes, which seemed full of unanswered questions today.

"I better get some breakfast ready, Edward and the children will be waking soon."

THE FOLLOWING DAY the weather had cleared. Nelma stayed home with the children, watching from her window and wishing they were out on parade. She found the other wives equally on edge with this change, and it was at her neighbor Ellen's house that she heard news of the inevitable arrests.

Though Frank had advised against protest, some of the local men would not respect his authority over the matter. They still formed a picket line. Ribs were broken and eyes were blackened. The sheriff used every opportunity to break the will of the strikers, but the men were prepared for this, and every day another group would set out to be arrested. After nine days, the injunction was lifted.

Nelma and her neighbors, Fran and Eunice, were gathered around Ellen's kitchen table, draped in fabric, creating a quilt. No one expected the strike to end before winter anymore, and those who heated with coal could not afford to keep their homes warm all day and night. Extra blankets would help moderate the bitter cold.

"Finally!" Nelma said. "We've won something. Tomorrow we should have the biggest parade ever."

"The companies are appealing; the courts could still reverse the ruling." Ellen said, who had become the skeptic of the group, always cautioning against optimism.

Nelma looked at her friend suspiciously, wondering if she was losing her nerve. "If they reverse the ruling, we'll fight 'em again, and again. Until we win in the end."

Nelma's statement was suspended in the air without support, where it faltered, and like a soap bubble, soon disappeared as if it was never there. Nelma was annoyed that no one else voiced any encouragement; she felt the women should be more hopeful in light of the ruling.

"We can't forget why we're doing this," Nelma said. "The companies know how dangerous those one-man drills are; they just don't care. Breaking up the two-man drill teams is just marking 'em for death."

"We haven't forgotten. It's just tiring, is all. We're eating just two meals a day, sometimes only one," Eunice sighed. "Why don't ya pass me that pink scrap over there? I think I can make something with it."

They were sewing a child's quilt, embroidered with elephant, monkey and parrot appliqués, sketched and cut by Ellen's daughter. As a group, they found a wealth of fabric in old worn out clothes, rags, and odd scraps left over from previous projects. Cloth that was too tattered for the quilt's patchwork exterior was torn and shredded to line the inside.

"How's your Mother doing, Nelma?" Ellen asked. "You know we don't hold it against her for boarding scabs."

"She's doing all right, I guess. I don't blame her much either. She needs the money. But don't think I could hold my tongue with those boarders, so I've been keeping pretty scarce over there."

"I heard her cow died?"

"No, that was the neighbor's cow. Ma's old girl will probably outlive us all."

Nelma's thoughts wandered to Frank, as they often did lately. She supposed that in an enlightened society it would be quite acceptable to have a male friend. And his overtures toward her were nothing more than a comrade in arms, a colleague in the fight for worker's rights. It pleased her to be seen as an equal by such a distinguished man.

The quilt was almost completed by late afternoon, with the fine needlework finished on the front-piece. Ellen thought they could finish and start another tomorrow, after the parade.

"You should have this quilt, Nelma," Ellen said. "Your daughter would love it, and my children are too old for its design."

"But what about Eunice?" Nelma said. "She has three children, and all boys, god forbid!"

"No, you take this one," Eunice said. "This is a girl's quilt. We have plenty of fabric for more."

Nelma was thrilled to have the quilt, it was a lovely piece, though she tried to temper her feelings so as not to appear too proud in front of her friends. She walked home along her familiar dirt street, lined with identical two-story houses, stopping in front of her own, pausing before going in. Her daughter tugged at her hand, wondering why they had stopped. Nelma wasn't quite sure herself. She had a pang of doubt and wondered what would happen if their struggle should fail. She saw a path of destitution, the mining jobs either gone or taken by scabs, her dream of breaking out of her mother's cash poor life shattered, her children's lot even worse. Her impatient daughter pulled free and ran inside their home. Nelma knew there was no turning back now. They must succeed.

THE NEXT MORNING'S parade lifted everyone's spirits. Her daughter, Lila, waved an American flag while her son happily babbled in the back of their wagon. All the girls' dresses were pressed, clean and white; all the boys marched proudly, little men wearing their Sunday jackets. Some were skipping down the street, as if on a holiday outing. The merchants watched from the doors of their stores, and even the guardsmen smiled at the return of the children. At the end of the march everyone sang songs, reluctant to go home.

Ellen invited Nelma over for coffee after lunch. "Let's talk before the others come to work on the quilt."

"Has anything happened?" Nelma asked.

"You notice the Kauppi's and the Tomlinson's weren't marching today? Their husbands went back to work. My Otto is talking of it as well."

"You mustn't let him! I'll send Edward to talk to him, or maybe Frank."

"Send Edward—Otto doesn't think much of Frank."

"But why? He's done nothing but help."

"It's all his socialist talk – Otto don't want no revolution, he just wants a union voice and a decent job. Besides, Frank's an outsider. When all this is over, he'll not be around; he'll have forgotten us."

Nelma had become so accustomed to Frank's presence in the house, she hadn't thought about his eventual leaving. She would miss him, but it would be nice to move the children back into their own room. Still, the strike was a long way from over. The company refused to negotiate, even as the national press took notice of their cause.

"He wouldn't forget us. A person can't spend so much of their heart and soul in a struggle such as this without it affecting him. Perhaps he'll meet a woman here. Perhaps he'll stay."

"Ah, Nelma. Sometimes I forget how young you are."

Nelma blushed in resentment. Ellen was ten years her senior, but had never made mention of it until now. She may be young, but she never thought of herself as naïve.

NINE DAYS LATER the Michigan Supreme Court reinstated the injunction, Edward went out to walk the picket line and didn't come back. The empty hours crawled towards the inevitable news. The anticipation of more trouble wore a hole in her heart. Nelma had seen the other men after their arrest. Often they were beaten, but let go the next day on bail. They couldn't afford to keep hundreds of men in the small county jail, and Nelma smiled at this, holding onto this piece of knowledge as a protective armor.

In the morning, Nelma left the children with the neighbor. She didn't want them seeing their father in such a state as the sheriff might have left him. The streetcar was filled with wives on a mission to pay bail and retrieve their men. Nelma recognized most of them, but wanted to share conversation with none of them. Eunice was sitting in the back with Mary, a sour tempered woman that neither liked. Saima was in front of them, a stout woman who perhaps liked her pasties and rhubarb pudding a little too much. Nelma chose a window seat up front, away from the others.

Edward had his problems, but she still loved him, and missed him when he was gone. She had known him years ago when he would walk with his father and Nelma's father to the streetcar station every morning. He had started working the mines when he was eleven years old as a drill boy running errands, then as a puffer boy, handling the small hand-powered air machines used to ventilate the drifts. He had worked his way up to stoping the mines and working the two-man drills with one of his boyhood friends. The one-man drill scared him though, enough so that he shared his fears with her in their bed at night. The day they put him on the one-man drill was the day he joined the union.

She took the through car to Hancock, then switched to the small yellow dinky, which took her over the swing bridge into Houghton, to the county jail. It was an imposing building, built of brick and sandstone. The lobby had tiled floors and high arched ceilings with chandeliers. She took her place in the line of women, clutching savings pulled out of kitchen mason jars, silenced by the immensity of their surroundings, feeling small and insignificant.

When it was her turn to speak to the clerk, she was determined to be strong, and spoke Edward's name loudly, hearing it echo off the walls, like a schoolyard bully mocking her words.

"I'm sorry, ma'am," the clerk said. "But Mr. Jokela isn't up for bail."

"Why not? How much is bail? I've seen how this works, I've been watching," Nelma said.

"His bail hasn't been set. He's been charged with assault and battery, resisting arrest, and violating the injunction. They've been harder on those who cause any trouble, who fight back."

"What trouble? You can't do this. Tell me how much the bail is and I'll pay it. I know my rights. You can't keep him here."

"I'm sorry, ma'am. You might want to think about getting a lawyer. You can see him tomorrow. Visiting hour is at three o'clock."

Nelma relinquished her place in line, stepped aside as the other women offered their support, then paid their husband's bail and went on through the ornate wooden door that she was barred from entering. Her neighbor Eunice pulled her away and tried to console her. Nelma's whole body shook with anger and fear and would not be calm. She tried to still herself, think of the children, think of pleasant things, but all she could see was Edward, locked away and probably hurt. As her eyes dampened, she rushed outside, not wanting the clerk to see her distress.

Nelma boarded the streetcar outside and got off at the next stop. She needed to think. Needed to walk. Without a clear idea of where she was headed, she hiked across the bridge into Hancock and outside of Hannah's family store. She stood in front of the big picture window, staring at a room full of clocks, each one measuring the time of Edward's imprisonment. She could think of nothing that she could do and was angry with herself for this impotence.

As Nelma turned to go, her friend ran out of the store and called her name.

"What's wrong?" Hannah asked. "You look upset. Did you come to see me?"

"Edward's been arrested."

"Oh, no! What did he do?"

"Nothing!" Nelma shouted. "He's done nothing wrong, and they wouldn't let me see him."

"I'm so sorry," Hannah said. She placed her hand on Nelma's arm. "What can I do to help?"

"I don't know. I need to talk to Frank. I'll let you know."

Nelma returned home and obsessed with cleaning the house. She scrubbed the floors, washed the windows, swept the entrance and shook out the bed sheets. Her daughter played in the yard and her son followed her around the house, mesmerized by all the activity. She polished the chrome on the kitchen stove, baked biscuits and bread, then pulled some whitefish from the icebox and prepared a small pan of kalakukko, the fish pie that Edward favored. Frank stopped by to collect more of his clothing; he would be staying at the hotel again tonight. He thought it improper to remain in her house with Edward gone.

"You all right?" Frank asked, concern etched in his face.

"It's just another small battle, another trial. Finns have a word for dealing with these times, it's called *sisu*. Have you heard of it?"

"What does it mean?"

"It means biting off more than you can chew – and then chewing it."

Frank smiled and placed his hand on Nelma's shoulder. "The union is sending a lawyer. He'll be here in two days. We'll get Edward out of this."

Frank's touch sent a warm spell of relief down Nelma's spine. It seemed that every day he found some excuse to touch her hand, her arm, her shoulder. His attentions pleased her to no end, and she found herself looking forward to them, wondering when he would touch her again. She almost asked him to stay, to spend the night, that she wouldn't care what people might say. They were friends, good friends, and nothing more.

SEPTEMBER 22, 1913

RUSSELL WOKE EARLY SUNDAY morning as the rest of the boarders heeded the call to church. While they put on their best clothing, often the only clothing not soiled by mine-work, Russell slipped into his boots, denims, and flannels. Oscar had invited him hunting, but they would have to be discrete, miners were not allowed firearms during the strike. He told Mrs. Huhta that he'd be helping a friend with farm-work today, and she cooked him a big breakfast, pancakes and hash browns, and sent him off with her blessing.

The Keweenaw was as well endowed with churches as it was with saloons. Every denomination, and within them, every ethnic group requested a building site for their own church, which the companies provided. On Quincy Hill alone, there were Catholic, Episcopal, Congregational, Presbyterian, Baptist and Lutheran churches. And this was just in Hancock. Russell had nothing against the religious, and lacking something to do, he would bide his time at the Norwegian-Danish Methodist Episcopal Church, two blocks from his boarding house. But the promise of fresh game was too compelling. If there was a time to snare a deer, Oscar reasoned, there could be no better time to go unnoticed then when the rest of the population was sequestered away in prayer.

Oscar's house was off the main line in Paavola, sheltered from the northern winds by a surviving stand of old-growth pine. He shared the house with his father and two younger brothers. His mother had died in the childbirth of a girl, the daughter she had always wanted. And though the girl survived, her father felt she needed a woman's influence in her upbringing, so she was sent away to an aunt in Detroit. Oscar hadn't seen her since she was a baby.

The two brothers were choirboys, and though they begged to go with Oscar, their father was firm on where they would be spending their Sunday.

The house had a similar layout to Russell's boarding house, with a kitchen, sitting room and front hall downstairs, and three bedrooms on the second floor. A large sauna was tucked into the back of the yard, next to the woodpile. This was definitely a man's home, with the remains of a woman's influence evident only in the floral print curtains hanging over the windows. The wood floor was covered in so much dirt that at first Russell had mistakenly thought there was no floor at all. The upstairs looked better kept, and Russell followed Oscar's lead of kicking the mud off his boots on the bottom step before proceeding up the stairs.

The hunting rifles were stashed between the walls of the sitting room and the kitchen, hidden from mining company officials, who served as employer, landlord, and unofficial lawmen. The firearms were retrieved by opening a trapdoor in the upstairs bedroom closet and hoisting them up with a piece of wire that kept them dangling out of reach. The guns were well oiled and maintained, though of a make Russell had never seen before. Each had an elaborately detailed stock, with a brass plate behind the trigger written in something he presumed was Finnish.

They would be hiking to a tree blind the family maintained halfway to Torch Lake, and Oscar's Father would help carry out any game they garnered by the afternoon. Oscar packed his satchel with a canteen of water, a flask of whiskey, and a log of summer sausage the size of his forearm. He handed a second flask to Russell. They finished the pot of coffee on the stove. Russell thought it tasted rather rank and wondered how long it had been there. Then they set off, out the back door under the stairs, past the sauna, and into the woods. The ground was littered with dead leaves, some brown, and some red, gold or burnt orange. The leaves made a rustling sound and Russell worried they would be scaring off game with their footfalls. Then he worried how they might explain themselves, if someone were to happen upon them in the woods.

About twenty minutes into their hike, Oscar pulled out a small glass vial, poured a gelatin-like substance into his palm, and spread it liberally over his face, neck and hands. He handed the vial to Russell, whose nose stung and whose hand involuntarily repelled the repugnant smell away from his face.

"What is this stuff?" Russell asked. "Decomposed skunk?"

"My uncle makes it, secret family recipe. It's the best scent block on the planet."

Russell dipped his forefinger and spread the gel on his neck. Thankfully, the odor didn't seem to persist long out of the bottle. "Are we close?"

"About another half hour."

The maple and oak turned to white pine and spruce, muffling their steps on a cushioned bed of pine needles. They rounded an abandoned pile of mine tailings, skirted an open mine shaft that Oscar said had been abandoned close to twenty years. Finally they reached the blind. It was a fine-looking platform, fifteen feet off the ground in a multi-stemmed ash tree on the side of a hill overlooking Torch Lake. They climbed up and through the center of the platform and rested their rifles on the floor. There was room enough for three or four full-grown men, and a series of rusted hooks driven into the tree served as a convenient spot to hang their satchels.

At each end of the four-sided platform, a long slot cut through the wood for sighting and shooting any hapless deer passing through. The blind was situated not too far from an obvious deer run, and Oscar promised that their only concern would not be sighting a deer, but selecting which one. Russell chose to sit on the east side, overlooking the lake, reasoning it was a pleasing view to rest his eyes on for the next several hours. According to Oscar, Torch Lake had been named by the French-Canadian trappers that first shared this region with the Chippewa. They would camp on the far side of the lake observing the eerie nighttime movement of the Chippewa, as they lit up the darkness with torches and paced through the village situated on the distant shore.

Russell let his mind wander, thought of the beer drinking ballads the men sang out west, examining the length of his fingernails, and trying in vain to pass some gas. Back in Chicago, Maria would mistake his silent moments as indication of deep thinking on the complexities of the world.

She would always be disappointed when he confessed there was nothing at all in his head, and she insisted that he shouldn't hide such meditations from her simply because she was a woman. Russell had an eye on Maria ever since they were kids, when they had attended grade school in Chicago. Maria lived with her family in a flat above her father's store, which had electricity and steam heat. Russell lived one block away, in a tenement that was gaslit and the only heat came from the kitchen stove.

As teenagers, they would meet in the library, where Russell lingered until his parents came home from the factory and fired up the stove. Maria used her sojourns in the library to avoid working in her father's store. Under the table they would hold hands, and before walking her home he would steal a kiss, out of sight from her father's disapproving eyes. Her father wanted her to marry up, and had tried to match her with the livery owner's son. That family owned a large tenement and was rumored to have much money hidden away. Maria had told the boy she could never marry someone with boots that smelled like horse manure.

Russell imagined bringing Maria up north, away from the city, and away from her father. Here they could raise a family and live in a clean house with no cockroaches or bedbugs. Every fall he would go hunting with Oscar and bring back enough venison to feed the family all winter. This was where he wanted to stay. This was home.

A movement in the brush caught Russell's attentions, and he readied his trigger finger, waiting for whatever it was to show itself. A jackrabbit ran out from the underbrush, already wearing its winter white, and darted into the woods. Disappointed, Russell took a swig from his flask. Again, something crashed through low bushes. This time it was a large buck, an eight-pointer, accompanied by two does. Russell sucked in his breath, and then slowly exhaled with cautious stuttered bursts of air. Oscar was aiming for the buck when Russell squeezed the trigger twice, missing both times.

Oscar's shot skipped the heart but passed through the shoulder. The buck fell on his front legs looking confused; the does vanished down the path. The creature was still alive when they climbed down from their blind, looking at them with fear in its eyes. Russell wondered what sort of thoughts pass through a deer's simple brain when faced with death. Did it understand what had happened, or was it just agonizing over the pain. Did it accept this as the natural course of things, or did it still harbor visions of escape? Oscar shot him again, this time through the head.

Russell was unsure of what to do next. He hadn't mentioned it to Oscar, but he had never dressed an animal before. Looking at the dead buck's open eyes, he wasn't certain how to cut it or if he even wanted to try.

Oscar wasted no time discussing the matter. With two swift slices, he cut away the deer's testicles and tossed them into the woods. "Fouls the meat, you know," he said. "Got to take care of that right away."

Oscar gave Russell a large knife and showed him how to gut and clean the carcass. "Be careful not to cut too deep," he said, running one hand inside the hide as he opened up the deer. "Pull out them innards – we'll leave them for the bear."

By the time they had finished, Russell had lost his appetite and finished his flask. He whistled and tried to sound appreciative. "More than enough meat to go around," he said.

"We'll hogtie its legs to a large limb and carry it back when my father comes," Oscar said. "My uncle's a butcher, he'll take care of the rest for us."

"Shame we need to hunt on the sly. It's not like we're the ones causing trouble around here," Russell said.

"Company rule is the law—though I'd sure like to take a few shots at those picketer's boots, see how fast they run home."

"They're the kind of people who'll never be happy. They whine about a job that's too hard for them."

"Well, they can picket all they want, but they'll just get replaced, and they'll be out on the street. It's a lost cause, you know. Companies need to make money, and I'm here to earn my share."

"Yeah," Russell said. "I don't need no union to speak for me, I can speak for myself—my mouth is big enough."

By the time Oscar's father arrived, they had the buck tied up and both flasks drained. Oscar's father seemed to keep his opinions to himself, parting with just a few congratulatory words, as if speech were a rare resource in need of conservation. The songbirds had long since flown south, leaving the woods in a somber silence broken only by the progress of the men through the forest. Oscar and his father took the lead, leaving Russell to hold the back end of the pole, which he balanced on his shoulders and held in place with his hands. After the first few minutes, Russell felt a cutting pain in his collarbone from carrying the animal's dead weight. The pain accompanied him throughout the hike, like an unwelcome guest, a burden that dulled but never went unnoticed.

They crossed the same path used on the way in, passing the abandoned mine shaft and once again entering the stand of maple and oak. Their walk must have varied somewhat though, since Russell didn't recall seeing a strange carving of bleached wood on their way in. The closer they approached, Russell realized it was a massive moose antler, the rest of the skeletal remains lay half immersed in decaying leaves.

"That moose been picked clean," Oscar's Father said. "I remember spotting it a month ago when it was first fallen."

"A wolf got it, you think?" Oscar said.

"Ya, you betcha," Oscar's father replied.

After a few minutes had put the bones behind them, the father started a ramble, half to himself, about the strikers messing with the natural order of things. "They be putting their faith in a bunch of no good agitating atheist socialists, that just want to stir things up and leave nothing but bitter hate behind."

"What happened?" Oscar asked.

"Bunch of no good lay-a-bouts threw a bomb in the Ahmeek steam hoist yesterday. Nearly blew off someone's arm."

Russell almost tripped over an exposed root. A bomb! What kind of mess had he got himself into? Though he had never been much of a praying man, he put together a prayerful plea right there, in the middle of the woods, thinking it just might take a higher intervention to straighten out this place.

When they reached the woods behind Oscar's house, Russell heard voices and wondered aloud if they should be more cautious in their approach. His friend assured him they had nothing to fear, the neighbors would be supportive and the boys would warn them if any mining deputies were about. Russell offered to run ahead and check, and let the weight of the animal fall off his shoulder as they lowered it to the ground. He had a sensation of weightlessness, as if he shouldn't stand up too quickly, lest he float up in the air. He had forgotten how much whiskey they drank, forgotten that perhaps his reflexes were not what they should have been when a heavy hand clamped down on his shoulder from behind. He winced in pain, the unknown man had struck the same spot that had carried the buck, then he spun around, prepared for a fight.

"Uncle Elias!" Oscar said, "This is my friend Russell. Did ya bring your carriage? Do ya think this beast will fit in it?"

"We'll need to cut off that rack first – it ain't no use to me."

It was approaching dusk by the time the uncle had left with the carcass. Russell was still covered in blood and wondered where he would clean himself up. The alcohol had left a ferocious hunger in its place, and he asked Oscar if there was any sausage left in his satchel.

"You can wash yer hands off with that hand pump next to the house. Help yourself to the food—then join us in the sauna. Father has it fired up and ready."

Russell eyed the windowless A-frame building. "I think I'd rather wash at a bathhouse, I'm not sure about this…"

"Ha. You're not sure 'cause you haven't tried it. It'll fix up that shoulder of yours, and no bathhouse will take you like this—ya look like a butcher."

Russell conceded and stripped his clothes off to soak in the tin tub filled with water. The sauna was dark and hot inside. Oscar brought in a bucket of water and poured it over the rocks. The steam enveloped Oscar's body, wrapping him as if with a wet blanket. Oscar's father passed around another flask.

In the morning, he vaguely recalled having stumbled out of the burnt air and climbing the steps to Oscar's guestroom upstairs. His clothes were now hanging at the foot of the bed, clean, folded and dry. He couldn't imagine that anyone in Oscar's family had washed them, yet what else would explain them there? Coffee was brewing downstairs; the aroma probably had woken him. He was surprised at how good he felt, no soreness in his shoulder, and no aching in his head. He might have to give Oscar's sauna a try again, especially after a night of drinking. Russell dressed and hurried down the stairs. Then remembering the state of the floor, he went back for his boots, and joined the rest of Oscar's family in the kitchen.

"G'morning," Oscar said, handing him a tin of coffee.

The boys were dressed for work as well, and their Father was back to his usual obtuse self, smoking a pipe and not wasting words. Today's fresh coffee tasted better than yesterday's stale brew, which they had finished before leaving for the hunt. There was no time to return to the boarding house before the shift started, and Russell was pleased to see an extra lunch pail waiting for him on the kitchen counter. He wondered about its contents and later found a pasty, just as well made as Mrs. Huhta's, prepared by the widow next door in exchange for help with her chores. Russell tucked in his shirt and assumed she also washed clothes.

The picketers had already been arrested when Russell arrived at the mine location, their shouts of protest faded as they were led away. Russell smiled with satisfaction. He left his flannels on his hook in the dry house and took his place on the man-car. They were tramming out a new area of the level today, and Russell complained to the mine captain about large spaces of the overhanging wall that were untimbered and unsupported.

"Don't you be telling me how to do my job," the mine captain yelled. "Timbering costs more money than trammers, so get your ass back to work and let me worry about engineering."

"Bastard," Russell mumbled under his breath, understanding and almost sympathizing with the strikers' cause. He had to dodge several rock falls throughout the day, and by the time his shift was over, his shoulder was bared and bloody from pushing the tramcar. He favored his back for the initial shove down the tracks, and the sense of wellness that had greeted the day was forgotten in a symphony of pain over the whole of his body. He thought of the buck they had taken the day before, about the fear and pain in its eyes, and felt himself no better than an animal, a beast of burden.

SEPTEMBER 30, 1913

THE MORNING SUN REMAINED lost in the misty horizon of an otherwise cloudless autumn sky. Just one more thing displaced during the strike, Hannah thought. The leaves had all started to turn after the first hard frost, as if God had turned a switch and illuminated the hillsides with brilliant red, orange, and gold. She thought it a fitting prelude to the time known as the "Days of Awe," when on Rosh ha-Shanah the righteous would be inscribed in the Book of Life, and all others had ten more days to repent. Hannah stood on the rocky beach in front of the synagogue, skipping stones on the water, and thought her chances of redemption were pretty slim. Her faith had a spotty record, no better than her erratic skill at skipping stones, but no worse than her Aunt Ruth, the source of her card-playing skills.

Several years back, her aunt had paid an extended visit from somewhere uptown of Detroit. From what Hannah was able to pick up from hushed conversations behind closed doors, her aunt was avoiding some kind of legal trouble. Probably related to gambling. Anyone can win a wager in poker, Ruth had told her, but it takes talent to win at pinochle. Ruth taught her everything she knew, from marked cards and false shuffles, to how to rifle the stack such that each of the four aces ends up in your own hand. She taught Hannah not to cheat, but to catch a cheat. An honest win will get you more respect, she had said. Hannah would sit and watch her aunt play at Sam's games, stuffing winnings into her boots or inside her brassiere. She died of influenza the next winter.

During today's service, the rabbi would once again tell the story of the binding of Isaac, the rescued boy, the ram in the thicket. Hannah wondered why her aunt could not have been spared as well. In the east, the sun finally broke free from the fog and cast away the shadows from the beach. Hannah threw one more stone, a flat piece of shale the size of her hand, and watched it skip three times across the water. She smiled at her success, then hurried back up to the road, and continued her walk to the baker, to purchase challah for tonight's dinner.

Holman's bakery was the only shop open this early, and the sweet aroma of bread and rolls pulled her in. She could probably find this place with her eyes closed. The glass display case inside was lined with sweet rolls, rye breads, and desserts. Hannah thought she might purchase a pie for tomorrow as well, an apple pie if he had one. After a few minutes, when Mr. Holman didn't emerge from the back, Hannah shook the bells on the door.

A small young boy peeked through the back door and called to his father, "Hannah's here for her special bread." Mr. Holman came through the door a moment later, carrying two round loafs.

"So beautiful! A work of art," Hannah said, knowing Mr. Holman took great pride in his work, especially the braided loaves of bread he created for the holiday. Years ago, Hannah's mother was short on time and had gone to the Finnish baker with a recipe for challah, baked with raisins to celebrate the Jewish New Year. Since there were no raisins available, Mr. Holman had substituted dried cranberries instead. The bread had become a success, and soon all the Jewish families in Hancock put in their orders for Mr. Holman's famous challah. No one baked their own anymore.

Hannah left with the two warm loaves and an apple pie teasing her appetite, moving her thoughts toward less somber subjects, and she wondered whether Aaron Cohen would be invited for dinner. He had become a regular guest at the Sabbath dinner table, and Hannah looked forward to his irreverent discussions on religion and politics. He was never condescending, like her brother, nor dim witted like some of the local boys Father often invited in vain hope of finding a favorable prospect for marriage. She enjoyed his company, but worried that he liked to push the limits of what Father would accept as subjects for debate. Whenever he treaded too close to socialist lauding, she would gently kick him under the table, and try to change the subject.

"Hannah," Mother called from the kitchen. "Is that you? Can you fetch some potatoes from the root cellar?"

Hannah put the loaves on the table and gave Mother a kiss. "*Shanah tovah*, a good year to you."

"Oy, you're always rushing things. The New Year is not until sundown. Now go to the cellar, we have a lot of cooking to do today."

Hannah lit a lamp from the kitchen stove, walked through the pantry, and opened the cellar door. There were no electric lights down the stairs, and the lamp cast a cheerful glow over the lake rock on the cellar walls. The potatoes were in a basket on the far wall, past the stored carrots, turnips and onions. The cellar held the family's wealth, more so than all their possessions upstairs, and more so than the dwindling earnings from the store or even her gambling. The dank starchy smell blanketed her skin, a harvest of suspended growth waiting for a feast. She wondered how much food was left in her friend Nelma's pantry. Tonight she would pray for the welfare of the strikers and wish she could do more.

FATHER CLOSED THE store in early afternoon, and arrived with gifts for the family. Something new to wear for the service tonight. A yellow cotton hat for Hannah, a new white blouse for Mother, and a necktie for himself. There was a subdued excitement in the air, both festive and serious. They walked down the hill towards the synagogue, past the houses of their neighbors and friends, for whom today was just another weekday.

The synagogue was still new, still a novelty to the congregation, barely one year old and built on land deeded from the Quincy Mining Company. The radiant copper dome was wrested from the very earth beneath them, from the mines that now bore the wrath of so many striking men. Hannah touched the mezzuzah before passing through the door and climbing the stairway to the women's section. Ida was already seated near the far wall, with her son playing at her feet. Hannah liked to sit in the very front of the balcony, where she could gaze at the nine stained glass windows, which glowed from the soft light of the setting sun. Today she rested her eyes on the dove bearing the olive branch of peace and the hands brought together in blessing. They were anonymous hands, anyone's hands. Yet Hannah liked to imagine they were her grandmother's hands.

Her grandparents were buried on the high hilltop across the portage and she wondered if they prayed for her now. They would have been proud to sit in this synagogue, and would have told stories of their childhood in Berlin. Much of the money for the building had been willed from their savings, a generous gift from the family store that grandfather had built up from his days as a peddler. They would have told of the superstitious customs they left behind: adding two candlesticks to their five piece candelabra to create a lucky number, or waving a kapporeh rooster over their head on the Day of Atonement, before slaughtering it and donating the meat to the poor.

The deep, sharp blast of the shofar echoed through the synagogue. It was the Jacobson boy holding the ram's horn, blaring out a series of short and long notes that comforted her with their tradition. The repetition of the sound, the repetition of the holiday, and the repetition of liturgy reminded her of the holidays as a child, when the congregation had gathered in the basement of the family store. The same basement where the weekend pinochle games now reigned. Due to hardship and falling attendance, the games had been reduced from weekly to monthly, and Hannah worried they might soon become just another memory.

Later in the evening, Hannah realized that she hadn't seen Aaron in the men's section, but supposed he must have been in the back, out of sight from her place on the balcony.

THE NEXT DAY, the Indian summer weather continued to prevail. Hannah lingered outside the synagogue after everyone else had gone in. She loved to look at the menagerie of colors on the hills across the portage, and was a little reluctant to spend the day inside in prayer.

"Hannah," Aaron called to her from behind. "Better hurry, one might think you're avoiding something."

"Don't be so sure you can read my thoughts, Aaron Cohen," Hannah said, consciously suppressing her excitement and maintaining what she hoped was a calm demeanor. "I'm simply admiring the view. Something you probably don't see in the big city."

"There are a lot of things here I don't see in the big city." Aaron winked and held the door for her.

The shofar was already sounding, and Hannah hurried up the stairs, finding a spot in the back, pressed between the old women bent over in prayer.

Hannah saw Aaron again in the afternoon, as the congregation gathered on the same rocky beach that she had skipped stones from the day before. He was standing with his back to her, close enough for her to touch, throwing his crumbs, together with his sins, into the water. Hannah emptied the crumbs she had bundled in her kerchief and said the ritual prayers, but her thoughts belonged to Aaron, and again she hoped he would be coming to dinner tonight.

She wasn't disappointed. Aaron arrived soon after the last service, bearing an odd shaped package, which he opened to reveal a large pineapple.

"I'm guessing this will serve as a new fruit in this climate – probably not too common here, eh?" Aaron said. "May the lord look kindly upon this house and our funny fruit."

"Tell me something, Aaron. How can you know so much of the liturgy and traditions, and yet treat them to such ridicule? Aren't you a little afraid?"

"Are you afraid, Hannah? I thought you appreciated my humor."

"I'm only afraid of this fruit—do you have any idea how to cut it?"

"Not a clue. Perhaps your Mother could help."

With Mother's guidance, Hannah skinned, cored and sliced the pineapple. Once, she almost sliced the tip of her finger, and several times she questioned the intentions of someone who would bring such a difficult fruit. Finally, she placed the uneven rings on the table next to the apples and honey. The whole house was warmed with the kitchen smells of roast chicken, garlic broth, coffee, and cocoa for the children. In addition to their own extended family and Aaron, Father had invited the Jacobson's, whose youngest son was the same age as Daniel, and the two children played in their own secret world.

After dinner and wine, Hannah left the noisy banter in the dining room for the quieter seclusion of the south porch swing. Father seemed to grant Aaron a certain respect despite, or perhaps because of his politics, and she wondered how well she judged Father's opinions. The night sky was overcast tonight, and Hannah was disappointed there were no stars out. She turned to go inside and was surprised to see Aaron standing in the hall, looking uncertain about opening the door.

"You were absent from last night's service, weren't you?" Hannah asked, curious where he might have been.

"I had work to do. There was an important meeting at the Tyomies Building; the strikers were discussing the latest turn of events in the courts. The injunction against the protests has been lifted."

"Work on Rosh ha-Shanah? I think you're more of a socialist than a Jew, I think you're just a great pretender."

"I think you pretend to disagree with my choices," Aaron said.

"I think you care more for a good story than you do for a good cause."

"I think you pay more attention to the good cause because of the good story."

Hannah was working on a retort, enjoying the verbal sparring, when Aaron leaned over and kissed her, putting an end to their talk. It wasn't a family kiss on the cheek, and it wasn't a gentlemanly kiss on the hand, but it was a lengthy kiss on her lips. And on the eve of the Jewish New Year, when her thoughts should be focused on finding forgiveness for the sins of her past, she could only think of the pleasure she derived from Aaron's affection.

Aaron became a regular visitor to the store, stopping by most days to talk and bring news of the strike. Hannah wondered if Father could see through the reason for his visits, or if he thought Aaron was simply becoming a good family friend. Either Father didn't notice the way she straightened her posture and polished her manners whenever Aaron came to visit, or he thought it best left unmentioned. Whichever the reason, Hannah was grateful.

"Even the words of the bible have socialist leanings, Hannah," Aaron said during one of his visits. "In Leviticus, He speaks of the Jubilee year, every fifty years, when all land and property is redistributed, a great leveler of wealth."

"You're just bending the words to suit your own politics."

"You should study Leviticus before being so quick to critique."

"What if a business should bankrupt itself at the expense of the demands of the worker. How does anyone benefit from that?"

"In the long run, everyone would benefit."

"How can you be so sure?"

"And how can you be so serious?"

Aaron took her hand and led her away from the picture window, away from the public view, to the private cul-de-sac behind the grandfather clocks and pressed his body against hers as they kissed. Hannah pressed her hands against the wall behind her, and tried to suppress desires she knew were inappropriate. There was a certain opportunity in Aaron, and yet she wasn't certain where it was leading, what it would mean if he fell in love with a girl so far from his home. Would he consider staying, or perhaps inviting her back to New York? Surely they would have a respected university there. Hannah straightened her rumpled blouse and returned to work, unable to banish foolish daydreams from her head.

The afternoon business lagged and Hannah begged to leave the store early. She needed to talk to Nelma, though she told Mother she would be out for a walk. It was not exactly a lie, and perhaps even a small mitzvah, a kindness to keep Mother from worry. The unspoken divide between the strikers and everyone else seemed to weigh on every relation and every conversation, even in matters of little consequence.

Hannah stepped off the streetcar in Calumet and found Nelma returning home with a satchel of groceries. She looked tired and thin, but smiled at Hannah as she approached.

"Can I help carry something?" Hannah asked.

"It's not much," Nelma said. "Just some bread and chicory to stretch out the coffee. Can you stay for dinner?"

"Not tonight," Hannah said quickly, noting the relief on her friend's face. "Our whole family always eats together during the holidays."

"Sorry. I'd forgotten. A cup of coffee then?"

Hannah agreed and held the door while Nelma went inside to put away her scant purchase. It felt trite now, coming to discuss matters of the heart when her friend was struggling with such serious matters as putting food on the table and fighting to win concessions from an uncaring employer.

"How is Edward?" Hannah asked, remembering his arrest and hoping that it had been resolved by now.

"We've got a lawyer now, thanks to the union. He thinks we should have Edward out any day. It's just a game between the sheriff and the union. Edward's stuck in the middle of it. But he'll be home soon."

Hannah noted a forced optimism in her friend's voice, a change in demeanor, as if she was acting. She wondered if it was a mistake to come. They seemed to have the house to themselves, and Hannah was relieved that Frank wasn't there. He had made her feel so uncomfortable during her last visit.

"I have something to tell you," Hannah said. "I have a gentleman suitor. We've been, well, we have feelings for each other."

Nelma smiled and raised her eyebrows. "What sort of feelings, Hannah? Are you in love?"

"Maybe," Hannah said. "I'm not sure. It's complicated. He's a reporter from New York. He's a socialist. You'd like him."

"So he's just visiting?"

"Yes. That's the problem. I'm not sure what I should do. I'm not sure what my parents would think."

"Don't worry what your parents think. What *you* want is what matters."

"I just want to be with him whenever possible. He holds me and kisses me, and though I know it's wrong, sometimes I wish I knew him even more intimately."

"It's not wrong, but it's not worth the trouble. If you get pregnant, you'll never go to the university, never have those adventures you dream about."

"You're right, it's just a fantasy. I would never—"

"But if you do, make yourself a nice strong cup of black cohosh tea, the morning after. Either that or pennyroyal. But remember, the morning after. Time is important."

Hannah left her friend's house even more confused than she had arrived. The discussion had left her with little desire to expand the boundaries of her relationship with Aaron, and yet she couldn't stop thinking about him.

ON THE EVE OF Yom Kippur, the Day of Atonement, Mother called Hannah into her room, reached under the bed, and retrieved Hannah's gambling winnings from an old biscuit tin. It caught her off-guard; she hadn't any hint that Mother knew.

"Why, Hannah? In our family store! Why?"

"I'm sorry," Hannah said, and she was sorry, not for the gambling, but for the look in Mother's eyes.

"What does this do for your reputation? The reputation of our store? As if we need more trouble."

"But there hasn't been a game in weeks, and—"

"Stop. You'll donate this money to charity. And you'll go nowhere without permission and escort until further notice. Now come help me with dinner."

Mother unpacked the tablecloth reserved for the last meal before the fast, and Hannah helped dress the table with candles and food. The kitchen filled with the smells of roast duck and squash, though Hannah had lost her appetite. They would eat a light meal before sundown, and not eat again for twenty-four hours. Tomorrow would be difficult, especially in the morning without a cup of coffee or even water to start the day.

Dinner was quiet, without the usual banter, and it seemed that everyone was casting blame on her. Sam refrained from his usual dismissive comments about Aaron and his politics; Father never looked her in the eye. She wondered how Mother had found out and regretted not finding a better spot for the money. All that cash, she had earned it, though Mother would never understand. That was the one thing she owned in her life, and now it was taken away.

They finished their food just as the sun dropped to the horizon, and dressed for the walk to the synagogue. The winds outside blew a cold blast of air across the Keweenaw, a reminder of the coming winter's harsh dominance. Hannah pulled her white shawl across her chest and kept a few steps behind the others. Was it so wrong, what she had done? It was just a game. Hannah felt defiant as much as she felt regret. She fell into step with Ida as they entered the front hall of the synagogue.

Hannah again took her favored place at the front of the balcony, overlooking the eternal light burning behind the bimah, where the rabbi would speak. Behind him the curtain over the ark would soon open to reveal the scrolls of the Torah, which would be draped in holiday finery. She studied the stained-glass windows, especially the last one, which formed a triangle. It represented some esoteric triad, though she couldn't remember what. It reminded her of three-handed pinochle.

The rabbi began with the chanting of the Kol Nidrei passage, forgiving those promises that may be made and left unfulfilled in the coming year. A recognition of the failure of the best of intentions. Hannah smiled, put her hands to her face and sighed. Aaron was against the south wall moving the whole of his body in prayer, looking more serious than she had seen him in weeks. She tried to will him to look up at her, but he remained absorbed in his own prayers.

Hannah went to bed early after the evening services; she found it easiest to sleep through as much of the fast as possible. In the morning, she remained in bed, listened to the low murmur of her parents downstairs, and noted the absence of coffee aroma that usually greeted her awakening. Knowing she couldn't have even a drop of water made her crave it all the more, and she lay in bed until Mother rapped on the door urging her to dress and ready for the morning service.

It was a long day with an empty stomach, and Hannah soon tired of the liturgy. Her patience wore thin. She imagined spending the fast meditating on a hill overlooking the portage, or perhaps resting in Aaron's arms. She remembered her childhood intolerance of the worn tired look of her parents and older brother who fasted while she ate a modest meal, when she was too young for the custom.

Her nephew, Daniel, played at their feet, and Hannah felt a pang of melancholy for his innocence. He caught her eye and started playing with her skirts, hiding and kicking and giggling until Mother gave them both a disapproving look. Ida pulled her son into her lap, winked at Hannah and whispered in the boy's ear to quiet him. Hannah heaved a sigh and looked at the rest of the women cramped into the front row of the balcony. Rocking and nodding to the internal beat of their prayers, she wondered what secrets they harbored, what regrets they needed forgiven. Elizabeth Blumson had captured the aisle seat and took advantage of the extra room to stretch her legs out fully. She had been widowed years ago while still in her twenties and there had been rumors of many lovers on the side, though it was difficult to believe such an old woman could garner the favor of so many men.

Hannah brushed her lips with the tips off her fingers and thought of Aaron's kiss. It excited her that such a man held an interest in her, and she wondered again where it might lead. Perhaps they would marry and she would attend a university on the east coast, buy fashionable clothes and visit the theater on weekends. Hah. Where did she get such thoughts? Not from Aaron, who never mentioned their future. Hannah laughed at her folly and tried to determine the time from the angle of the sunlight through the windows. The rabbi was reciting the story of Jonah and the sinful people of Nineveh. Hannah wondered what they had done to draw such threats of retribution. The rabbi never mentioned the specifics.

Finally the shofar marked the end of the holiday, just as Hannah was becoming accustomed to her hunger, her atrophied stomach, and her parched mouth. The thought of food seemed almost alien, a sacrilege to her body which felt weightless and pure. She turned to join the weak shuffling crowd as they descended the stairs. She hugged Mother before joining the rest of the family outside.

Aaron was in the front yard, looking strong and rested. She wondered if he had fully observed the fast. He caught her look and smiled, before weaving himself away in the crowd. She regretted he would not be breaking the fast with her family. She wondered how much longer he would remain in the Keweenaw, and how much longer the strike would last. It seemed to go on and on until, like the fast, it became a normal part of their days, a constant rhythm in their lives.

OCTOBER II, 1913

ERIK TOMLINSON'S STREETCAR stationhouse was built one block from the Keweenaw Central Railroad station, in open defiance of the mining company's former dominance on local transportation. The mining company owned the railway, but the Houghton County Traction Company owned the streetcars, the electric grid, and even the Electric Park Resort located halfway between Hancock and Calumet. Erik had nothing against the mining companies or the railroad, and had even labored in the Quincy Mine years ago. But it hadn't worked out.

He was hired under the contract system, paid to cut so much rock within a period of time, purchasing supplies from the mining company and claiming his paycheck on settlement day. One month, he and Nelma's Father had worked some exceptionally hard rock, and the drift they were required to cut was several fathoms short of their target. Erik ended up owing the company five dollars, which he paid with potatoes grown in his backyard.

Erik decided to put an end to his days underground and took a contract with the Houghton County Traction Company to build and operate a streetcar station in Calumet. The upstairs housed his wife and seven children, while the downstairs offered streetcar passengers a waiting room and confectionery counter offering candy and soda products.

Nelma sat in Erik's stationhouse waiting room, with Toivo in her lap, and her daughter Lila beside her with a handful of candy. They had become regular commuters to the Houghton County jail, which still held Edward on various charges that Nelma deemed excessive and verging on extortion. Clearly it had not gone unnoticed that she and her husband housed a union representative, and while the other men were out on bail within a day, Edward was still confined to his jail cell three days later.

Erik was a fine boned man whose bow tie partially obscured a pronounced Adam's apple that bobbed in and out of his shirt collar. Nelma couldn't imagine him swinging a pickaxe or manning a drill underground. He seemed to belong behind the confectionery counter, selling sweets, streetcar tokens, and offering homilies to all that would listen.

"You should come by for dinner tonight," Erik said. "Mary hasn't seen you in ages, and she'll be here with her kids."

Mary was one of Erik's daughters, a homely, washed-out blond imp when Nelma had seen her last. The kind of person who perpetually looked like an adolescent, awkward with her body and her place in society. But Erik's invitation was difficult to decline. Behind his humble demeanor and kindhearted words was an unmistakable authority. An authority wrested from the shared history between them, bequeathed to Erik from her dead father, a patriarchy of male comrades.

"Depends how late it is when I return. Edward's seeing the union lawyer today," Nelma said. "We hope to have him out on bail today or tomorrow at the latest."

"You've all been in my prayers. Perhaps we can see the both of you tonight, Lord willing."

Nelma smiled and gathered her children, as the streetcar was pulled up outside. Lila was excited, and looked forward to the outing, relishing the ride on the streetcar as if it were her first, though she had been on it many times. They took the seat directly behind the conductor, with Lila by the window. The streetcar was nearly empty; the midafternoon was an odd time for passengers—too early for a shift change and too late for lunch.

Nelma had met with the union lawyer in the morning. Frank had brought him over and filled him with expectations of the "best brewed coffee he'd ever have the pleasure of drinking." Claimed the coffee at the hotel paled in comparison, a cup of weak tea water at best. Nelma had just roasted some green coffee beans and the aroma had welcomed them into the kitchen. The lawyer had worn a black suit and tie, black hair, and black mustache. When he smiled, the lawyer exposed a blackened tooth in the corner of his mouth. He was a serious man, and Nelma had been so taken by his appearance that she had forgotten his name, and in her mind she simply referred to him as "the union lawyer". The lawyer was confident they could have some of the charges dropped and a reasonable bail set by end of day.

Nelma looked out the window as their streetcar rumbled past mining locations, towns and woods. Frank had expressed constant amazement at their streetcars, contrasting them to the urban trolleys back east, which rarely left the city limits and never ventured into the country. Nelma loved riding the streetcars almost as much as her daughter. They provided affordable transport for all, with windows to keep out the weather, and heaters to melt away the long winter chill. Even the small yellow dinky that serviced the local lines was a bit of an adventure, with its rocking and rumbling over the tracks and trestles.

Several chattering women waited on the platform at Osceola, and they continued their meaningless prattle until finally getting off at Frenchtown. The Quincy Number Seven shafthouse loomed on the horizon, then ducked out of view as they descended into a steep valley. The streetcar crossed over the railroad lines and steered clear of the mining location, though Nelma could make out the rockhouse, blacksmith house and Number Four steam hoist before they turned away and descended Quincy Hill.

In Hancock, they switched to another streetcar, which didn't progress more than a few blocks before it was stopped at the swing bridge as a freighter passed through the portage. Its rusty hull rose high above street level and it seemed as if a floating city was going by.

"Mama, why don't they wave to us, like the passenger ships?" Lila asked.

"It's just a job for them, not a holiday," Nelma said. "They're probably counting the days before they can go home. Same as your daddy used to count the hours underground."

Copper ingots were piled high onboard, gleaming like gold. The sailors stared at the cityscape before them, looking tired or perhaps just resigned to their fate. Nelma wondered how long since they had seen home, and if anyone was waiting for their return. She had heard some speak of the waters of Lake Superior as if it were an inland sea, rife with its own trials and risks of death.

A loud horn blast signaled its passage and the center section of the bridge slowly started to swing back into place. Lila had once asked if she could ride the bridge as it shifted, and was disappointed that no one had ever tried.

After climbing back in their seats, the trip to the courthouse was just a few blocks on the other side of the bridge. Lila pressed the stop button when they approached the building, and Nelma lifted her son onto her left hip as Lila hopped out before them. The lawyer should already be waiting, and she hoped that he had improved Edward's mood, which had been dark and angry these past few days.

They met in a cold, bare room that joined the courthouse with the jailhouse next door. Edward seemed small and passive in the uncluttered space. Both he and the lawyer smiled when she walked in. Lila ran to her father's lap. The guard in the corner indicated it was allowed, with a slight nod of his head.

Nelma returned their smile cautiously, nervously. She looked first at Edward, then at the lawyer. "Has anything been decided? Have you seen the judge?"

"Good news," the lawyer said. "They've dropped the charges of resisting arrest, assault and battery. The charge of violating the injunction remains, but they wouldn't set bail until tomorrow. Edward needs to spend one more night here, but he should be out by morning."

Nelma let the words filter through her mind and forged a smile. She was relieved that Edward's situation would no longer be special, that they could comfort themselves at being in the good company of the hundreds of other men who were at home, awaiting trial for violating the injunction.

Yet there was also a touch of apprehension, as she studied his hands, which were clenched tightly in his lap. Would he be angry when he returned, would he take it out on her?

Lila gave her father a sticky piece of hard candy she had carried all the way from Erik's stationhouse, and little Toivo gave his father a wiggly hug. Nelma brought Edward up to date on the neighborhood gossip. Nothing much had really happened, but she felt it would comfort him to hear. Ellen's husband still remained loyal to the strike, and Anna's husband had been injured the first day he returned to the mines, leaving him bitter and anxious to rejoin the union effort. She decided not to mention Erik's invitation, since she thought Edward wouldn't approve of her visiting anyone who opposed the strike, even an old family friend.

When they made their way back to Calumet, Erik insisted they go upstairs, where his wife, Agatha was waiting with coffee and rye bread, still warm from the oven.

"Nelma, dear, how have you been?" Agatha said, "Any news on Edward?"

"He'll be out tomorrow," Nelma said. "They'll listen to a lawyer, though he didn't say anything I haven't been saying for days."

"You will be staying for dinner, of course. Help yourself to some bread. Mary should be here within the hour."

Nelma cut and buttered bread for her children, the decision of where they would eat had apparently already been made. Agatha cooked and spoke of her children, a long monologue that Nelma endured while feeding Toivo. One son was a streetcar conductor, another was a blacksmith, and Waino had opened a restaurant in Copper Harbor with his wife. Nelma remembered taking a fancy to Waino when they were young, before she met Edward. One daughter was finally pregnant, another had moved to Detroit with her husband, and the youngest was the real tailor in their family business. Mary lived just down the street and of course would be stopping in tonight. Nelma found herself jealous of the Tomlinson family's quiet fortune. It seemed they were untouched by the strike and lived in a happy vacuum without trouble or strife.

Mary's voice preceded her arrival as she climbed the stairs. "Mother, I've brought some blueberry pie, so don't bother with dessert. Nelma! What a nice surprise." Mary arrived with twin boys in tow. She had gained a little weight, inflating her bony frame and starting a trend that Nelma suspected would continue until all the sharp angles and lines would be replaced with generous curves and fleshy rolls. Yet she seemed to have gained a new confidence in herself that was absent when Nelma had seen her last. Nelma thought she was a less annoying person, and in their children they found common ground for discussion. After a generous dinner of ham, cabbage rolls and bread, Nelma set aside her intention to leave early and settled in the sitting room amid children's toys and coffee cups.

Later, Agatha interrupted their discussion of the children's affections and habits. "Nelma, we've forgotten the hour and it's already dark. You'd best be going home now, but I do hope you'll stop by again soon."

"Where did the time go?" Nelma wondered aloud and turned to Agatha. "Thank you so much for dinner. We'll stop by again soon."

Nelma slung little Toivo's sleeping head against her chest and hurried Lila down the stairs and out the back door of the stationhouse. Deputies on horses passed down the street, and though she had done nothing wrong, she thought it best to wait until they turned before she walked home. The night air was cold and stiff against her face, her shawl no longer enough to warm her, and she knew tomorrow she should be unpacking the winter coats, darning wool socks and mending the children's mittens.

EDWARD WAS OUT on bail the next morning, as the union lawyer had promised, and he greeted her with an emotional attentiveness that she hadn't seen since he courted her years ago. He closed her in his arms like a child clutching a stuffed bear and kissed her on the lips with an earnestness that had her forgetting all the late nights he had come home smelling of whiskey and perhaps the faint smell of perfume. All the times he had slapped her in his drunkenness seemed to be distant and rare, all the days he had silently skulked and ignored her were understood and forgiven. She remembered the boy she had fallen in love with at her father's house, with his deep blue eyes and golden hair streaked with strands of copper, his strong hands that promised sanctuary from all harm.

In the afternoon, most of the neighborhood gathered around Nelma's small kitchen table, overflowing into the front hall, and it felt as if they were on holiday, the business of the strike set aside in honor of Edward's release. At dinner, they celebrated with his favorite fish pie, *kalakukko*, and even Nelma drank half a bottle of beer, supplied by Frank who soon left to spend one more night at the hotel.

Later, after the children were put to bed, Nelma lingered at their door where the smell of talc and clean flannel filtered out from their room, cradling the darkness with a sense of security, a sense of safety that Nelma willfully believed to be true. Edward surprised and groped her from behind, his strong hands exploring, squeezing, unbuttoning and pulling her into their bedroom. She smiled and for a moment believed that this would be different, that this would happen with the romantic tenderness that her friend Hannah had heard whispered of at weddings. But soon Edward became frustrated with the petticoat and instead of asking for help, he violently tore off her bloomers, ripping the delicate lace she had picked out this morning especially for him. He turned her around and pinned her against the wall, pressing her cheek against the rough plaster, tearing her inside with the same brute force he had used to disrobe her. When he was done, he sat on the edge of their bed and lit a cigarette, flicking the ashes on the floor. Nelma gathered herself in a blanket and went downstairs to the kitchen to wash up.

She hated him for this. For the first time, she allowed herself an anger unmitigated by guilt or subservience. How dare he treat her this way. Nelma took a dishrag, dampened it with water, and cleaned herself. These private acts belied any kind words he offered her in public. For all the virulent complaining he directed at the mine bosses, their lack of respect, their arrogance, and their deliberate disregard for his physical safety, he failed to see the hypocrisy in how he treated his wife. She vowed that something would have to change. With the victory of the strike, there would have to be a victory at home.

EVERY TUESDAY and Thursday night, Edward and Frank would visit the homes of the strikers, making plans and keeping alliances. Nelma would watch them walk down the street from the sitting room window, sometimes able to see the doors of their neighbors open and swallow them in, sometimes they would disappear down a side street towards town. After she was certain they were out of sight, she would pack up the children and walk the dirt roadside to Erik Tomlinson's stationhouse. It had become a welcome respite from the strike, which Erik and Agatha tactfully never mentioned, and they would discuss the weather, the children, the politics back in Finland.

Erik and Agatha were devout Lutherans, and while they never pressed Nelma to renounce alcohol, tobacco, or playing cards in her home, they would often quote stories from the good book to entertain the children, both hers and the grandchildren who would also be occasional visitors. Their home and their family became an extension of her own, the grandchildren calling her Aunt Nelma and accepting her authority on matters of childish dispute.

One Tuesday, Nelma was helping clean up the dessert dishes while Lila and Toivo played in the sitting room.

"Agatha, I do wish you'd share your recipe for the rhubarb pudding," Nelma said. "My children won't eat mine anymore, they claim it's too bitter, that it's not half as good as yours."

"Why don't you come a little earlier on Thursday and we can make it together. I've never written it down. You know how it is. It's just something you pick up."

Nelma considered how she might leave her house without being dependent on the time that Edward and Frank left for their meetings. She might as well simply tell him where she'd be. She couldn't imagine Edward would make a show of things with Frank around. Nelma looked at the clock in the sitting room. It was late again, but she doubted the deputies would bother her. It was the men they would be most concerned with.

She packed up her children and walked down the familiar staircase. The bottom step creaked in the undisturbed silence of the stationhouse waiting room; the streetcar lacked much evening traffic since the strike began. Outside, a group of mounted deputies rode by, but Nelma wanted to get her son into bed and tired of hiding from these men every visit. They were outsiders, guards brought in from the Waddell-Mahon Corporation in New York, deputies that worked for both the sheriff and the mining companies. Even the Tomlinson's disliked them and derisively called them Waddell men, as if it were an insult.

Two mounted deputies stopped alongside her. "What business do you have at the stationhouse? We saw no passengers leave the streetcar in the last hour."

"It was simply a social visit—my children were playing, we forgot the time. We're heading straight home, sir." Nelma despised offering these men any respect, but didn't want any trouble, especially with her children by her side.

"You're Edward Jokela's wife, aren't you? That union rep is staying at your house."

"Who stays at my house is none of your concern."

"Ma'am, I beg to differ. Is there anyone else at the stationhouse tonight? You're not holding a union meeting there, are you?"

"I told you, it was a social visit. Now if you don't mind, I need to take my children home. It's late and they're tired. Good night."

Nelma started walking down the street, holding her daughter's hand firmly, resisting the urge to look back. She didn't hear them following her, but didn't feel at ease until she opened the door to her house. She scanned up and down the street, saw no one, and went inside.

Edward and Frank sat at the kitchen table, smoking cigarettes and turned in their seats, as if they had been waiting for her. A deck of cards was spread in front of them. She suspected they both ceased their talk when she had opened the door.

"Nelma, it's late," Frank said. "You shouldn't be out with those deputies about. They wouldn't think twice about stopping a woman. Many have already been arrested."

"I'm here, aren't I? Let me put the children to bed. I'll be right down again." Nelma decided against mentioning her encounter, nothing had come of it, and it left her feeling confident that nothing would.

"Where have you been?" Edward said. "We thought you might be at Ellen's house, but she hasn't seen you since this morning's parade."

"I've been visiting with the Tomlinson's, they had invited us over for dessert." Nelma hurried the children up the stairs, thankful that Edward didn't seem to have anything to say about her visit. Perhaps she misjudged him on this, perhaps he wouldn't mind.

ON THURSDAY, she took the children to the Tomlinson's, looking forward to the promised rhubarb pudding recipe, looking forward to their company. Frank and Edward said they'd stop by on their way home, to make sure there wasn't any trouble. Agatha waited in the kitchen, surprising the children with freshly made ice cream. Little Toivo had never eaten ice cream before, and tentatively probed it with his chubby fingers. Lila mined the chocolate dessert with a steady and circular path of her spoon, in constant motion between the bowl and her mouth until she had emptied the dish. Little Toivo tried to follow suit, but most of the ice cream ended on his face and lap. Nelma studied Agatha as she prepared the rhubarb pudding, writing down the measurements, commenting that the brown sugar surely made all the difference in the final taste.

As promised, the men arrived shortly after dark, and escorted her defiantly past the five mounted deputies who sat waiting out on the street.

They looked down at Nelma and her family, and silently followed them with their eyes. One of the horses impatiently kicked the ground with its hoof and flared its nostrils. Another bared its large irregular teeth. Nelma thought the rider owned a similar set of ivories; he was the same insolent man who had questioned her the other day, though at the moment he kept his mouth shut, his lips pursed. She wondered if they were disappointed that she hadn't broken any law, frustrated there was no crime they could punish.

One of the deputies shouted "Let's go," and all five men whipped their horses into action. They rode round and past Nelma's family, kicking up pebbles at their feet, leaving her confused as to their intent. Two men stopped out back, another blocked the front entranceway, and the final two dismounted and slammed open the stationhouse door. Edward tried to pull her away, but she stood her ground, horrified at the scare they must be causing upstairs.

Frank urged them all to go home and approached the man guarding the front door. At first, they talked politely, as if they were old friends meeting on the street, as if he were asking about the wife and children. Frank held the appearance of a gentleman, an inquisitive bystander, perhaps a visitor from abroad. One of Frank's hands rested on his walking stick, a restive picture of civility, while the other began an angry conversation, gesturing wildly in the air, pointing and accusing. Their voices became louder, and soon it was apparent that neither was listening to the other, as both shouted their demands. The guard threatened with the butt of his rifle, and Frank stumbled backward, almost falling, losing his hat to the street.

"They've been arrested for conducting illegal meetings at the station," Frank said. "They've been accused of inciting striking miners. I explained that I'd be the first to admit to a union meeting, but that this was obviously a mistake, that this was nothing more than a gathering of friends."

"Bloody hell," Edward said. "I say we get some of the boys and show 'em what justice is about."

"We'd better go home or we'll be arrested too," Frank said. "This isn't a fight we can win."

"But they can't do that!" Nelma cried. "They don't even support the strike." She let her daughter's hand fall from her grasp; little Toivo clung to her side, understanding nothing but fear. Nelma covered her face with her hands and raked her fingers through her hair. For a moment she forgot everyone around her and it seemed she was standing alone. She wondered if the Tomlinson's blamed her and cursed the day they invited her into their home. Edward put his hand on her shoulder and said they really should go. Nelma looked back to see Erik led out of the house, walking with a pious deference to his accusers. His eyes were cast down and she doubted he knew she was still there, his vision not yet accommodating the dark. She turned to go, knowing that he would continue to remember her in his prayers, and this weighed her with a guilt that was all the more debilitating.

OCTOBER 31, 1913

IN THE GLOW OF HIS HEADLAMP, Russell stood mesmerized by the glitter. Small chips of copper and rock were snapping off the walls like bits of metallic confetti. They seemed to emit a light of their own, a surreal underground glimmer. He tried to catch them in his hand, like a child's first encounter with snow, marveling at the lightness of the chips, thin as paper and no larger than his fingernails.

"We gotta go." Oscar shouted from behind him. He had just returned with an empty tramcar.

"Look at this," Russell said. "Have you ever seen anything like it?"

Oscar took hold of his arm and pulled him back down the drift. "Now."

Russell turned to look at his friend – there was fear in his eyes and urgency in his voice. They rushed back towards the shaft. Oscar called out to others as they went, but everyone already seemed to understand, dropping their tools and leaving them as they ran. At the shaft, a mancar stood waiting and all thirty men clambered in. One of the miners signaled the engineer above, and the mancar began to creep upward, slowly at first and then gathering speed. The men sat in anxious silence during the long ride. There was none of the usual light-hearted jostling around, the knees of a man on the step above pressed uncomfortably into his shoulder, but Russell dared not move. He looked up at the cables that pulled them, but the apprehension in the eyes of those above forced his gaze back down. For Russell, it was the fear of the unknown, the nameless thing that gnawed at his consciousness. A tingling sensation crawled up Russell's spine, forcing an involuntary shudder.

He wanted to ask what it was that had spooked them so, what was the thing everyone else knew, when a thunderous blast reached up from below and blew the mancar towards the side of the shaft wall. Russell gripped the railing and waited for the mancar to drop. He was certain he was about to die. Pump rods and pipes that carried water out of the mine swung like vines and slammed into the mancar. The light on his headlamp and those of the others were extinguished. In the darkness, a fine mist from the broken pipes showered over them but still the mancar moved upward. The cabling seemed to have held. After a few minutes, another blast shook them and vibrated through his very bones. Russell swore that if he survived the day, he would never go down the mines again. It was time to find another line of work. Even laboring in a Detroit auto factory seemed appealing. Russell anxiously waited for the next blast, and tried to determine how much farther they had to go before they saw grass.

The mancar slowed and Russell could see light filtering from above. He could see the entrances to each abandoned level above him now. Each was one hundred feet apart and he counted six more levels to go. Superstitious, he vowed to suppress any sense of relief until he actually stepped into the sunshine. Four more levels to go. The steady updraft of the mineshaft seemed to falter, and Russell braced himself for another blast. Two more levels. He had a vision of the whole mancar collapsing back into the earth the instant they reached the summit, and smiled at the irony. When the mancar stopped and the men climbed out, he still sat smiling in disbelief. He was the last to get out.

"What the hell was that?" Russell said.

"That," Oscar said, "was an air blast. Those metal chips flying off the wall were a sure sign of one. I'd never seen it before, but I'd heard about it. You ever see that, it's time to bail."

"But what is an air blast—what happened down there?"

"It's a shakeup is what it is. Like an earthquake. Hanging wall shudders and collapses. Shoots out a blast of air. Sometimes even the foot wall moves."

"Damn. I'm not going back down there again."

"Not today we're not. I think we've earned ourselves a drink."

"I'd say we're past due." Russell felt a rush of adrenaline inside that made him hypersensitive to everything around him. The distant October sun, the crisp leaves underfoot, the stench of the nearby smelters. They walked to the dry house to change into clean clothes, passing engineers and captains rushing the other way, back to assess the damage. He thought about the mine rats, stranded down in the darkness, and was saddened by their probable demise.

They chose the pub closest to the streetcar stop, overlooking Quincy Hill and farther out, the southern hills hugged Portage Lake like a woman sleeping against the backside of her lover. Oscar reminded Russell of the Halloween party his girlfriend, Lisa, was hosting tonight, and encouraged him to come. Russell hadn't planned on going, but now thought a bit of frivolity might take the edge off the day.

"It should be a good time," Oscar said. "Lisa ordered some kind of Halloween planner and she's been decorating her father's house all week."

"I don't need no costume, do I?"

"Some of the women will probably be wearing somethin' or other, but I ain't planning on wearing anything special beyond a clean, dry pair of trousers."

Russell finished his second beer, wiped his face with his sleeve, and told Oscar he'd meet him at his house later. From there they would take the streetcar to Laurium. Despite the two beers, he still felt agitated. Russell opted to walk to the boarding house. Calm his nerves a bit. Think about how it would feel to go back in the mines tomorrow. Wondered what it would look like.

The streets were quiet, and Russell kicked a stone before him to see how far he could send it at each pace. Occasionally, a carriage would pass and the driver would tip his hat. By the time he had walked back to the boarding house, the air blast had faded into a good story to tell friends. Exaggerating his ignorance for comic effect, but describing the half-hour in the mancar pretty much as it happened.

The other men from his shift were late for dinner. Mrs. Huhta made small mention of their absence and assumed they were still at the bar. She had felt the air blast several miles away and didn't need to be told what had happened. After dinner, Russell stopped by the bathhouse for a long hot shower before dressing and taking the streetcar back to Oscar's house. The roadways were filled with more lawmen than revelers, mounted deputies patrolling for trouble, breaking up clandestine strike meetings, sending suspicious characters scuttling home for refuge. It made Russell feel protected and important, on the right side of society for perhaps the first time in his life.

The party was a short walk from the streetcar-barn in Laurium, down a sidewalked avenue lined with trees and large houses, a better neighborhood than either his or Oscar's. Lisa's family house was all lit up with electric lights, the front porch lined with small carved jack-o-lanterns, each aglow with its own candlelight.

Lisa opened the bevel-glassed front door and led them on a tour of her transformed home. Russell studied Oscar's lady-friend. An orange mask obscured most of her face with crepe paper and rhinestone glitter, revealing only her soft, red lips. Her smile revealed a small gap between her two front teeth, an intriguing space like the one Maria had when she was younger. He imagined Lisa and Maria building a friendship over the years, hosting future Halloween parties and festivities for their children. He imagined a home of his own, perhaps not as opulent, but still with a telephone and electricity, a parlor for guests and a pantry full of food.

Lisa insisted they each wear a masquerade mask before joining her guests, several dangled from her hand. Russell chose one that seemed the least embarrassing, and strapped on a simple black-feathered eye mask. Oscar chose something more flamboyant, a full devil's face complete with cardboard horns. Lisa commented on how positively intriguing they both looked, as if they were collectables for her party, before guiding them down the hall. There were paperboard devils hung on the walls and crepe paper lanterns suspended from the ceiling. Already a crowd of almost twenty had gathered in the sitting room, where small tables were covered with tablecloths embossed with black cats and witches, and topped with paper-mache ghosts filled with candy. Russell hoped no one noticed how out of place he felt, and nervously followed as Oscar and Lisa navigated through the room. Two men with large, waxed mustaches paused to greet them before continuing their conversation.

"The strikers used to be hard workers," said the man with a jack-o-lantern mask pushed up on his forehead, "but they're foreigners – they don't know our language, customs or laws. Is it any wonder they've been waylaid by these union agitators?"

"We're a country of foreigners," Oscar interjected, "them strikers don't deserve our sympathies. They know what they're doing."

"They're just afraid of change, is all," the man said. "Years ago they were just as fearful with the switch away from hand-drills. The company needs to stay competitive, or we'd all be out of a job."

"The strikers need to give up while they still have jobs to go back to," the second man said. "You heard what the company said yesterday. They'd sooner let the grass grow in the streets before they'd recognize that rogue union of theirs."

"Must we talk about those people tonight?" Lisa complained. "It's Halloween. Come into the kitchen for cake. If you get a piece with the coin baked in, you get a prize."

Russell pulled Oscar back as several guests followed Lisa into the kitchen. Lisa's father was a mine captain; he was bound to know something.

"Have you heard anything about the air blast?" Russell asked Oscar. "Do they know if the mine is safe?"

"The engineers have already been down there," Oscar said quietly. "No signs of damage below the fiftieth level, they found a minor cave-in on the forty-ninth. But that was already mined out and abandoned. No one worked there."

"Will they want us back tomorrow?"

"No one's going back so soon. I think they've shut down for the weekend."

The weight of the day came back to bring down his mood and sober his spirit. The man with the jack-o-lantern mask emerged from the kitchen with a plate of frosted cake and sat down to a game of pinochle with three ladies. Another man with a pair of baggy trousers and long pointed beard pulled out a flute and played a giddy tune that brought several people to the floor clapping. "I don't think I'll be staying much longer, Oscar. I don't play the card games they play. It's been a long day."

"Give me a few more minutes with Lisa—I'll walk with you to the streetcar station."

"Don't ya bother, I can find my way."

Russell gathered his jacket and left his mask on the banister as he slipped out the front door. The day could have ended tragically, he told himself, but no harm had come to anyone. He was welcomed into the home of one of the wealthier families in Laurium. It really wasn't such a bad day.

He was halfway to the streetcar stop when he cast his eyes up at the sky and found the heavens filled with the most amazing natural display he'd ever witnessed. He had heard of the northern lights, but always considered them a tall tale at worst, an exaggerated light show at best. Now, there were ribbons of blue and green waving, breathing, and pulsating above his head in a mesmerizing dance. They had the hypnotic quality of a campfire, magnified a thousand times above his head. In her last letter, Maria had asked what stars looked like at night. Tonight he would write her about this. He could imagine her wonder at her first glimpse of this show. He could imagine his whole life spent in a place that shared such magic.

Russell sat down in the frost-bitten grasses on the side of the road, drew his knees up to his chin like a child, and watched. He forgot the time and the place, the strike and the air blast, the party and even Maria. It was beautiful. Everything else receded from his mind, and the voices at first seemed to haunt from a dream in the half sleep of morning. Accusing voices, angry voices, but voices that threatened someone else, somewhere else, and it wasn't until they came closer that his attention was brought back to the ground.

Three men surrounded another miner just a hundred feet up the road. They didn't appear to have noticed Russell. The short man seemed to be the ringleader, the one who interrogated while one of his partners stood with a shotgun aimed straight at the man's groin. "You don't got a union card, mister? You're not one of them scabby dogs crossing the picket line, are ya? I'd never think twice to shoot a scabby dog, you know. You sure you don't have a union card on ya, mister?"

Russell sat frozen with fear. Three men and a gun were no match for two unarmed miners, let alone one. He was in danger if he stayed, but dared not risk being noticed in an attempt to flee. The men continued to taunt the miner, who begged for mercy as they pushed him down the road, closer to Russell.

"Tell ya what, mister. You see how it feels to be hunted like a dog by those so-called deputies. They ride down on my children yesterday, for playing marbles in the street. Trampled my wife's autumn garden, and tore apart the wash she had hung up on the line. I'll give you two minutes to run your sorry scabby ass down the road before I shoot ya."

The miner started running, but the strikers didn't give him more than a few seconds before they felled him with a shotgun blast and left him bleeding in the road as they ran away. Russell hurried to the man, who had been shot in the thigh. The seeping blood reflected the eerie glow of the northern lights, creating the illusion of an oil slick on the man's pants.

Russell stood over the man, and offered his hand. "Can you walk if ya lean on my arm? I saw what they did—I was just down the road."

The miner sat up and tried to look at the back of his leg. He winced in the pain of the effort. Russell wasn't sure if he had been heard, but didn't want to repeat himself quite yet. A stray dog approached with his nose to the ground, perhaps sniffing for food. The dogs had become proficient at salvaging a miner's lunch pail whenever the strikers would snatch it and smash it to the ground. Russell kicked at the animal and it scurried away with an indignant yelp.

The man turned his eyes to Russell for the first time, and mumbled a word of thanks. Together they hobbled to the stationhouse, where the stationmaster called for an ambulance. Russell stayed with the man until the ambulance arrived, a modified surrey pulled by a team of two stout horses. The stationmaster offered Russell a soda from his icebox upstairs, and asked about what he had seen.

"They were out looking for a fight—if I hadn't stopped to look at the sky, it might easily have been me they shot." Russell said.

The stationmaster sat in quiet thought for a minute while Russell sipped his drink.

"It seems many have been tolerant of the strikers, like unruly children who used to be well-behaved," the stationmaster said. "They do have valid grievances. I've been down there myself with the petty bosses. I'm sure you have too, mister. But this violence will be the death of their cause. I fear how it will all end."

The streetcar pulled up just as Russell was finishing his drink. He thanked the stationmaster for his kindness, climbed in and took a seat next to the electric heater. Russell rested his head against the darkened window, and drifted into an uneasy sleep.

He dreamt of the strikers attacking that man, over and over again. Sometimes they attacked him, and sometimes he slipped away into the night. Once he fought back, knocking the shotgun from the striker's hands and hitting him with the butt of the rifle again and again as the man pleaded for him to stop. He dreamt he was falling, slipping down a mineshaft coated with blood and woke with a start. The streetcar was descending Quincy Hill. Russell pressed the electric stop button and looked down at his pants. They were his only dress pants, light grey cotton, cuffed at the bottom, and they bore a large bloody stain from the injured miner he had helped.

NOVEMBER 9, 1913

IT HAD BEEN SEVERAL YEARS since Hannah had traveled this way. She had come in the summer with Nelma. They were looking for blueberries and had come across the trapper woman's shack. It was an odd four-sided building, not quite square, with no two sides alike. There were two walls of split cedar, one with bark and one without, another fashioned from lake rock, and the back was built into the hillside. No one was home at the time, but Nelma had insisted that if she was ever in need of a fur pelt, she could do no better than Keras Kilpela. Hannah had committed the route to memory, certain that one day she would return. So much had changed since then; it hardly seemed to be a real memory anymore. It almost felt like a story from some other person's life.

Back then, the trail had been easy to follow; now it was obscured by a layer of sour fermenting leaves. Occasionally she would step on the sweet mash of a rotting apple, and would try to wipe her boot clean with a twig or exposed root.

The day had started out incredibly fair, the kind of warm weather one might expect in early September, not early November. Hannah wore her fall cotton jacket, with an s-curved shape embarrassingly out of fashion. Since she had come of age, the shape of the corset had become more in line with the shape a woman wore naturally, instead of a posture that forced a woman's chest one way and her back-side the other. Her jacket fell awkwardly in places where her pose provided nothing for it to hang upon.

Hannah paused at a slight rise of sparse birch to try to get her bearings. It looked so different from the summer, but she was certain she would find her way. The winds had picked up and the clear sky that had greeted the morning became covered with a fast-moving tumble of clouds.

Hannah buttoned her coat and imagined how warm she would be with a fox-fur stole around her neck or a wolf-fur muff around her hands. She still had a little gambling money set aside, and the university now seemed like a distant dream. She should have been studying for mid-terms by now, not idling in her hometown for one more year. An illicit shopping trip seemed just the thing to raise her spirits.

Since Aaron had invited her to see a show at the Kerridge Theater, a Broadway show direct from New York, Hannah had obsessed with what she might wear. Every piece of clothing in her wardrobe was woefully out of date, immature, or both. She knew father would never part with any of their meager funds for a new outfit, and she couldn't purchase one herself without raising questions. Instead, she would borrow a dress from Ida. She would still need something more though, something that would present her in the manner she wished to be seen. Not a small-town merchant's daughter, but an intelligent woman capable of conversing on any topical subject of the day.

At the moment though, she just wished she could find the right trail to Keras Kilpela's shack. She had been hiking about an hour. It seemed she should be there by now. The trailhead was clear behind the streetcar station, but soon narrowed in the fallen leaves until Hannah wasn't quite sure if she was imagining the trail or if it still existed. If she looked to her right or left for more than a minute, the patterns in the leaves seemed to create the illusion of a trail in every direction.

Reluctantly, she decided it was time to go home. She could come back tomorrow with Nelma, who would certainly know the way. Turning around with a measured glance behind her, to make sure she was facing the opposite direction, Hannah set off the way she had come.

The hike seemed to take longer on the way out than on the way in, but Hannah refused to believe she was lost. It wasn't that far to the station, it was just a trick of the mind, a different way of measuring time when you grudgingly turn around than when you're looking forward to your destination. The winds began to whistle through the trees. A large fat snowflake danced around the path before her, and was joined by another, and another, and then a whole flurry of snow filled the woods. It seemed that winter had just remembered it was lax, a bit late for this north country, and was trying to make amends.

Hannah wished she had brought a hat. How silly not to have worn a hat this time of year. She approached another slight rise in the land, the clean lines of birch trees looking far too familiar. The ground was already covered with a thin veneer of white, concealing any footprints she might have left before. It was probably a different stand of birch. She had been walking too long to have come full circle. But if this was the same stand of birch, was she headed in the wrong direction then or now?

Where was the streetcar station? Hannah felt a tingle of fear spark from one extremity to the next. Her parents had given her the day off, another day off from their store, which barely needed one person to tend to the slow pace of business. They wouldn't think to look for her until dinner, and it was probably just past noon.

"Help! Auttaa!" Hannah cried out in both English and Finnish, sinking down against a tree, huddling in her thin, unfashionable coat. "Please, help!"

It might have been hours that had passed. It might have been one. Hannah's only measure of time was the thick accumulation of snow rising all around her. When the snow stopped, Hannah reasoned, she could easily find her way back to the station. No risk of doubling back in the snow, she would make her own footprints to stay her course. Hannah sat in her small stand of birch, waiting for the snow to stop, though she knew that when the snow starts falling in these parts, it could be days or even weeks before it pauses.

Lumi, lumentulo, lumikinos. To pass the time, Hannah tried to remember all the derivations the Finns had for snow. How many different ways were there to describe a snowflake? The flurries intensified. Soon it was hard to see more than ten feet away. *Lumimyrsky, pyry, lumipyry.* Was this a blizzard, a snowstorm, or a whirling snowstorm? What had she been thinking? She should have brought Nelma along, though how would she explain her need for a fur pelt while the strikers were rationing both food and fuel. Hannah was tired of the strike. She wanted to get on with her life, and wished others would do the same.

Hannah didn't remember dozing off, but when she opened her eyes, she was confronted with the eyes of a woman who could only have been Keras Kilpela herself. It was hard to figure her age. She could have been anywhere between fifty and one hundred years old, but had an almost childlike smile, with laugh-lines that fell into place across her leathered face.

"Odd place for a nap," she said. "You want to come to my place and warm up?"

"Thank you, I was so cold," Hannah said, extending her hand in introduction.

"Cold and foolish," Keras Kilpela said. "Follow me."

They hiked in a direction that Hannah hadn't even considered, casting ever more doubt on her decision to trek into the woods alone. Ten minutes later she was inside the odd house, warmed by the woodstove, marveling at the blankets of fur hides thrown over the sofa like cheap throw rugs.

"I thought I knew the way," Hannah said. "Nelma Jokela had shown me your place years ago. I wanted to buy some fur." She caressed the soft furs with the back of her hand. There was probably mink and fox, and the large hide on top could only have come from a bear. "Do you know Nelma Jokela? She was probably Nelma Huhta when you saw her last."

"I know all about Nelma and that damn strike she's in."

"I don't understand it either. Why can't they find a compromise, why—"

"You need to rest up, girl. Stop your yabbering. Besides, I didn't say she was doing anything inappropriate. You can't fault a person for doing what she thinks is right. Here, have a sip of coffee and a slice of bread. Made it myself. Bark bread, ya know? Best kind there is."

Hannah sat up and arranged the furs around her lap, excited by the sight of so much luxury. In her hunger, Hannah bit off a large chunk of the bread, examining its coarse texture while she chewed. It had a robust flavor with an odd aftertaste, something she couldn't quite identify.

"What kind of bread did you say this was?" Hannah asked. "Some kind of rye?"

"There's rye in it," Keras said, tending to the fire with a long metal pipe. "But it's mostly bark bread. Nelma never told you 'bout bark bread?"

Keras shuffled over to a large bin in the corner, returning with a handful of white flour. "Plenty a pine trees 'round my camp here. Usually take one down every summer to help tide me over till next year. Need to strip the bark off a young sapling and scrape off the white innards. Heat it over the fire to get rid of the resin, then mill it out yonder Got me own grinding stones. Got everything I need here."

Hannah thought the bread might taste better with a bit of jam or butter, but didn't intend to push the woman's hospitality. She was short, a good foot shorter than Hannah, and kept her hair pulled back in two thick braids that fell well past her middle back. She seemed to relish having company, talking constantly with a grounded, reasoned voice that was neither masculine nor feminine. She was nothing like Hannah imagined she would be.

Hannah wondered how to broach the subject of purchasing a pelt. Keras returned the flour to the bin and puttered around the small cabin, humming to herself. If it wasn't for the braids, she could easily be mistaken for a small man, with baggy wool pants tucked into a pair of high moccasins. The cabin was lined with shelves filled with pots, mason jars, and surprisingly, a large amount of books.

"Have you taken an opinion on the strike?" Hannah asked. "Most folks I know are pretty tired of it all. Not that we're not sympathetic, mind you. It just doesn't seem to be solving anything. Nobody's making any money. Everyone's struggling."

"Every corner of society gots its own inbred deceits. I don't try an understand it. Just prefer to stay clear of it," Keras said. "Here – have a bite of sausage. I'll need to get you back to the station before the snow gets too deep. Just got one pair of skis."

"I'd love to purchase one of your furs before I go," Hannah said, feeling the need to direct the conversation. "Did I mention I was looking for your cabin? I wanted to see some of your furs."

"Not many people buying much these days," Keras said. "What did ya have in mind?"

"Something fashionable, but useful. Maybe a small pelt for a hand muff, or a stole wrap for my neck. I've brought money, I have ten silver dollars."

"My furs wouldn't cost you that much, I'll be fair with ya. But I think you'd be better off buying a nice pair of wool mittens, girl."

"I'm tired of being practical. I'm tired of holding my breath waiting for this strike to end. I want something nice to wear to the theater."

"You'll need to find someone else to stitch it up for ya. I just sell the hides. But they're good quality. I could give you a nice fox for your hands—let me see your hands. I try and raise a litter every spring. Keeps the cost down. I'll let you have one pelt for five. You can tuck it in your blouse on the hike back. It'll keep ya warmer."

Hannah brushed her hands across the three hides Keras laid before her. Red fox. Smooth as silk. Hannah felt a warm desire as she imagined stepping off the trolley, hands bundled in the muff, one arm looped through Aaron Cohen's. The third pelt seemed to have the best shape.

"I'll take this one. I like this one the best. What do you think?"

"I think we better get going now, or you'll be snowed in for the weekend."

Hannah tried to gauge the weather from the single windowpane in the corner. The glass was nearly opaque and it was difficult to discern much beyond night and day. The winds had quieted. Hannah reluctantly stood up from the sofa, leaving behind her impression in ripples of fur.

Keras lent her a men's grey hat and a wool shawl for the walk back to the station. Outside, the clouds had cast the shadows of twilight over the woods, though Hannah wasn't sure of the time. She followed in the footsteps that Keras left behind, keeping the snow off her ankles, rather than try to walk beside her. For a short woman, Keras Kilpela had a sure, fast gait that challenged Hannah to keep up. In under an hour, they were within sight of the station. There was no stationhouse, just a platform and small shelter. A streetcar labored through the snow in the distance. Hannah was uncertain how to say goodbye. A polite farewell seemed insufficient, and yet anything more seemed inappropriate since they had just met. Keras solved her dilemma with an uninhibited embrace before taking her leave.

Hannah traded the borrowed clothing for the warmth of the coal-heated streetcar that took her back to Hancock. The streets were empty and the winds howled and battered the window with missiles of snow. Hannah felt embarrassed to have been caught so unprepared by the storm and walked home from the streetcar as quickly as the weather would allow her.

The house was filled with the warm smells of Friday night when she opened the front door. She wondered whether she should conceal her prize pelt for another time, or proudly show it off. She could hear her brother and his wife, Ida, conversing in the kitchen, and decided to stash her fur upstairs before joining the Sabbath preparations.

"Hannah, where have you been? And in that thin coat?" Mother looked up from a pot of lentil soup that filled the air with comfort.

Hannah hesitated, unsure how to explain. "You know that trapper woman, the one with a cabin in the woods near Arcadia? I tried to find her, but then the weather turned…"

"You should know better than that. Here, have a cup of hot cocoa—Sam has been entertaining us with his newfound political calling."

"It's not political," Sam protested, "it's just pragmatic. The strikers have organized, so why shouldn't we?"

"The meetings have been very social these past few nights," Ida said. "A social club with politics."

"We've been working: printing pamphlets, ordering buttons, and making plans. Tomorrow we'll cover every lamppost with placards up and down the peninsula. Tomorrow the people will know of the 'Citizens Alliance'. Tomorrow's our big day."

"Sounds like you're trying to stir up some trouble," Hannah said.

"We're trying to end some trouble," said Sam. "I've had it with all the violence in the streets, all the idled miners, everyone complaining and hoping the economy will get better. We don't have to watch from our empty storefronts as the union bleeds away the life we once had here. We can have our parades too."

"I don't want you involved in any vigilante business," Mother said. "Be sure you're doing the right thing."

"There's women involved too," Ida said to Hannah. "It was Mabelle who came up with the button idea. You could help too. It would be fun."

Hannah looked at Mother for an opinion, but if she had one, it was well hid. This did sound interesting, and Hannah craved a change in the dreary routine of going to the store every day and pretending that the business would return if they just waited long enough. They hadn't had a gambling night in weeks and Hannah was bored. She thought of her friend Nelma and once again felt as if she were lost in the woods, uncertain which way to go. There was a loyalty between them that bordered on being a sacred trust, and yet she worried that it hobbled her views, making it difficult to find a belief of her own.

"Maybe I could help a little—though I don't want to be out hanging posters."

"You can come to the next meeting and decide for yourself," Sam said.

"Enough talk," Mother said. "Hannah, I need some matches for the sabbath candles. The sun is going down. Sam, where is your Father?"

LATER, HANNAH LAY in bed listening to the winds from the storm whistle through the portage. She had been so foolish today. She could have perished, frozen in the woods, lost until spring. She felt so ashamed. The snow fell without relenting, without resting, without pausing to gather strength. She could imagine the storm clouds growing at the edge of the peninsula, appearing out of empty turbulent air like a magician's trick. In the summer she would watch storms born out of the nearly inexhaustible supply of Lake Superior water. Benign currents of clear air would become turbulent and stormy as soon as they hit the Keweenaw Peninsula.

Hannah turned the black and white button her brother had given her over in her hand. It was a simple tin button, the bright letters of the "Citizens Alliance" emblazoned against a beige background. Sam's plan was to put a button on every butcher, barber, storekeeper, and lawyer. Everyone who wanted the reporters to go home, the strikers to go back to work, and the old life to return, would get one. They had ordered one thousand buttons, and optimistically hoped to order even more.

Hannah slipped the button under her pillow and turned off the small lamp on her nightstand. The snowflakes glowed in the streetlight outside her window, and she watched them dance in eddies created where the winds slammed into her house. Farther out in the street a white deluge poured from the sky, each flake blindly following the next.

How does one go about stopping such a storm? Hannah wondered. How does one go about stopping such a strike?

NOVEMBER 11, 1913

NELMA PAUSED TO WATCH THE snow cover the stain on the sidewalk. Flake by flake, it obscured the black stain, with the subtle undertone of red, a memory of blood. Ellen had said it was a scab's blood, that a fight had broken out last night and gotten out of hand. One of the men had fallen and hit his head, and never again stood up. Nelma had asked who started the fight. "Does it really matter?" Ellen had said.

The stain was almost completely covered, and by the time the snow melted in the spring, it would be gone. Nelma tried not thinking about the violence in the streets these days, tried not thinking about these acts that she would have condemned before the strike. She would have probably mourned this man's death, demanded justice, and be shocked at the cruelty of the act. But this was the moral equivalent of war, she reminded herself. A revolution. She agreed with the socialists—the Boston copper bosses had stolen the rights of the copper from the people. The land was a public trust, and should be treated as such.

Nelma gathered a wad of saliva in her mouth, spat it out, and walked home.

"Well?" Edward asked when she walked in the door. "Did they give you the job?"

"It's mine," Nelma said. "There's no pay, of course, but we get an extra ration of food from the commissary each week. And any fresh food that's at risk of spoiling."

Nelma turned her attention to her son, barefoot and dirty, playing with two spoons on the floor. They had no boots that would fit him, and though it was already November and she knew the snows were inevitable, she still had no plan for keeping his feet warm through the winter. Perhaps she could double him up in socks when there was a need to go outside. She had plenty of hats, and Lila's old coat would fit him for another year.

The job at the union commissary was more than a lucky break, she knew. Frank had told her they would be looking for local help before he announced it at the union meeting. She had been first in line, and returned with a job, a loaf of bread and some chicory to stretch out the coffee supply.

THE NEXT DAY she went straight from the daily parade to the union commissary. Lila and Toivo would stay at Ellen's house, at least for today. She promised Ellen a cut of her extra ration from the store in return for caring for the children. This she hadn't told Edward. He needn't know every detail of everything she did. Especially if he was likely to make a scene.

The commissary had been open just a few days, taking an empty storefront next to Heimo's Tavern. Fifteen thousand miners had walked off the job this summer, and though it was unclear how many remained, no one could deny the hunger of so many families. Three carloads of meat had arrived on the morning train, and half of that had been sold by evening, traded for the benefit coupons handed out to the strikers at union meetings. Nelma's job was to tally the coupons traded in and help keep the shelves stocked from the backroom.

The snow was nearly a foot deep as she trudged the narrow path to the storefront. Mrs. Kallio and her friend turned their backs and walked to the other side of the street when they saw her. Mrs. Kallio's husband ran a small general store over on Pine Street, and she knew there would be hard feelings about the loss of business there. The commissary's brick façade still wore a shadow of neglect, as it had been empty since the previous owners had packed up their belongings and moved out west, one month into the strike.

Inside, Frank had traded his usual walking stick for a broom, which he used to sweep up the remnants of a broken window. Newspaper and rags formed a temporary barrier to keep the cold weather outside.

"A brick," Frank said, when he saw her. "Surely they could be more original than that? And in this season, I would have preferred a simple message fastened to the door."

"Did you see who threw it?" Nelma asked.

"The window was already broken before the parade started this morning. Ah, well. Nothing else was disturbed. Did you see Estelle on your walk in? She'll be your partner most days. I'll just be here to open the store."

"Estelle is taking the streetcar from the far side of Red Jacket – it might take her a bit longer. I can manage until she's here."

"I wouldn't want to leave you here alone. I'll wait. Be out back unpacking if you need me."

Nelma stole a glance at his retreating back when she was certain he wasn't looking. Sometimes Frank seemed downright smitten with her, and other times he might have been talking to someone else, a stranger even. Nelma wondered if she was just imagining his affections, or if he was toying with her, a big city man enjoying the friendship of a union man's wife.

The storefront was a small claustrophobic space belying the cavernous storeroom to the rear. Crates and boxes piled behind the counter, against the back wall. Shelves were lined with canned and dry gods shipped from exotic places Nelma didn't think she could place on a map. Coffee from Haiti, rice from Rangoon, Valencia oranges from California. From the east were canned corn, peas and tomatoes, but Nelma didn't think these would sell. Most folks kept their own gardens, with the harvest saved away in mason jars in the cellar.

Estelle opened the creaking door as Nelma was surveying the goods. She brushed off the snow and hung her coat on the hook behind the counter.

"Did ya see the signs this morning?" Estelle asked, wide eyes gracing an otherwise plain peasant face.

"What nonsense you talking about, Estelle?" Nelma asked, "You've never been superstitious before."

"I mean signs, written signs. They calling for a 'Citizens Alliance.' Put an end to the strike. I think them copper bosses are up to no good, stirring the locals against us."

"They already against us. Don't ya see it when you walking down the street? We're threatening their social order, demanding a piece of their pie."

"Don't you ladies worry about that Citizens' Alliance." Frank had emerged from the back storeroom. "It wouldn't take hold with people that have no grievances. The local merchants couldn't put a candle to the suffering our union members are enduring. They don't have a cause."

Frank put his hand on Nelma's shoulder, gave her a concerned glance. "There's a phone next door—give a call to the union hall if you see any trouble. We'll have someone keep an eye on the store at all times."

Nelma was again left wondering about Frank's intentions. No one else touched her like he did, but it was the touch of a comrade, the bond of one socialist to another. As he gathered his cane and closed the door behind him with slow deliberation, Nelma studied Estelle, but failed to see any questions in her eyes, any judgement or jealousy. Nelma decided there was nothing of note in his interactions with her, nothing even worth daydreaming about.

The afternoon bore a steady stream of customers, most of whom Nelma knew by name. Edward stopped by with some union men and shoveled the walk outside the store. By closing time, Nelma and Estelle had worked out a balanced partnership, with Estelle restocking shelves from the back storeroom, and Nelma working the ledger. Hard coal was a big seller as the snow continued to pile up outside. Potatoes, lard, flour and yeast were popular items as well.

Edward met her at closing time and walked her home under streetlights obscured by the winter storm. The winds blew the snow sideways, around and ahead of them, as if it was racing down the road. Edward walked beside her silently, deliberately, fulfilling his role as a husband, but not offering much beyond his presence. Nelma looked forward to the day Edward would bring home a paycheck again, yet the job gave her a sense of independence that she never had before. She wasn't sure she'd ever want to give it up.

The children were as full of energy as Nelma was tired. Lila raced ahead through the snow and Edward scooped Toivo from Ellen's arms and carried him home. Though the distance was short, Toivo's stocking clad feet were cold as ice when they put him in front of the stove. Perhaps someone with the union might have a pair of child's boots to lend.

Dinner was late. Nelma gave the children a snack of bread to keep them from complaining. She mixed in some bully beef, from an enormous fifteen pound can, with the potato stew and hoped it would suffice. She had never tried it before. Her life seemed to be full of new tastes and experiences these days, and as tired as she was, she realized how happy she was. Odd to be happy in such hard times.

Nelma worked Tuesdays and Thursdays at the union commissary, and other days she would wonder if they were keeping the ledger up to date and making proper note of those items that ran low. On days she worked, Ellen would bring the children for lunch and Fran and Eunice would linger well into the afternoon, even if they had nothing to buy.

Some women would grumble about having to parade every day in return for the strike benefits. One would complain, "Is it really making any difference?" Another would try explaining her absence to Nelma: "My children were sick; I had to tend to the children and now we have no coupons."

"But what about your husband, why couldn't he parade?" Nelma would say. "It's really not much to ask, and it's not even up to me." Nelma disliked being put in the position of enforcing the union code. She gave her a pound of flour even if she did doubt the woman's sincerity.

"They're gonna nationalize the mines!" Fran burst in one day, speaking to Nelma, but loud enough for everyone to hear. She never seemed able to speak without an audience. There had been rumors for months and everyone was receptive to any thread of hope in their struggle. Most felt that the government would be a better boss than the companies they had now. Fran quickly acquired a crowd of listeners.

"Of course they will," Estelle waved her hand knowingly. "Tell us something we don't know—tell us when."

"I read it in here," Fran said, brandishing a newspaper. "A government man says right here: 'If any corporation takes the ground as his own and fails to take into consideration the welfare of society, that will cause society to modify those titles to property, as it has the perfect right to do.' That means the government's taking over the mines!"

The paper quickly traveled around the storefront. Estelle looked dubious, and still wanted to know when it all would happen. Ellen had to read it twice to Edla and Impi, with their weak understanding of English. Nelma felt a rush of excitement. The strike was really accomplishing something important, something historic, and she was a part of it.

Still in good spirits at the end of the day, she purchased a small sugar-cured ham for dinner. Tallied it up on the ledger and waited for Edward at closing time. Estelle's sister stopped by after cleaning houses in Laurium, and the three of them discussed the current state of fashion, as seen in the closets the sister had cleaned that day. But as the dark thickened outside, they grew tired of waiting for Edward and set out together. They parted company at the streetcar station, where Nelma continued down the road to her house.

Edward was home and in foul spirits even before he noticed Nelma's ham. "That sure better be a surplus ham you toting there," he said. "We can't afford spending coupons on meat for no good reason."

"We're still in good shape, and we've only had meat once this past week," Nelma said. "I thought you were going to meet me at the commissary tonight?"

Edward banged his fist on the table. "I was. I'm sorry. It's been a hard day. Half my old crew's gone crossed the picket line, and the other half's left town. Usually we'd all get together for Otto's birthday, but no one else showed up."

Edward trudged upstairs. Nelma watched his back and felt a tinge of pity for him. At least she still had her friends. The ham went into the icebox for tomorrow; she wouldn't have time to cook it for tonight's supper. She stoked the kitchen stove with wood, noting that the wood box was nearly empty. There was still plenty of seasoned logs outside to be split, though Nelma worried there might not be enough to make it through a hard winter. Unless the winter was mild. But a mild winter in the copper country was about as rare as a charitable copper boss. Nelma put on her coat and left to fetch the children from Ellen's.

Her daughter squealed in excitement when she walked in the door. Ellen's daughter had given her a tattered old doll, one she had long since outgrown. Little Toivo tugged at her skirts, incorporating his sister's excitement as his own.

"Lila found that in an old chest when we were going through the winter clothes," Ellen said. "You'd think she had found gold."

"You've made her day," Nelma said.

Nelma scooped up her son, relishing his little hugs, and dressed both children for the short but cold walk. After closing the door behind her, she removed her mittens and placed them on Toivo's feet, wrapping her own hands in the folds of his coat as she carried him home.

ATTENDANCE AT THE morning parades was visibly dwindling, both in the women's ranks up front, and the men's formation in the rear. Those strikers that remained were the truly committed, the union men and women who were undeterred by long months without sign of compromise from the mining companies. Nelma daily adjusted her opinions of neighbors based on whether or not they attended the parades and rallies, whether or not they supported the strike. She carried a tin can loaded with stones and kitchen waste to pelt at anyone known to cross a picket line. Her patience ran low with those weak-kneed losers who abandoned the union and returned to the mines without any concessions. To hell with them all.

By the next morning, another six inches of fresh powder had fallen, piling high on the ever-rising road, slowing the progress and the spirit of the parade. Nelma and Ellen pulled the children in a sled, where they sat bundled in a tumble of blankets. They paused on the corner of Pine Street as a team of eight horses pulled a giant wooden roller over the snow-bound road. The roller towered above them as the horses labored by, panking the snow, ironing another layer and leveling the snow-bound road for traffic.

"You been to Hancock lately?" Ellen asked as they waited. "Seen all them Citizens' Alliance handbills across the city?"

"They're up here too," Nelma said. "There's one right over there in the shoemaker's window. It don't mean nothing. They haven't done anything."

"I don't like it. But at least it makes it clear who has our sympathies and who don't. I saw that Weinstein girl wearing one of their buttons on her lapel yesterday. I knew I wouldn't be shopping at their store anymore."

"You mean Hannah? Hannah Weinstein was wearing a Citizens' Alliance button?" Nelma felt there must have been some mistake. Hannah was her pal.

"You were friends with that girl, weren't you?" Ellen said. "You went to school together? It was her all right, wearing her little button. They should just call it the Copper Bosses Alliance."

"Yea, we were friends," Nelma said, fingering the necklace Hannah had given her. "A long time ago."

It had only been a few weeks since she had last seen Hannah, but she didn't want Ellen to know. It seemed there was no longer room for neutral friendships. She might be judged unfavorably, with Hannah as a friend.

By what measure is someone considered an ally? Nelma wondered. Was it possible to stand firmly on the other side of an issue so vital to her very being and still be considered a compatriot? Could Hannah be so wholly unsympathetic to her cause and still be her advocate?

When Nelma's father died in the mines, Nelma had stolen a copper ingot and hid it under her bed, her intentions wavering between revenge and remorse. Hannah had devised the plan to wrap it in Nelma's father's shirt and throw it down an abandoned mine shaft, depriving the copper mine bosses of their bounty and mourning her father at the same time. She always thought that Hannah had understood.

NOVEMBER 12, 1913

RUSSELL SAT ALONE ON A BARSTOOL at Shute's Saloon. The beer filtered through his tired body like a wave of relief. The fatigue remained, but felt comfortable and welcome. By the second beer, the gnawing ache in his shoulder seemed distant, and his thoughts of visiting the company doctor slowly disappeared. Russell didn't need anyone telling him whether or not he was fit to work. If the strike ended with him out due to injury, he knew there would be no place held for him. His job would be gone. It still might be gone when the strike ended, but enough people had left the district for him to hold onto hopes of a permanent position. Maybe even a shaft-sinkers job, where he'd pull in the big bucks along with the respect of the mine captains.

Russell could see how differently one was treated according to one's position in the mines. A trammer like himself would be lucky to get acknowledged on the streets, instead of roughly brushed aside by the likes of that drunken mine captain at the other end of the bar. The man in question worked down in the South Range. Russell had picked up that much when he had pushed past him on the way to the toilet. He was loudly proclaiming how the union leaders were frequent guests at the local whorehouses, ignoring his friend's observation that he was just jealous that his best girl was now favored by one of them. Russell ordered another beer. Perhaps his third, he had no inclination to keep track.

A wind-blown man with two chipped front teeth sat on the barstool to Russell's left, shook out his hat and dusted the bar with plump snowflakes.

"Join me for a whiskey, mister?" the man said.

"Sure thing," Russell said. "You work the Quincy? I ain't seen you here before."

"I worked the L.C. Waldo up till yesterday. Name's Jack. Been sailing the great lake for near twenty years now."

The bartender presented the two men with their shots of whiskey, his starched white jacket wrinkling as he worked. Russell studied the man beside him in the plate glass mirror behind the bar. His face was chiseled and bronzed, his eyes glowed with an eerie excitement. He nodded to Russell's reflection and downed his drink, before Russell could bring the glass to his lips. Jack was already ordering another round. Russell wondered who'd be paying. He figured the whiskey alone would cost about twenty cents.

"How long you out on the water, working a job like that?" Russell asked. He'd never been on a boat in his life and wasn't of a mind to try, but thought a little conversation might have Jack feeling more generous about picking up the tab.

"Ya get to shore every few days, usual," Jack said. "But I don't think you'd be wanting a job like mine. I'm not sure I'm still wanting a job like mine after this weekend."

Russell felt he had some boasting rights about tough jobs, and was about to prove it when the back-delivery doors flew open and two deputies on horseback stampeded into the bar. The cold November snows blew in behind them. The bartender shouted obscenities at the men and their horses, ordering them out of his building. One man who had fallen to snoring on the table behind the billiards woke with a speechless, confused expression. The horses snorted and shook up the place, trying to navigate the crowded barroom. One bumped into a table and sent several bottles crashing to the floor, which startled the frightened animal.

"Don't you people be worrying none," one of the riders said. "We're just cleaning your premises of some of them undesirables."

Three men who had been sitting quietly in the corner looked up at the deputies like a pack of trapped animals. They were all young men, blond hair, blue eyed with features so similar that they might have been brothers. One ran for the front door, but a deputy blocked the entrance. The remaining two didn't put up a fight, but stood defiantly, insisting they had done nothing wrong. The deputies allowed them their coats before they were handcuffed and led away.

"What the hell was that about?" Jack said.

"We got a strike in the district," Russell said.

"So you're on a picket line then?"

"Not me, I don't want nothing to do with their union. I'm just working my job and making good money. They might call me a scab, but I got nothing to be ashamed of. They the ones causing trouble. You got a problem with that?"

"Not at all," Jack said. "Takes a strong man to take a stand." He turned to the bartender and ordered another round.

"It's hard work, thousands of feet underground. These are some of the deepest mines in the world," Russell said, striking what he imagined was a proud pose. "You gotta be good with the risks working something like that, but the wages are better than any other job I'd ever had."

Russell raised his shot glass, waited for Jack to follow suit, and poured the harsh drink down his throat. He had a good feeling about his new friend; he was a good listener.

"So how come you left your ship?" Russell asked. "You looking for work on dry land?"

"I'm surprised you haven't heard," Jack said. "They had two rescue boats battling the gale trying to get us out."

"I don't spend my money on newspapers," Russell said. "Nothing of interest in them for me."

"We left Two Harbors on Friday, before the storm warnings were raised. The temperatures were fair for November, probably sixty degrees. By afternoon the lake was high and a gale blew a hard rain that turned to snow. We were taking on water. They say the winds were blowing o'er sixty miles an hour. Close to midnight, the pilothouse was swept overboard, and the captain almost went over himself."

The bartender wandered over with the third round of whiskey and stood back a ways, polishing a glass till he likely wore it thin enough to break. He was looking down the long bar, trying to appear disinterested, but Russell could tell his ears were cocked in their direction, like a cat with its ears turned back.

"We had no lights and no navigation, save one hand compass I had stashed in my duffle. Otherwise we would have been lost. The captain managed to turn the boat around and head for Bete Grise Bay, but we never made it. Got tore up by the rocks on Gull Island. Split the whole thing in two. Imagine that, eh? Over four thousand tons of steel broke up on Gull Island. I thought sure we were done for."

Russell soon lost all awareness of the world around him. There was just him and the sailor's story. Jack seemed to grow several inches with the enormity of the tale he told. Russell's own troubles seemed to shrink in comparison. His own job seemed safe and unassuming.

"But that were just the beginning of our ordeal," Jack continued. "We were holed up in the windlass room for four miserable days. No one knew we were there. The boat froze over until we were trapped in a cave of ice. Nothing but two cans of preserves for twenty-three men. We were just waiting to die. Twenty-three miserable cold men waiting to die."

"Damn. That storm was fierce," Russell said. "Seems like you never should a been on that water this late in the season. Damn."

"Four cursed days listening to the winds howling, like wild animals circling in for the kill. Didn't think anyone knew we were there, and if they knew, couldn't see how they could do anything about it, the lake was so fierce. We took to burning everything in sight, just to keep warm. We threw charts, journals and furniture into the captain's bathtub, watching the flames and watching the smoke filter up through the hole in the ceiling. Wondering how long it would take to die."

"But they found you," Russell said, anxious to hear how it all ended, like a child listening to a bedtime fable. Mesmerized by the sailor, his whiskey and his story.

"Yep, they found us. A steamer saw us through a break in the snow and sent a man to shore. He hiked for hours until he finally reached Eagle

Harbor, but their lifeboat was down for repairs. They tried to get to us in a damn surfboat. Lucky no one got killed before they turned back. A full day later they got their lifeboat back in business about the same time the Portage Canal crew reached us. They chopped their way through the ice with pickaxes, put us on the lifeboat and brought us back here. I've been drinking pretty steady ever since. Drink to life, my friend! Drink to life."

Russell raised his shot glass high and turned to see if anyone else had heard this ordeal. Disappointed to find no audience, he emptied the whiskey down his throat. He composed a small speech in that slowed moment in time that inebriation occasionally creates.

"My friend," Russell said with exaggerated fanfare, "You need to get yourself a new job. I've been here but a few months, even so, I know I could get you a job in the mines tomorrow like that." Russell tried in vain to snap his fingers. "You need a new job, my friend."

"Maybe so," Jack said. "But I'll probably hire onto another steamer in the spring."

"And whatcha gonna to do until then? Tell you what. I'll meet you back here tomorrow. Same time. I'm sure I can get you a job. Tomorrow, okay? I gotta go."

Russell fished two bits from his pocket, left them on the bar, and weaved his way out of the saloon. The furniture was still in disarray from the horses. Buttoning up his coat, pulling on his hat, slipping into his mittens on the way out, Russell lumbered home against a relentless head wind. The cold on his face gave him the illusion of sobriety, but his foot falls wavered along the road before finding rest at Mrs. Huhta's house. The front hall was still lit, but the rest of the house was dark. It was late. Russell's last thought before collapsing into bed was that the morning would probably be rough.

It was. Mrs. Huhta's insistent pounding on the door stubbornly penetrated his dreams until he finally awoke. Reluctantly, Russell rolled out of bed and dressed on the cold, bare floor. Dressing didn't require much effort, he just pulled on the same clothes as yesterday over his underwear. Downstairs the other boarders were already done with breakfast and finishing up their coffee.

Luckily, he didn't have a headache, just a vague disoriented feeling that had him thankful for the predictability of his daily routine. His job didn't require much thought. He finished up the last of the pancakes, potatoes, and coffee. What the bitter drink lacked in flavor, it made up for in potency. Russell lagged behind the other men, but still made the train in time. He preferred to take the ride in silence, by himself at the back of the car. He would ask his buddy Oscar about a job for his bar friend; he held no desire to start conversation with anyone on the train. Oscar would be his best bet, anyway.

The picketers offered an anemic presence amongst the snow drifts, hardly even a nuisance anymore. Russell was glad to see that the strike appeared to be running down. Though he had never seen the Keweenaw before the unrest began, he still adopted the wistful memories of his neighbors, talking about what a nice place this had been. A tidy, well-kept place where a good man could raise a family. A place where the company would provide jobs, libraries, bathing houses, hospitals and homes. A virtual paradise, albeit a bit frozen most of the year.

Russell found Oscar in the dry house, stripping off his flannels, stepping into his hob-nailed boots, getting ready to go down where the temperatures still hovered in the eighties. Russell told his friend the tale he heard in the bar last night, and asked if he knew of any work.

"There's always work around here—especially trammers," Oscar said. "I'd send him over to the number three shaft tomorrow. Have him get there good and early. Daniel's the shift captain, and he's a good man, unlike the ones we stuck with. He'll give him something. Hell, maybe I'll go over there tomorrow morning!" Oscar gave Russell a jab in his shoulder and Russell winced in pain. "Hey, man. That was bothering you yesterday, weren't it? You should have someone take a look."

"It's nothing," Russell said. "My other shoulder's just fine. I just need to lay off it a little while."

Oscar gave him an understanding look, grabbed a handful of carbide crystals for his sunshine lamp, and headed over to the man-car. Russell lagged behind, changing slowly and nursing his shoulder. The skin there had grown as much callous as the sole of his foot. Two more days till Saturday, and Saturday would just be a half shift. I should be able to make it, he told himself.

Russell took the last seat in the man-car just as the surface captain was giving the nod to send the men down. They had started a new level this week, where the rock was hard and the copper was scarce. Oscar said it didn't seem to be following any vein, but the captain never listened to him. Hell, what did they really know anyway? Best not to think too much. The man-car shuddered as it ran over the newly laid rails that had replaced the ones warped by that air blast a week or so ago.

When they came to a stop, Russell remained seated for an extra minute to load his lamp. He got out and caught up with Oscar several yards ahead, passing one of the drill boys relieving himself on the rock wall. At the end of the drift, there was still plenty of rubble left over from yesterday's blasting for them to get started. The passage was narrow and low, causing the men to work hunched over as they shoveled and lifted the boulders into the tramcar.

The dull pain in his shoulder soon numbed in the monotonous work. His mind too became numb with the repetitive tasks of shoveling, hoisting, and pushing. He thought only of simple things, physical things, the next boulder to fetch, the angle to position his good shoulder against the car, where to place his footfalls securely. Occasionally he would think of Jack, of how good it felt to help another man in need, of how grateful he would be when he passed on the tip that Oscar had mentioned to him.

At the end of the day, he paused at the sump pool in the shaft to wash the grit off his face, rinse the rock dust out of his teeth. He settled into his seat on the mancar and waited for the hoisting engineer to bring them up top. Most of the men were too tired to talk, and those that spoke had nothing to talk about other than their work. There was no time at the end of each day for recreation, and any time spent at a tavern was time taken away from sleep. Russell's shoulder hurt. Last night's whiskey still wore on him, but he obliged himself to seek out Jack and pass along his news.

The snow blew for the sixth straight day, the packed level of the road rising high above the train tracks he took to work and back. He stood on the platform watching the engine struggle through the snowbound tracks, plowed twice daily since the storm began and still the white plague was winning. The icy wind infiltrated his clothing, under his hat, through his mittens, against his legs. Thankful to climb into the heated car, Russell rode to the top of Quincy Hill, just long enough to leave a damp residue of snowmelt dripping inside his collar.

Shute's Saloon was a short walk from the train stop, but the winds blew so hard that Russell felt as if he would move backwards if he didn't keep up his pace. Inside the first of two doors, in the small anteroom that served as a buffer between what lay without and what lay within, Russell stomped the snow off his boots and shook the icicles off his hair. He opened the next door into the familiar barroom, perhaps even more welcoming than his crowded rooming house, and looked around for Jack.

He was already at the bar, sipping his whiskey, and had found someone else to lend his story an ear. Russell decided not to interrupt. He took a stool several spots down the bar, and listened.

"Drink to life," Jack once again exclaimed, "Drink to life."

"Pal, you need to get yourself another line of work," the new man said, "I can get you a job in the lumberyards tomorrow. A good job, no need to waste your life away in these mines. That's work not fit for an animal."

To his horror, Russell watched the whole scene play out almost as it had the day before. The lumberman paid for the drinks, the sailor accepted the offer of work, and they both parted as if friends for years. Russell pulled the hat back over his wet hair and waved the bartender away when he came to take his drink order. He felt used, like a secondhand pair of boots, and jilted, as if some society lady had laughed in his face. But most of all, he felt alone and homeless. His binds to this place loosened, his dreams soiled, his future mocked. He waited a few minutes after the lumberman had left, walked to the door, and went back to Mrs. Huhta's.

NOVEMBER 16, 1913

HANNAH RETURNED HOME FROM Sam and Ida's house hugging borrowed clothes wrapped in paper, her hands warmed in her new fox-fur muff. Ida had lent a skirt purchased just last spring while visiting family in Detroit. The skirt was a narrow jet-black wool design interlaced with thin ribbons of foil, providing a subtle glitter in the proper lighting. She rushed upstairs to the full-length mirror in Mother's room, where she unpacked the skirt and held it up to her waist.

Maude Adams was playing Peter Pan at the Kerredge Theater Saturday night, and Aaron had two seats in the first balcony, front and center. They would have an evening without chaperone; Hannah already felt a rush of excitement. Sam would accompany them to and from the theater, of course, but once inside, they would be alone. Hannah modeled the new skirt and practiced the limp wrist pose that Ida had taught her. She imagined Aaron taking her hand, guiding her to the lobby, where they would engage in small talk and polite conversation until the first bell sounded.

"Hannah!" Mother called from the kitchen. "Come downstairs, I need your help."

Hannah reluctantly scooped up her clothes, and left them and the muff on her bed. At the bottom of the bare wood stairs she left her jacket on the coat rack, took a deep breath, and held it for a minute before continuing into the kitchen. Mother didn't look up from her task of peeling and slicing potatoes. "The teamsters stopped by with our order," she said. "I haven't had a chance to put it away."

Hannah remembered the large orders they would place before the strike, when Mother didn't look worried all the time. Now her face looked withered like a piece of dehydrated fruit left in the cellar too long. Today there was a pail of lard, a pound of sugar, and a gallon of kerosene. Plus the potatoes Mother worked on. No meat, no coffee, no pastries. There was whitefish in the icebox and elderberry wine in the cellar. With this, they would have Sabbath dinner tonight.

Hannah set the table with the china and silver, candles and wine glasses, bread and butter. Sam and his family arrived with a loaf of challah bread that Ida had baked, and Hannah discretely put away the loaf she had just set out. Mother's was better shaped and probably better tasting, but she knew it would be improper to point this out. If she had even half of Mother's skills, she would give Ida some pointers, but her breads always came out weighty and dense, lacking the light buttery flavors Mother knew how to bake in.

The sun set fast in the shadow of the South Range hills, rushing the family through preparations that were much more leisurely in the summer time. Mother ushered the family around the table, lit the candles and closed her eyes while reciting the prayers. As a child, Hannah would be mesmerized by Mother's hands as they fluttered around the flames and commanded an unquestioned authority every Friday night. Even now, Hannah knew, it was Mother that brought Sam back every Sabbath evening, perhaps his own home lacked the familial magic that Mother wrought.

Dinners had become livelier since Sam had joined the Citizens' Alliance. Mother would quietly poke fun at his enthusiasm, while Father would wear a perpetual look of concern. Hannah had missed the last meeting. She had been helping Mother with some inventory.

"Was Stella dominating last night's meeting?" Hannah asked. "I find her a bit overbearing at times."

"I think the times have moderated her behavior a bit," Ida said. "Her tea parties aren't so important with this crowd. We're more serious minded for her petty gossip. She didn't have much to say."

"We had the sheriff in attendance last night," Sam said, his voice imbued with importance. "We're setting up a call service with the deputies.

We can report any disturbing behavior directly, and we can help by keeping an eye on the key agitators from the union."

"What is this?" Mother asked. "You're not skulking around in the dark watching over our neighbors?"

"Not skulking," Sam said. "That's what the union men are doing. We're simply walking the streets, just a friendly walk down the street every day. Nothing wrong in a little gentle persuasion to keep the peace."

"It's a fine line between activism and vigilantism," Father said. "Be sure you know where that line is."

Sam conceded the point and the helped himself to the last of the canned peaches and cream. The men moved into the sitting room and Ida tended to her son. Hannah helped clean up in the kitchen. After clearing the table, Mother washed and Hannah dried. She wiped a plate with soap bubbles curdling along the rim, placed it on the shelf and reached for another. Mother was usually quick at this chore, so Hannah was surprised to see her hesitate.

"Aaron Cohen is a courteous gentleman," Mother said. "Very proper, if not a bit outspoken in his politics."

"He takes his job seriously," Hannah said. "I like that about him."

"I worry," Mother said. "He's a bit evasive about how long he plans to stay."

"I don't think he knows. It depends on the strike."

"You've become fond of him, haven't you?"

Hannah's face warmed; she wasn't sure where Mother was taking this conversation. "He's different than the local boys. More interesting."

"Should Father have a talk with him? What exactly are his intentions?"

"No, please Mother. It doesn't need to be so formal. This is 1913! Things are different now."

"Maybe. But I think you need to know. If he doesn't talk about the future, is he not planning ahead, or are you not in his plans?"

Hannah felt exposed. It was as if Mother could read her thoughts and see her anxieties. Whenever Hannah tried to talk about her hopes and expectations, Aaron would deftly change the subject. She imagined herself moving to New York or Boston, and studying at a university in the east. He had opened her eyes to a world that she longed to join, with women doctors, lawyers and suffragettes, though she was uncertain how. She preferred to think that Aaron shared her vision and was equally unsure how to proceed, but Mother's words fed her doubts.

Later, when she retired to her room and thought about the next night, she cast those concerns aside. Aaron did care for her, and somehow they would work things out. Hannah went to sleep to the muffled sound of the wind throwing inch upon inch of snow against the houses, trees and streets.

When the sun broke above the horizon in the morning, snow was still falling. The lower sash of her window was completely frosted over, creating small rainbow daggers scattered across the walls of her bedroom. Coffee brewed downstairs. Hannah put on yesterday's dress, the worn gray one with fabric buttons from neck to toe. She needed to do the wash, and was grateful she would have Ida's outfit to wear tonight. Laundry could be put off until tomorrow.

Saturday breakfast was now burdened with a tension between Mother and Father, who disagreed on keeping the store open on the Sabbath. During more prosperous times, the Saturday business was when most of the big money items were sold. Women would bring their husbands in to show off the sofa or Oriental rug or special china they had picked out earlier in the week. Hannah would repeat the same glowing assessments she had first delivered to the women, but she would speak them as if for the first time, to convince the men who carried the wallet.

But these games were no longer played out on Saturdays. Most of the business came on weekdays, and none of the larger items had been sold since the strike began. Mother felt they should close the store on the Sabbath now. It brought in no business and it no longer seemed appropriate to work on the day of rest. Father feared losing any business to the union commissaries. He feared what any change might signal to miners, union and nonunion alike.

Father drank his coffee and left to open the store, without a kind word to Mother on his way out the door. Sam now spent Saturdays with his new Citizens' Alliance friends, some who wouldn't have given him the time of day before the strike began. They were all united, with a mission that often took much of the afternoon to discuss at the Bosch Brewery in Houghton. Hannah sat at the breakfast table on the edge of uncertainty. Wondering whether spending the day at the quiet store would pass the time any quicker than attending synagogue with Mother, shivering in the cold balcony that separated the women's section from the men's.

In the end, there was little choice. Mother made it clear she would not be attending synagogue alone. Hannah buttoned her boots and followed Mother through the deep snowdrifts that lined the roads, covered the sidewalks and loomed over the streetcar tracks below. The tracks were the only piece of ground that required snow removal, to allow the streetcars along its steel rails. The streets were simply panked down by giant rollers, creating a firm, but ever-rising path for hoof and foot to trod upon. After last night's snowfall, Hannah figured the panked ground had risen several more inches. She guessed the distance between her boot and the streetcar tracks below could easily accommodate the full length of her body, and then some. The wall of packed snow lining the tracks seemed smooth as a wall of plaster.

In the synagogue, Hannah sat close to the far wall, pressed between Mother and the widow Blumson, who gave way to snoring before the curtains of the ark parted, exposing the decorated Torah scrolls inside. She looked back to Mother, whose head was bowed in prayer, and examined her face as if that of a stranger. Hannah studied the thin, almost translucent skin, the chestnut hair pulled back tightly under a kerchief, the closed, dry lips, unrecognizable in their lack of expression. Who was this woman? How well did she really know her, beyond the routine of their daily existence? Hannah tried to think of someone she could claim to know intimately, whose secrets and desires, failures and shortcomings were as well known as her own. She thought of her family, of Mother and Father, her brother and his wife, her neighbors and Nelma, and they all seemed to be strangers today. Strangers who shared the same path now and then, but never truly revealed where they wanted to go. Strangers every one, and then she thought of Aaron. She closed her eyes and tried to imagine him from the inside out, and thought him to be a like minded soul, with a clear direction in life, and not wearing blinders on his journey. She wondered how much longer they would tread the same road, and whether she really wanted a future downstate at the University of Michigan. Perhaps going east, and closer to Aaron, was where she wanted to be.

Beneath the women's balcony, the Cantor started singing the familiar strains to "Shema Yisrael" and the widow Blumson woke with a snort. The curtains of the ark closed, the Rabbi spoke his benediction, and soon they were all filing down the wooden stairs, already stained from the snows of its first winter last year.

At home, the sluggish hours seemed to pass with great reluctance. It seemed as if the clocks were all running a little slow. This was the first Sabbath spent at home since Hannah and Sam were children. In those days they would look toward Mother to judge how much they could get away with, without violating the day of rest prescribed by Jewish law. Traditionally, they could eat, but not cook; walk to synagogue, but not ride the streetcar; pray, but not play. As much as Mother wanted to spend the Sabbath at home, she too seemed unaccustomed to the great expanse of empty time. Finally the sun was set and dinner was prepared. Soup and stuffed cabbage, biscuits left over from yesterday.

Hannah rushed upstairs after dinner to change her clothes. She put on her white blouse with the frilled collar and studied its compatibility with Ida's borrowed skirt. Unhappy with the combination, she undid the wealth of tiny cloth covered buttons and instead tried the plain blouse with the contoured waist. Studying her profile in Mother's mirror, she wished Ida were here to help her choose. She heard Aaron come in downstairs, and paused to listen to him talk with her brother.

"Welcome, Comrade Cohen," Sam said. Hannah bristled at his sarcasm.

"You shouldn't mock what you don't understand," Aaron said.

"I don't need to be party to your cause to see what it's done to my hometown. These socialists and union men came to a peaceful, affluent society and turned it into a war zone."

"It was the local men who called the strike, the union headquarters in Denver thought it premature."

"Damn right it was premature. The union barely has twenty percent membership," Sam said. "The mining companies have no obligation to negotiate with them."

"The union has well over fifty percent membership," Aaron retorted. "The mine companies just don't want to recognize the union."

"I don't know why Father puts up with your rhetoric," Sam said. "Nor why Hannah thinks so well of you."

Hannah went back to the frilled blouse and labored over the buttons as her brother continued to spar with Aaron downstairs. It was a mistake to have Sam drive them to the theater, but Mother was insistent.

"Perhaps they have an open mind," Aaron said. "Perhaps it doesn't seem unreasonable to request an eight-hour day, a three-dollar daily wage, a formal grievance system."

"And don't forget the abolishment of the one-man drill," Sam said. "That's the rallying cry, isn't it? What these people don't seem to understand is the one-man drill is the only thing that will secure their future. Without it the mines will go bankrupt."

"It's not just the money, Sam. The mines kill a man every week of the year, and over ten times that are seriously injured. A just society would value a man's life over a company's profits."

Hannah hurried down the stairs and hoped to put an end to the debate, which she thought Aaron had handily won. They dressed in their winter coats and Hannah sat herself between the two men as Sam held the reigns to the family carriage. He raced the horse at a pace that would surely vex Father, but she didn't dare criticize now that they had turned to less combative small talk. He moderated their speed as they approached downtown, and then checked the horse to a walk.

They came to a stop in front of the Kerredge Theater. Aaron helped her out of the carriage and shook Sam's hand before taking her inside. Hannah had never been in the building before. The floor was laid with red sandstone, likely taken from the Jacobsville quarry just out of town. Ornate electric lights cast a soft glow on the white plaster walls, and beyond the theater doors, the orchestra played a lively tune, though much of the audience still loitered in the lobby.

Aaron took Hannah's coat, stuffing her muff into the right sleeve, as they made their way to the coat check. Hannah stifled a giggle when she saw the black velvet necktie neatly knotted around his collar, the latest fashion back east.

After the first bell rang, they climbed the stairs to the balcony, the usher pointing out their seats in the front row. The stage was cloaked with a heavy burgundy curtain, framed by gilded trim. An ornate pressed-tin ceiling hung over their heads, illuminated by blue glass wall sconces spaced along the outside walls. Hannah felt she had stepped into another city in another world. How could all this opulence have been hidden behind the ordinary exterior without her knowing? Of course, she remembered the excitement when the theater had first opened, but that was over a decade ago, when she had been a child. Too young to be allowed inside. And somehow the occasion to visit had never presented itself until now.

"It's beautiful, don't you think?" Hannah felt she was gushing, and studied the expression on Aaron's face for his response.

"It's very nice. Much newer than the theaters in New York, which all have retrofitted gaslights converted to electric. You've never been here before?"

"I'm sure I visited years ago," Hannah lied, embarrassed.

Hannah sat down and adjusted her skirt, covering her ankles and smoothing the rippled cloth on her lap. Aaron was reading his program, so she opened her program booklet, while stealing an occasional glance his way. She checked her hair with her hand, tucking a loose strand behind her ear. The second bell rang and the lights began to dim. Aaron reached over and held her hand, with an awkward smile. Hannah saw that he was as nervous as she, and this emboldened her. She squeezed his hand gently.

They sat in the darkness, listening to the orchestra, until the lights sprang to life, illuminating the fanciful world of Never Never Land. When Peter Pan sprinkled his fairy dust on the children and they flew, actually flew out the stage window, Hannah was completely absorbed into the story. At the first intermission, they remained in their seats, discussing the life that Maude Adams must lead. Dressed as a boy on stage, traveling the country, perhaps treated as near royalty at the finest hotels. She wondered how she got started, and if this was something she herself could ever do.

In the next acts, Hannah rediscovered the magic of childhood beliefs in mermaids, Indians, pirates and fairies. When Tinkerbell drank the poison destined for Peter Pan, she joined those around her in a collective gasp, horrified at her impending death. Peter Pan implored the audience to show their belief in fairies. They responded with thunderous applause. Hannah's eyes welled up with emotion, gratified at her ability to make the world a better place and save a fairy's life.

At the last intermission, they filed down the stairs, back to the lobby, where she imagined herself the star, greeting well wishers, graciously accepting accolades and commentary on her performance.

"Quite a show, don't you think? This town is full of surprises—almost makes me want to move here," Aaron said with a wink.

"The costumes were fabulous."

Mr. Rosenblatt and his wife approached from the first-floor entrance. "Ah, Miss Weinstein, Mr. Cohen. Enjoying the performance?"

Hannah noticed Aaron's eyes fix on Mr. Rosenblatt's Citizens' Alliance button, and hoped he wouldn't say anything confrontational. She felt she had just returned from holiday, and was forced to consider the unpleasantness that had persisted for nearly four months. The magic of the evening was broken.

They returned to their seats at the second bell, breaking away from the exceedingly polite and superficial conversation with Mr. Rosenblatt and his wife.

"Have you been to their meetings?" Aaron whispered. "You're close to those in the Citizens' Alliance, aren't you?"

Hannah remained silent, unwilling to talk about it here, in public.

"Could you invite me to one of their meetings? As a reporter?"

"Of a Yiddish, Socialist paper? Ha!" Hannah whispered back, looking straight ahead, hoping he would change the subject.

"Can we talk later?"

"Fine, later," Hannah conceded as the lights once again dimmed.

The last act was just as magnificent as the first, reclaiming the suspension of time, the cessation of adversity, if only for an hour. Hannah again allowed herself to be immersed in the story. Her hands remained alone in her lap.

After the finale, they waited outside, under a sky that had been swept clean of its overcast to reveal a piercing display of the stars. It seemed like weeks since she had seen them last. Earlier, she had asked Sam to allow them a little time to themselves after the show, a little time to linger before he picked them up in the carriage. Now, as Aaron pried her for information, she regretted that request.

"Could you at least let me know when the next meeting is?" Aaron begged. "No one need know where I found out."

"Aaron, they'll know."

"It would make a terrific story, a more balanced story if I could find out more. Who are the members? Are the Boston copper owners involved? Or their managers or agents?"

"It's just the folks around town, butchers and wagon drivers, doctors and lawyers." Hannah said.

"Lawyers?" Aaron raised an eyebrow. "Which lawyers? Some of them have had steady clients in the copper mines. Steady clients mean steady cash. Where does the money come from for all your handbills and buttons?"

"I don't know and I don't care. It's just neighbors, just people around town. Can't we talk about something else?"

"I'm sorry." Aaron's expression softened. "I need to stop working for a night, don't I? Look, here comes your brother with the carriage."

He reached one arm around her back, pulling her closer than he probably needed to escort her to the street. Something that she would normally enjoy. Something that she would usually see as playful. But tonight she wondered if perhaps she was being used.

They dropped Aaron off at the Scott Hotel before proceeding back to their family house. Even at the horse's slow pace, the cold air was sharp and biting. Her face became rigid in the cold. Odd how the beauty of the clear winter night could be the cause of such bitter temperatures.

"Was it a good show?" Sam asked, checking the horse's gait.

"Wonderful." Hannah answered, thinking about the costumes and the stage sets and then the conversation with Aaron. "It was mostly wonderful."

Sam pulled the horse to a stop in front of the house, walked around and escorted her inside. He caught her eye as she slipped off her coat.

"You're not wearing your Citizens' Alliance button, Hannah. You should have worn it. We need to show it off everywhere – even at the theater with Aaron. It's a statement, you know that. You know what we've been saying."

"Oh, Sam..." Hannah began, but then decided she was too exhausted to protest. "I'm sorry. I must have forgotten. I'll put it on tomorrow."

Hannah lingered in the foyer as Sam went back to the carriage. She put her face to the window, staring. Outside the stars continued to shine in the still of the night. They seemed frozen overhead, stationary outposts in the sky, and yet somehow they moved at unfathomable speeds. A heavenly slight of hand that created daylight out of night, change without movement.

NOVEMBER 27, 1913

LAST NIGHT'S TRAIN DELIVERED THE weekly stock to the union commissary. Every new shipment seemed like holiday gifts to Nelma. There were the usual staples: Chicago hams, coffee and flour, Bayer Aspirin and Lifebuoy Soap, but there were always surprises too. Today she found bottles of Canada Dry Ginger Ale and Coca-Cola, cans of candied yams, and a whole case of pecans. She wasn't exactly sure what one would do with pecans, but was certain she would have to try them.

Nelma opened the store ledger and tallied one can of pecans before placing it on the counter. She would wait for Estelle before opening it up, and they could sample its contents together. There were two ledgers in the commissary, one for purchases and one for inventory. Frank had walked her through the system on her first day. It seemed complicated at the time, a real test of her rusty mathematics skills, which had barely been exercised since grade school.

Now the ledger system was a simple task she looked forward to. Checking the purchases against the inventory, and reviewing the back room for accuracy when the numbers were running low. She remembered having a head for math when she was in school. She remembered the pride in easily handling multiplication, division and fraction problems that caused others to stumble. It felt good to have that pride once more.

Estelle broke her thoughts as she entered the building, bringing with her a burst of cold air and snow. She hung her coat behind the counter, stomped the snow off her boots, and sat on the stool next to Nelma, silent and brooding.

"How's your mother?" Nelma ventured to ask. The old woman had fallen ill last week. She was cranky enough when healthy. Theirs was a family of all girls and Estelle was the oldest. She had been expected to carry the load since her father was blinded in an underground explosion. He now earned a fraction of his former pay at a company broom factory but hadn't worked since the strike began. No one would walk him across the picket lines.

"Oh, she's gotten her strength back," Estelle said. "Strong enough to beat me with her birch twigs if I don't get the sauna heated up the way she likes. I think the only reason she labored to have seven children was her foresight of having seven indentured servants."

"You shouldn't talk like that about your mother."

"And your mother, Nelma? Has she spoken a word to you since the strike began?"

"It's not like that at all, Estelle. We get on just fine." Nelma suppressed a pang of regret over the wall that had grown between her mother and herself. She understood her mother's need to make ends meet, but still found it difficult to excuse. She couldn't endure a visit to that boarding house filled with scab labor. They had rarely met since the start of the strike.

"Look what I found," Nelma said, holding up the pecans, trying to change the subject. "Have ya ever had these nuts before?"

"I wouldn't of known they were nuts if you hadn't told me," Estelle said, smiling. The tension dissolved between them. "Let's open it up and see what they taste like."

IT WAS A BUSY morning at the commissary. The cured hams were selling fast as Thanksgiving was only a couple days away. Usually they tried to clear out the back room before opening up the new shipment, but today there wasn't enough time to do that. So they sold the hams right out of the crates.

Edward stopped by over lunch with the kids, and together they ate the last of the smoked whitefish. There had been a change in him over the last few weeks. A subtle difference that she couldn't pin down to any particular day or event, but still the man who stopped by today was nothing like the man who would take out his frustrations on her at the drop of a hat. He seemed more civil, more distant. It made her suspicious. She had no understanding of how he spent the long hours she was away at the commissary. It wasn't another woman she suspected; it was something else.

"You should pick out a ham for Thanksgiving," Edward said. "Find a good one before they all been picked over."

"It ain't like a bushel of apples, silly," Nelma said, smiling to cloak her sarcasm. "They're all pretty much the same. But I'll set one aside after I'm finished with my sandwich."

"Ham and yams and a loaf of bread. I'm already looking forward to a bite of meat."

Nelma looked hard at her sallow faced husband, and wondered if he was really becoming kinder, or if he was just getting tired and worn down, like a wild horse that's had the spirit broken out of him. She realized she was no longer attracted to him. Estelle had little Toivo on her knee, and Lila was seeing how high she could stack the cans of pecans. It was a different kind of home here at the commissary—just as comfortable as the house, but usually without the children. And when they did come, she sometimes felt more like their aunt than their Mother. She still loved them dearly, but while she was here, it was usually someone else who would wipe their nose, tie their boots, and cut their bread. Nelma was surprised at how much this pleased her.

THANKSGIVING MORNING there were no parades and the commissary was closed. Nelma was up early, roasting coffee beans and kneading bread. She thought of her mother and could imagine mirroring her every move, going through the same motions, cooking the same foods. As she turned the dough over in her hands, she realized this would be the first Thanksgiving they would celebrate apart. Last year she had taken her family down to her mother's house, with two pies and a wild turkey that Edward had downed with a lucky shot. Her younger sister had played with

Lila, while Toivo shared the kitchen with the women as they cooked. She wished this Thanksgiving could be the same.

Frank was usually the next to wake, with the syncopated rhythm of his cane coming down the stairs, but he had taken the train west last week. Gone to visit his family in Denver. She missed his easy company, so different from Edward, so worldly and mature.

Nelma placed the dough on the kitchen stove to rise, covered with a worn dishrag, and poured herself a cup of coffee. The sun was slowly changing the dark dawn sky to a deep blue. The holiday lacked the sense of festivity that it usually brought. It would just be the four of them for dinner, and even with the small ham, there wouldn't be much to eat. The meat would be good though. It had been several weeks since they last had any red meat. Still they had been lucky. One neighbor's baby looked to be withering away since the strike began, and Ellen's daughter hadn't been back to school since she had been shot at the strike parade months ago. She felt uncomfortable measuring her fortune against the suffering of her friends, yet there was little else to use.

Edward lumbered down the stairs, down the hall and into the kitchen. He mumbled "G'morning," poured himself a cup of coffee, and went out back to split some wood. Nelma shook off her lapse into self-pity, and went upstairs to check on the children.

Toivo was already up, playing with the bedsheets in their room. Lila still slept soundly. Nelma scooped up her son and took him downstairs for breakfast. There was some crusty bread left over from yesterday, and she softened it in hot water before tearing it up for her son. Unhappy with the result, Toivo pushed the soggy mess onto the floor, and then cried in hunger. Nelma picked up the crumbs from the floor, brushed them off and placed them on the tray before him. Once again, he pushed them onto the floor. Frustrated, Nelma picked him up as she went upstairs to check on her daughter.

The sun was well above the horizon and though there were clouds, there was no sign of snow in the air. It looked to be a milder day than they had been having. Lila was usually up with her brother, but today she continued to sleep soundly. Nelma felt a quiver of fear, a momentary feeling that all was not well, a reoccurrence of a mother's need to touch her baby to make sure she still breathed. Instead, she quietly left the room, closing the door behind her.

Back downstairs, Toivo resumed his hungry cry as soon as she set him down. Nelma felt like leaving the house until he calmed, but looked through the cupboard for something else to feed him. There were a few cans of fruit, but she was saving those for tonight's dinner. In the root cellar, she found some wormy apples from the bottom of the bushel basket, and cut out the bad parts with a paring knife. This finally satisfied her fussy son and gave Nelma some peace.

Outside the back door, Nelma found a stack of freshly split wood, but Edward had wandered off somewhere. Possibly Toivo's tantrum had driven him away toward other chores for the morning. Nelma piled the wood into her arms and walked it over to the kitchen wood box, and let it tumble in. Two more trips and she had finished refilling the box. Edward could take the rest downstairs when he returned. She hoped he wasn't off drinking.

Toivo played in his corner, a makeshift playpen constructed from a broken crib. Nelma sat down to read a copy of *The Saturday Evening Post* that Frank had left behind. She browsed slowly through its contents, reading a short story and an article on how to buy coal. She tried to enjoy the quiet of the morning, but concern for her daughter loomed behind every thought. She checked on the rising dough, decided it was ready, and fired up the stove with some more wood.

Nelma punched down the dough, divided it in half, and shaped it into two breadpans. Then she placed them in the oven, allowing the aroma of the baking bread to mix with the coffee and wood smells already sifting through the house. She remembered waking up to these smells as a child, especially on holidays. She was surprised they hadn't rousted Lila out of bed by now, and went upstairs to check on her again.

Lila was still sleeping, but not as deeply. Nelma watched from the bedroom door as she tossed from one side of the mattress to the other. Something was wrong. Her daughter never slept this late. Nelma reached over to place a hand on her forehead and recoiled as if touching a burning stove. She was hot as fire.

Nelma picked her up and rushed her downstairs, laying her on the couch. She filled a towel with snow, rolled it up, and placed it on Lila's forehead. She thought of the aspirin locked away in the union commissary. She thought of the company doctor who would probably not take her call. She felt her eyes dampen and cried out, "No!"

Toivo looked up in surprise, but continued to play with the spoons and soggy breadcrumbs on the floor. Rushing into her boots, she ran outside while still buttoning her coat, running to her neighbor's house. Perhaps Ellen could help.

The two of them returned with a canister of herbs. Lila was now awake and unhappy. "Why did you wake me?" she demanded. "I'm so tired. My head hurts."

"Hush, child," Ellen said. "Let me make you some tea."

"I don't like tea."

"You'll like this," Ellen said.

Ellen prepared a mixture of native hemlock and sarsaparilla; Nelma changed the cold compress on Lila's forehead. When the tea was ready, Nelma cradled her daughter's head while Ellen held the cup. It took several minutes of patient encouragement before Lila finished and they let her fall back to sleep on the couch. The two women watched over her for a time, remembering other illnesses their children had recovered from and assuring each other that this time would be no different.

After Ellen left, Nelma cursed Edward with every vulgarity she could think of, in both English and Finnish. Where was he? She needed his help. There was food to prepare, and Toivo to watch and Lila to tend. She took back any kind words she had thought of him lately. All that charm could be spent in the outhouse for all she cared. Today she needed help.

A slow-footed shuffle at the front door announced Edward's return later in the afternoon. Lila was still feverish and moaning on the couch. Nelma heard him come in, but kept her back to him. Refused to acknowledge him. Smelled the liquor on his breath. He'd probably been visiting Otto's still.

"Got us a turkey, Nelma," he said. "Today we'll have us a proper Thanksgiving."

Nelma turned, reluctantly. It was a good-sized bird, young and probably tender. "It's too late to cook a bird like that today. It needs to be plucked. Put it in the icebox. I'll cook it tomorrow." She glared at him. How could he be so unaware of her anger and of their daughter's illness? "Lila is sick with fever. She needs ice. Can you get her some ice?"

"I could get her ice shavings from the Ice House. They just started harvesting ice from the portage this week." Edward said. "I'll be right back."

"Don't you be stopping anywhere else, Edward." Nelma warned. "You already been gone most of the day. I need you here."

Edward was already out the door. Nelma stood with her hands on her hips, shaking her head. She felt like throwing something, but didn't. For all his good intentions, he rarely got things right. She made another cup of tea for Lila and poured a cup of coffee for herself. *Things never turn out the way you expect*, she thought.

LILA'S FEVER BROKE two and a half days later, the same day that Frank returned. He commented on the weight Lila had lost and how tired she looked. Nelma sat on the couch, combing the tangles out of her daughter's hair. Edward was outside splitting more wood, uncomfortable with so much inactivity after several months on strike. Nelma had saved the turkey for Lila's recovery, and its long cook time filled the house with a hungry aroma.

"How was your trip?" Nelma asked.

"The trains were timely until we came back to this Michigan snow. We left Chicago on time, but still managed to arrive several hours late."

"I missed your company," Nelma said. Then quickly added, "We all missed you. You've become a part of our family."

"I missed you too," Frank said. He walked over and gently kissed her hand. Nelma could smell the slightly sour travel clothes, the musky aftershave, and the soapy residue on his hands. Lila giggled and pushed off her mother's lap to play with her brother. Frank continued to hold her hand, standing at her side, as if studying her.

Nelma looked into his face, curious of his thoughts. She imagined him leaning closer, as if to share a secret. He could kiss her on the lips if he wanted, Edward wouldn't ever have to know. The longer he stood there, the more certain she became that they were both thinking the same thing. At first, she would push him away, but not very hard. She would see an apology forming on his lips, a look of surprise in his eyes. She would wonder if he was surprised at his own actions or at hers. She wouldn't want him to speak, wouldn't want to hear an apology, wouldn't want to break the magic. Edward opened the back door and Nelma's fantasy dissolved. Frank withdrew his hand and turned to go.

"That should do it," Edward shouted from the next room, stomping the snow off his boots. "We're set for wood for a while."

Nelma stood up and walked towards the kitchen, not looking at Frank behind her nor Edward in front of her. She busied herself at the oven, basting the turkey, cutting up some cheese for the children to snack on, making another pot of coffee. She could hear Frank and Edward in the next room, discussing the latest rumors of the strike.

What had just happened? she wondered. *What happens next?* She had her children to care for, and they needed their father, perhaps more than she needed a husband. It couldn't be wrong to accept the affections of another man, she decided, as long as she didn't upset the commitments of her family.

The days that followed carried with them a strange tension in the air. She became afraid of Frank whenever he shared a room with her, but thought of nothing else when he was gone. At the strike parade, she marched with revitalized vigor, an energy that others perhaps mistook for hope, or knowledge of something to bring an end to the strike. But the strike and Frank had become almost one and the same for her, and she loved them both equally, and without desire to bring either to closure.

She wished there was someone she could trust to share her feelings on this matter. She could think of no one who could take this knowledge and not hold it against her. She worried that Estelle might use the information as a political wedge within the union, and Ellen never really liked Frank all that much, so there would be no joy in confiding with her. Her family would of course never want to know.

One night, as she lay awake next to Edward's heavy sleep, she imagined visiting Hannah to discuss her complicated relationship. They would sit on the south porch swing and figure the whole thing out. It would seem funny, no doubt, and after a time they would lose themselves in a fit of laughter.

Nelma rolled out of bed and opened her top dresser drawer. It was too dark to see well, but she would know it by its feel: a small metal chain with an odd shaped silver pendant. There it was. She drew it out and traced her fingers against the foreign script. *"Why the word life?" Nelma had asked when Hannah gave her the necklace. "Life is a wonder," Hannah had said. "Some people spend their whole time on earth trying to figure out what it really means, and never find out, but we always celebrate it." They had felt so close then, so special. "Friends for life," Nelma had said.*

Nelma threw the necklace back in the drawer. Angry at herself. Embarrassed by the fit of sentimentality that had taken hold. A true friend wouldn't be parading around with a Citizen's Alliance button on her lapel; campaigning against everything she was fighting for. Still, as she went back to bed and drifted into sleep, she tried to imagine how someday they might make amends.

The next morning a distant sun cast its frigid light over snowdrifts and dreary clapboard houses. Nelma pulled on her robe and quietly stepped downstairs, her husband and children still sleeping in their cramped bedroom. She stoked the stove, put on water for coffee, and sliced bread for toast. Soon after the coffee was ready, the two men came down to join her. Sometimes they were like brothers, like old friends, and she found herself resentful of their relationship.

Nelma wondered what they would eat today. Perhaps Edward could catch some fish on the frozen portage lake and they would feast on fish pie. Nelma put on her boots before stepping down in the cold cellar to search through bushel baskets of dwindling potatoes, yams and onions. A sparkle of light reflected from her propane lamp. Curious, she lifted the lamp above her head looking for the source of the reflection, revealing a wainscoted wall of steel. Strange. She stepped closer and the odd vision became a cache of rifles. Over a dozen rifles propped casually against the wall behind her vegetables.

An angry jolt of fear teased her scalp. If anyone found this, they could be evicted. Strikers in the South Range had already lost their company houses. What were Edward and Frank up to? She grabbed two of the rifles and raced up the stairs, pushed the cellar door against the wall and slammed the weapons on the tabletop.

"What is the meaning of this?" she demanded. "How dare you put my children at risk."

DECEMBER 3, 1913

RUSSELL PROCRASTINATED UNTIL THE pain in his shoulder hurt so bad that even Oscar couldn't stand his complaining any longer. Go see the doctor or I'm telling the shift captain, he had said. The doc gave him a sling and put him on a week's unpaid rest. Russell tried to barter his room and board with Mrs. Huhta, but she rebuffed his efforts. She said that sweeping floors and washing dishes was women's work, and his shoulder wouldn't allow him to shovel snow or split wood. He felt crippled and uncertain on how to spend his idle time.

"You should see my pastor down on Quincy Street. He'd welcome any help with his charities," Mrs. Huhta said. "I'm sure the reverend at your Methodist Episcopal Church has his charitable projects as well."

"I'm not sure what help I could offer," Russell said. "If I'm not fit for any work around here, what could I hope to do for them?"

"Don't belittle yourself. I've never seen our pastor turn away a helping hand."

The other men had left for the morning shift and Russell sat at the kitchen table drinking coffee, while Mrs. Huhta scrubbed the pots and pans in the sink. Her two daughters flirted with him throughout their breakfast until Mrs. Huhta gave them a stern look, and sent them on their way to school. Russell nursed the coffee in his cup until all that remained was a cold and bitter sludge at the bottom.

Without a clear idea of where he wanted to go, but feeling unwelcome at the boarding house, Russell put on his coat and boots, and stepped outside into the cold. The distant sun bore down on the clean white snow covering the city. Russell lowered his eyes against the icy glare of the cloudless sky. The sunlight seemed cheerless and distant; in place of its warmth he felt only frozen currents of air.

He passed his church, barely slowing his gait to glance at the nondescript white entrance door, the beveled glass windows, the tall steeple crusted with snow. It didn't seem the same, without the Sunday crowd lining up for the weekly sermon. Russell wasn't sure what the protocol was for visiting a church during the working hours of the week. He had never done it before and knew no one else who might have either.

Shute's Saloon would be open now, and not nearly as awkward. He could walk over and be greeted by name, no matter what the hour. It could even be therapeutic, he reasoned, if he drank left-handed. He had been saving a couple dollars every week to offer Maria a decent wedding in the spring, rarely drinking except on weekends. He could afford this now, he told himself. Hell, he deserved it.

Russell doubled back to the other side of the street. Past the church and the streetcar station. Up the steep incline of Summit Street, now unsuitable for horses during the snowy winter months. The sunshine cheered his mood now, lighting a path he usually tread in darkness.

Russell stepped inside the corner saloon, tucked beside houses and churches, barely distinguishable as a drinking establishment. He let his eyes adjust to the dim electric light, noting the lack of windows, save one small casement in the front. He had never been here in the daylight. A coal stove next to the bar heated the dark interior. There was a woman behind the bar today, *probably Shute's wife*, Russell thought, and a couple old men in the back, engrossed in some sort of dispute.

The barkeep was a pretty woman, the kind who grew into her looks as she aged and was generous with her smile. Her dark hair was laced with grey, and Russell wondered what Maria would look like when they grew old together. He tried but failed to imagine her in any way different than now, at least as captured in the picture he always carried with him, with creamy skin and dark eyes that almost looked oriental. It worried him that he couldn't imagine her in this future, as if it might have some bearing on what might really happen. But he couldn't quite imagine his own face years from now either, so he shrugged it off.

"What can I get you?" she asked before he had a chance to sit down. "Bottle of Bosch beer?"

"Beer and a pickled egg would do me fine. Call it a meal."

The barkeep smiled at his joke and returned with his beer by the time he had his coat off.

"I've seen you in here with Oscar before, haven't I? What's your name?"

"Russell. Russell Toll, ma'am."

"Looks like you're laid up with a bum arm."

"Bum shoulder, actually," Russell winced as his injury seemed to pain him with merely a mention. "I work with Oscar down at the Number Seven shaft. Don't quite know what to do with myself."

"Well you make yourself at home here while you're healing. First drink's on the house. We got a crew of older men usually come in around noon playing cards. They should be here soon and I'll introduce ya."

"Appreciate it," Russell said, already feeling better about himself.

The card players arrived on schedule. A disorderly assortment of former miners, barkeeps and timber men. Pinochle was their game, and at the barkeep's gentle insistence, they welcomed him into their circle. They played for the rest of the afternoon, gambling with penny antes, rotating newcomers in to take their turns. Offering good-natured jabs at each other's abilities and ordering another round whenever the last bottle went dry.

Ollie was the undisputed authority in the group, a stature earned from years as a surface captain, and before that, a contract miner. Others might walk away from the table after finishing a hand, but Ollie never relinquished his seat and no one challenged his position. He painted an interesting picture, with the hair on his head clipped shorter than was currently in fashion and the steely gray hair on his chin reaching half way down his barrel shaped chest.

"Don't understand how that judge can call himself a lawman after what he did in that courtroom yesterday," Ollie complained. "One hundred and forty-nine of them bastards, every one of them guilty as sin, and every one of them let off without even a slap on the hand."

"He's probably lined his pockets with union money," one of the men said. "There's no other accounting for it."

Russell had to have this explained to him. They were a gang of strikers.

Riotous, moral-less, un-American union men arrested for violating the law and let off without penalty. Russell rubbed his eyes for a moment and saw a vision of red. Blood red dripping like tears, falling to the floor and causing slippery mayhem wherever it flowed. The blood began to take on the form of a man, a man with a rifle, and the rifle was aimed at him. Russell opened his eyes, shocked to find everything as it had been.

"It's a bad sign for our community," Ollie said. "Now you didn't hear this from me, but I hear them Citizens Alliance people ain't gonna stand for any more of this nonsense anymore. Things gotta change around here. Things gotta get back to the way they were before."

There were several grunts of agreement, a few more snipes at the strikers, and then the conversation turned to the meld that the bald-headed man lay down. The interior of the saloon maintained a timeless quality without a clear view of the sun. As the day wore on, the surface workers were the next wave of men to filter into the bar. Their hands and faces were cleaner than the underground shift that arrived later. The card players finished up their game, with promises to play better tomorrow and salutations to their wives waiting back home.

Russell didn't see any of the men from his crew and was disappointed. He wanted to put a good face on his injury and show that he hadn't been beaten down, that he wasn't to be written off, that he would be returning in another week. He bundled up and hiked down the hill to Mrs. Huhta's, his usual evening hunger muted by all the beer in his stomach.

The onset of night, at barely five o'clock, brought back his normative routine, the return to the boarding house after a long day in the mines. He felt as if he had been on vacation all day, and recalled his school days when he and the boys had skipped school, but he still managed to meet Maria and walk her home from class. She must have known what he was doing but never let on. He wondered if Mrs. Huhta would be so kind about his stay at the saloon today.

The table was set and the other boarders were lingering around the kitchen when Russell came inside and hung his coat and hat. One of the boarders gave him a questioning glance, cocking his head slightly, raising his eyebrows. Never saying a word, yet inviting Russell to answer with the story of his day. The smell of the simmering stew was compelling. Russell wanted to revel in the aroma and let it stir up memories of his childhood home. They never had much, but every Sunday his mother would fill their hungry stomachs with a hearty beef and potato stew, even if the only beef to be found was the flavor in the broth.

"Look what the cat dragged in," another boarder, Thomas, announced Russell's presence to the rest of the kitchen. "How's that shoulder treating you?"

"It's about the same," Russell lied, the simple actions of playing cards and raising a glass of beer seemed to have aggravated his condition, whatever it was.

"Better hope you don't have none of that bursitis my brother had down in the mines," Thomas said. "He hasn't been able to do much of anything for o'er a year now. It still ain't healed up."

Russell caught himself rubbing his shoulder and thinking about what Thomas had just said. The doc hadn't mentioned anything about bursitis, but he hadn't mentioned anything else either. No diagnosis. Just instructions to rest up and nothing more.

Mrs. Huhta brought the stew over to the table and asked everyone to sit down. She looked steady into Russell's eyes for a moment, silently judging him for his afternoon of drinking, before handing him a letter. "This come in today's mail for you," she said. It was from Maria; he recognized her flowery script, the familiar wax rose seal in the back. There was an absence of perfume, he noted, and he resisted the urge to bring it closer his nose. He tucked it inside his shirt for later.

Mrs. Huhta took three bowls reserved for her family into the sitting room where she would take her dinner with her two daughters. She bowed her head in prayer, and not a single man in the other room brought a spoon to his mouth until she was done. When she finished, the men ate with the silent concentration of hunger satiated by good food. Thomas asked for some bread to be passed, and Elias shared the pitcher of water with those seated next to him. But conversation was generally forgotten until each had their fill.

After the dishes had been cleared away, Russell rushed upstairs, closed the door to his small room and tore open the envelope with a scrap of steel he kept under the bed for this purpose. He read the letter slowly, savoring each word, tracing the plump well-formed letters with his finger, pausing at the end of each sentence to think about what she had said. Maria mentioned the happenings in the family store, her mother and father, her brother who would be visiting for Christmas. She wrote with a light, chatty tone throughout her message, but the bloody heart of the letter was placed at the very end. There had been a death in her family, the childless aunt who had favored her, and she was uncertain about setting a date for marriage until her grieving had passed. As if one had anything to do with the other. As if this dead aunt should have any influence over their decision to marry.

Russell re-read the letter a second time. Then a third. It was a very cool letter. There was no mention of how she missed him, or when they might meet again. Like she always did before. How could she do this to him? His anger competed with feelings of abandonment. He had met this aunt once, an old teacher whose prospects for marriage became thinner the longer she taught, until she had found herself beyond that age where any suitor could reasonably propose. Is this what Maria wanted? Or was this just an excuse, a thinly veiled exit strategy out of a marriage that she no longer wanted?

Russell retrieved the billfold of money he kept under his mattress, counted out two dollars, and vowed to keep drinking until every cent of it was spent. He marched down the stairs, grabbed his coat and headed straight back to Shute's, deliberately avoiding any discussion or explanation with his fellow boarders.

Light from the saloon's small front window escaped out onto the snow, casting a cheery glow in the dark, depressed landscape outside. Russell lingered outside the door. He imagined the jovial company he would meet inside. Happy men, with wives to go home to. Men with families in town, brothers to give a hand, Mothers to lend an ear. Just yesterday he had imagined himself one of them, part of a community, a future wife and home pulling him through his days. He wasn't sure he wanted to join this crowd when he felt a hand upon his shoulder.

"Hello friend," a voice said from behind.

Russell turned to face Jack, the sailor he had met a week or so ago. His face still seemed etched by the wind, a chiseled expression with deep furrows in his brow and around his mouth. He seemed different today, though. Somber. Perhaps sober.

"So you're still in town, eh?" Russell said. He remembered overhearing Jack's conversation with the lumberman. He remembered his conflicted feelings from hearing his mining position declared unfit for man or beast. "Have you found any work?"

"I had a job for a time in the mills. But the lumber ran out quick as the snow falling outside. They couldn't drop any more trees with snowdrifts above their heads. Were you going inside?"

"I guess I was."

The two men found a space near the end of the bar, all the seats were taken, but they were able to hail the bartender over their way. Russell took in the energy of the crowd, the men in for their first round of drinks and those who had been there since he had left for supper. His melancholy was forgotten, his hesitation now seemed unfounded.

"Where you staying?" Russell asked. "Have you got a place?"

"Down in Painesdale. It's a bit of a ride from here, but this is where all me friends are."

Friends that buy your drinks, Russell thought wryly, but without blame. Since when was he such an expert on friendship, anyway? His girl was probably out dancing around with some other fellow in Chicago right now, while Jack offered a sympathetic ear and promised to buy a round. Maybe he was a bit rash about this sailor. *Maybe.*

"I'm out of work for a time myself," Russell said. "Overworked my shoulder in the mines."

"Doesn't sound serious," Jack said. "I broke an arm once when we were taking on green water on Huron. Got swept overboard, but I had tied on deck, so luckily, I was pulled back. Broke an arm in the whole affair, though."

"Hell, I've been laid up myself a few times," Russell said. He told of the time in Washington he had been beaten up by some thugs trying to push him out of his lousy fruit packers' job. Or the time he had broken a leg his first time on skis. They went back and forth like this all night. Commiserating and competing, consoling and belittling. Jack was true to his word and bought the first round, and they pooled their funds the rest of the night. Jack started arm-wrestling other fellows at the bar, and Russell lost two quarters on bets but won three more before they both called it quits for the night.

Russell felt he had rediscovered a friend after a falling out, despite knowing they had met only once or twice before. "You remember that crazy night with the deputies in the bar? They had those union men cornered like a sad trio of lame animals."

"Those sorry fellows never even put up a fight," Jack said. "They was a bunch of cowards. I wouldn't trust none of them to look after my back."

"I'd trust you," Russell said, with a sudden sense of sobriety. "Anything happen, I mean anything, you can call on me."

Jack eyed him with a studying look, before shoving him out the bar door. "Don't be so damn serious. But you know, I'd let you know the minute anything bad was going down. Without hesitation. See you tomorrow."

RUSSELL QUICKLY became comfortable with his new schedule. He'd play pinochle in the afternoons and spend his evenings with Jack, who had found a day job at the Painesdale general store. By Thursday he had spent almost half of his savings on beer. By Friday his shoulder was feeling better and on Saturday he had thrown away his letter from Maria, at Jack's urging, to dispense with his bitter feelings. They had done it at Shutes. Tore up her pretty stationary and thrown it into the trash. When he collapsed into bed later that night, he stole a peek at her picture, the one he carried in his wallet since his arrival. It didn't have the usual effect on his mood; the confident feeling of being loved was gone. His last thought before drifting off to sleep was that it was just as well.

He awoke to a loud rapping on his bedroom door. Annoyed, he rolled over and placed his pillow over his head. The rapping continued. Mrs. Huhta should know he slept in and attended the late service on Sundays. He peeked out at the window across the small room. The worn cotton curtains never quite met in the center, and always a bit of sunshine would leak in the morning. But it was barely light out.

"What? Who's there?" Russell finally managed to bark out.

The knocking stopped. "It's Jack. Open up."

"Give me a minute," Russell said, pulling on his pants, raking his hair with his fingers, before opening up the door. Jack walked in, wearing the same clothes as last night. Not that unusual, except it looked like he had slept in them. His face was unshaven, and his complexion looked pale and sickly in the morning light. "What the hell you doing here? I can't believe Mrs. Huhta let you in."

"I promised I'd come," Jack said. "Remember? I'd let you know if anything happened."

Russell looked hard at Jack's face, and something about it scared him. He had the look about him of a caged animal, a desperate feeble look that was unsettling.

"You know how I said I got me a room down in Painesdale? Well, I was a bit late getting back last night. There was another fellow from Seeberville say he'd give me a ride in the family roundabout. So we stayed until closing time. The streetcars were shut down by the time we left.

"It was quiet and still when I got back. Most houses were dark, but it looked like the Dally's had a light burning. Don't know what they were up to, though I know sometimes Mrs. Dally will stay up late reading. She runs a boarding house right next to mine. Real nice lady. She'll use any excuse to stay up late with a good book. Waiting for a boarder, baking a loaf of bread, just about anything."

Russell wished Jack would get to the point and leave. He started to doubt the urgency of Jack's long-winded tale. He walked over to the window, scratched himself, and combed his hair.

"Well I just stepped in the door when I heard it. I never heard nothing like it before. Sure, I heard a rifle shot, but this was like a war. It didn't stop. Glass

146

was shattered. Wood was splintered. This sounded like an army. I fell to the floor, I'm ashamed to say. But I fell to the floor when I should have run out to help Mrs. Dally."

Russell struggled to find the right words. Something to obscure a raw fear inside, a sense of a world outside the comfortable parameters of sanity, like a child's dream of being lost in a dangerous place. The only words that came out, however, were "What happened?"

"I don't know what happened. There's usually deputies out on the streets. Mrs. Dally was okay, but Mr. Dally got shot right in the head. Two of the boarders died in their beds. They was a couple of brothers come home to work the mines. In the house next to them, they shot a girl. A little girl in her own home. This is crazy. This ain't right. I'm leaving on the next train. I got a sister in Detroit. I can't stay here anymore."

Jack stood awkwardly by the door. Nervous. Like he half-expected someone to shoot up this house as well.

"But what they do?" Russell asked, "What them people do?"

Jack didn't offer an answer, and Russell didn't expect one.

"I gotta go. I'm sorry."

Jack shook his hand and left. Russell could hear him run down the stairs and out the front door. He didn't want to go downstairs and see the trouble mirrored on everyone else's faces. He didn't want to stay in his room here either. Finally, he opened up his wallet and took a long look at Maria's picture before ripping it in half, and then half again until there was nothing left but a puzzle of confetti dropping to the floor.

DECEMBER 10, 1913

HANNAH KNEW SHE WAS DREAMING, but didn't want to wake up. She was skiing, her feet tied to a pair of long boards with a single strap binding, tarred and waxed on the bottom. Perilous on the copper country hills. Aaron was leading the way, followed by Hannah, her brother Sam and his wife Ida. Nelma was taking up the rear. The skis slid smoothly through Aaron's tracks: push and glide, push and glide. In her dream, she had the rhythm down unlike any waking attempts. Her arms planting the poles just so at each stride. The trees around them were pregnant with snow. The sky above was cloudless and blue.

Then there were two explosions behind her, the echo of gunshot breaking the winter quiet. She turned, in the slow motion of a nightmare, to see her brother bloodied in the snow. As Ida approached, she too was felled by a gunshot. Hannah looked to Aaron for help, but he just stood there looking perplexed, his hands probing a chest wound and then extending to her, the blood staining the clean white snow before he collapsed.

Now Hannah wanted to wake up, but she had to first find her friend, her dear friend Nelma, who was the last to join them for this outing. Nelma stood defiantly behind them and lowered her rifle slightly, pausing and then swinging it over her shoulder. "You'll never understand us," she said before turning and skiing away.

Hannah was awake now; open eyes staring at her bedroom ceiling. Examining the hairline cracks in the paint above, while her heart beat madly and the whole room appeared at an odd tilt. She knew it was a bad dream yet still was disturbed by its dark message. She remembered the Painesdale shootings. Three miners and a neighbor girl gunned down in the middle of the night. Two of the miners had been regular guests to her pinochle games. Both were good men, handsome and with a sense of humor. The details of the dream fell away leaving only horror and dread. The feeling of being personally singled out by tragedy. Last night, Hannah had gone to sleep hoping all would seem clearer in the morning and was deeply disappointed.

She lay in bed for a long time before dressing. She felt detached from time and it wasn't until she had finished combing her hair that she remembered the day. Wednesday. Downstairs, she heard her parents talking, the samovar gurgling, and the hiss of the fire as someone threw another log in the kitchen stove. She tread cautiously down the stairs, as if this too was a dream in danger of turning ugly.

"Hannah, dear," Mother said as she entered the kitchen. "You're finally awake. I think you have a predisposition to sleep if no one knocks on your door."

"It's late?" Hannah asked, helping herself to a cup of coffee.

"Almost 8:00," Mother said. "We've already eaten. Father's just been to the store and back. He posted a note explaining we'd be closed all day."

"It's an odd morning," Father said. "Merchants and saloons have posted notes. They're even closing the mines so everyone can attend the rally."

"Everyone should attend. They must!" Hannah said, gripping each arm with the other. "I placed Citizens' Alliance handbills everywhere I could think of, even outside the union commissary. No one dared stop me."

"The Book of Job has much to teach us," Father said. "Job's bewilderment at the chaos, the injustice, is our bewilderment. We must have faith that all will be well."

Hannah had never heard Father quote scripture before; she was surprised that he would find comfort in it. Mother perhaps, but Father was more likely to go through the motions with all the enthusiasm of a child taking his medicine.

After breakfast, Mother sent her on a walk to pass the time. Hannah was impatient for things to get in motion, and Mother grew tired of her anxious energy. Later, she would be needed in the kitchen; Sam had invited many neighbors and friends for a mid-day potluck. The rally was to start after noon, after the services for the murdered miners. There would be marches in Calumet and marches in Houghton. These would be citizen marches, supplanting the strikers in the streets. Outside, the city seemed to be holding its breath in expectation. The streets were as quiet as on Sunday, when their Christian neighbors went to church. She climbed Quincy Hill, seeing nobody along the way. Hannah wondered if Nelma was remorseful, if she was ready to give up the strike. She hoped the next time they talked there would be no uncomfortable, divisive subjects.

Even the December snows had taken notice of the change, no longer falling from the sky, waiting to see what would happen next. At the top of Quincy Hill, she could see the whole city of Hancock below, the lift bridge across the portage, and the city of Houghton on the other side. The hillsides beyond the city were barren of any trees for quite a distance. There was a line beyond several folds of the land, a dark line of growth, where the old forests that once covered the peninsula resumed. Without knowing why, Hannah found hope in these distant trees. Perhaps it was their ability to persist, or perhaps they simply represented someplace away from here.

Crows circled the Quincy Mine location, casting their screeches against the mineshaft, filling the void with their harsh sound. They annoyed her, spoiling the quiet. She wondered why the crows spent their winters here when all the other birds fled south early in the fall. She wished they would go away.

Hannah took a deep breath and turned back down the hill. She zigzagged through the residential streets, planting the heels of her boots in snow rendered suitable for foot traffic only. The horses were kept away from these steep snow-clad streets until late in the spring. At the end of this street was a stone stairwell, behind the synagogue, providing access to the street entrance below. The younger men were expected to shovel it every Friday, before the service started at sundown. There hadn't been any significant snowfall since the weekend, and the steps were still passable. Aaron stood at the bottom, as if waiting for her.

"I wouldn't expect to find you here on a Wednesday morning," Hannah teased, trying to hide her pleasure at finding him there. Despite his politics, despite his evasiveness of their future, and despite her resentment, she couldn't suppress the flutter she felt in her chest whenever they met.

"Likewise," Aaron said. "I was just taking a walk along the portage. Waiting for the rally. The calm before the storm."

"So you're coming? As a reporter or as a citizen?"

"I'm just an observer, an outsider. I'll be there, hoping for a peaceful demonstration, but expecting a riot."

"How can you suppose such a thing? You know what's transpired. It's been the strikers, the union organizers that've been rioting and murdering. I knew the men that died. The strike must end." Hannah turned to go as her eyes dampened. She was tired of discussion and inaction. Tired of the edge of discontent that hung between people. She wanted it all to stop.

"There's too much hatred in the air," Aaron said. "I know you feel it. Promise me you'll not forget the plight of the strikers in all this anger."

"Anger!" Hannah stopped to face him. "How can you speak of anger, as if it's a child's feud. Four people have been murdered, killed by this cause of yours. It's time for the outsiders to leave. Time for everything to return to normal."

"Hannah, you know in your heart the strikers are not murderers. These are your neighbors, your friends. Remember what they've been through, and why."

"What about us? Who will be shot next? After miners crossing the picket line, will they shoot merchants doing business with the wrong people? It's time for the strike to end, and perhaps it's time for us to end as well." Hannah marched away, determined not to let him see the uncertainty on her face, the glistening eyes, the flushed cheeks that formed an ill match with her bold words. She strode down the street until she came to her street corner, where she glanced over her shoulder and was disappointed to see he hadn't followed.

Back home, the house was in a state of orderly commotion. Mother was preparing a stew at the stove while Sam was working on placards to carry at the rally. Ida was trying to keep her son, Daniel, from interfering. The kitchen table was crowded with food. Bread and jam, deli meats, smoked fish, and potato salad all circled the samovar, which served as a gurgling centerpiece, offering Mother's dark roasted coffee.

It was a community in mourning, and it reminded Hannah of the shiva when her grandmother had died. The gathering of food and people. The strange mixture of sadness and excited gossip. Sam had come home with a fiancé, their first introduction to Ida. They had all formed visions of her based on his letters. None were accurate. She was not immediately attractive, a stout woman without any sense of pretense. The family was at ease with her from the start. There was no competition for her parents' affections, as Hannah had feared. Yet neither did she fade into the furniture, a wallflower without presence.

Grandmother passed on not two days after Ida's arrival. Stealing Ida's limelight, though she took it all with modest grace. Ida helped in the kitchen, creating an exotic dish from her family's Sephardic background, insisting Mother abdicate the kitchen to the other women, freeing her up to comfort Father with his loss. Every day, Hannah would awaken to the arrival of more food, contributions from the other Jewish families in their community. Their gentile neighbors would often stop by, bewildered at the festivities, unaccustomed to the somber celebration of life that followed its ending.

Hannah wondered if anyone else saw the similarity of ritual in today's preparations, but suspected her family would take offense if she offered this opinion. Abe and Sol, friends of her brother since childhood, stopped by with their wives, each bearing covered dishes whose aroma preceded them. There was enough to eat for lunch and dinner. All would be welcomed back following the march. The expanse of food created a feeling of wealth and well being that had been absent all these months of the strike. They seemed to offer promise of change, or a return to times past, times of prosperity and peace.

Soon the house was filled with people from all over town. The men gathered in the sitting room, talking roughly, while the women remained in the kitchen to clean up. Children were outside, playing with the placards, shouting their own juvenile derisions at imaginary strikers. At quarter past twelve the house emptied without announcement or planning. Probably somebody started the exodus, but by the time it registered with Hannah, the sitting room had been cleared out and the Citizens' Alliance march had begun.

The whole town seemed to be streaming towards the bridge to Houghton, where they would join others in a march to the Amphidrome for a rally. The only precedent for such a gathering seemed to come from Fourth of July parades and the occasional circus. The collective memory of these events created a festive mood as neighbors called to neighbors not often seen, and old friends joked and jostled each other in the crowd. Hannah found herself wishing Nelma were here to share in the fun before she recognized its absurdity.

There was a dark shift in mood as they crossed the bridge. Maybe it had been there all along, but it was roused by angry proclamations as they joined others on the Houghton side of the crossing. "Oust the red agitators! Go to work or get out of town!" A group of men in front of the gathering waved pistols and shook their fists in the air. Hannah remembered Aaron's talk of a riot and was shamed by their presence, for a moment, before she defensively rediscovered her angry indignation. They had every right to be marching in these streets. They had every right to be mad. They had every right to hate the union strikers for all that they had done.

She walked with Mother and her friends; Ida had stayed home with her son. Hannah was suddenly very aware of her position in this circle as the youngest by several decades. She looked for some of her old school friends, but none were nearby. She had remained close to nobody, excepting Nelma, and now Nelma could just as well be on the moon. She needed to get away from this place. She should be downstate right now. Going to the university, making new friends, creating a new life. This one was suffocating. Her family had cast her in a mold that was several years out of date, but no one seemed to notice.

They marched down Sheldon Avenue past the storefronts, all closed for business. Some were guarded by their owners, stoically watching from the sidelines. They walked past the Bosch brewery, the food cooperative and the county courthouse. Someone started a chant, "End the strike! Do what's right!" and soon everyone was raising their fists in the air as they approached the Amphidrome.

The crowd pressed; everyone was anxious to get inside. Hannah became separated from Mother; who drifted ahead as if tugged by an unseen current. The doors to the building were open, but they were too few to accommodate the crowd. Hannah doubted all would make it in. Women and men squeezed from all angles, they seemed to lose any sense of proprietary. Hannah crossed her arms across her chest, but soon found herself trapped in that position. There was no one around her she knew, no one with whom she should be in such close company. She tried glaring, but her looks went unnoticed, and the mass of people became even tighter, like a knot that might never come undone. "Excuse me," she tried, tentatively at first, then louder, but those around her just shrugged, smiled. This was wrong, this was frightful, why would good citizens act this way?

Hannah's pulse pounded against her chest, and throbbed in her throat. Could no one else sense the danger? What if she fell, slipped underfoot – she feared no one could stop for her. The front doors were now only a few feet away, and the pressure around her grew even greater. She couldn't continue like this, blown like a snow squall against a mountain. She needed to get out. Inch by inch, she mapped a path to the edge of the door, where she could slip off to the side. Either that or be flattened completely. She hoped for the former. She tried to resist every shove against her chosen path, and slowly made progress.

When she found the door, there was a tug on her arm and Aaron's strong hand reached through and pulled her the final steps away. Hannah let her lungs expand and contract, grateful for their unrestricted movement.

"Thank you. It was oppressive in there," Hannah said.

"I decided against going inside, when I saw you so tightly bound in that crowd." Aaron said. "It looked like you were trying to find your way out."

They stood near the edge of the snow-covered docks, the frozen portage stretching out to their right, the crowd still pushing into the Amphidrome on their left. During past winters, her brother would play hockey on the frozen waterway. Inside, she had seen circus players and politicians, but never with an audience such as this.

"Do you think it poses a risk? So many people close together? Or was I just being foolish?"

"I think you were being wise. So what is your feeling on this? Is it an angry mob or a civil gathering of like-minded citizens?"

Hannah wondered if she was being interviewed, if her thoughts would make it onto a piece of newsprint. "A little of both, I think."

"There are thousands here, room for a wide range of opinions."

Hannah understood that Aaron was trying to create an opening between them. A piece of common ground. She looked away and noticed someone standing alone on the hill overlooking the amphidrome. It was too far away to discern anything other than the outline of a skirt, so she only knew it was a woman. She worried it might be Nelma, judging her involvement against their friendship. But this was something she had to do. This was an atrocity, a dispute that had gone too far. Hannah was empowered with an assuredness that she was doing the right thing. Bringing an end to the strike was now a cause she believed in and she was ready to fight for it. Hannah felt strong with her own convictions. For the first time ever, it seemed, she owned her own opinions and didn't need anyone's approval.

"Thank you, but I just wanted to get some air. I'll be going in now." Hannah turned to go, and then tentatively added, "Perhaps you'll want to join me, as a reporter?"

"Not this time, I'm not sure I'd be welcome."

At the doors were some of Hannah's classmates, and Hannah called to them, eager to join, embracing the throng. Inside she heard the speakers had already started, stirring up excitement, a call to action. The union men were compared to poisonous slime, to mutineers and criminals. "They're not like us," someone said, "They have no remorse. We'll never understand them." At the edge of Hannah's consciousness, a vision of misunderstanding tried to surface. Something to do with Nelma. Hannah paused and tried to remember. But the recollection, like her friend, seemed to have crossed over some divide where there would be no easy return.

DECEMBER 10, 1913

NELMA WATCHED THE CITIZENS' Alliance Parade snake through the street below, and tried to reassure herself that the strike would be won. She was on top of the steep hill overlooking the Amphidrome, where the frozen boardwalk was a popular sledding destination for children. Nelma had often come here as a child, bringing her younger sister and sometimes the neighbor boy, who never seemed to mind the company of girls. He had left the county shortly after the strike had begun. Frightened by the rioting, he would likely return to reap any benefits once the strike was won.

Months ago, when the Waddell thugs had shot those Croatians, these so-called citizens were silent. The Seeberville murders were no less criminal than the Englishmen struck down in Painesdale, so she couldn't help wonder if Ellen was right in her assessment that the relative worth of a man largely depended on the language he spoke. Were their lives really worth less to these people because they or their parents didn't speak proper English? If their words were thick with accent and their grammar flawed, did this make their lives less valuable?

Lila had wanted to come, but the parade spoiled any prospects for sledding. Nelma had come to see how many of her neighbors she recognized below, to see the size of the crowd. It was quite big, but too far away to identify any faces. They would probably be boasting in the next day's paper, a scourge against the strikers, a victory against the agitators. It brought the bitter taste of bile into her mouth, and Nelma turned to go home.

The streetcar was empty when it pulled up to the station. In the middle of the day, everyone was either at the Citizens' Alliance parade or hiding at home, talking in conspiratorial tones of the neighbors whom they once were social with. It didn't matter which side of the conflict they were on, the fear and the angst were the same. Nelma felt this tension between people whenever she ventured outside her usual circle of friends: buying coal, visiting the icehouse, or walking streets absent of commerce.

Edward and Frank were out when she returned, gone without having mentioned where they were going. She sent the neighbor girl home, who had been watching over her children, and went downstairs to search through the meager remains of the potato harvest for dinner. The guns were still where she had first noticed them, stacked along the wall behind the bushel baskets, but they no longer made her as nervous. They almost comforted her. What had started as a shock of fear had turned into a bond of trust with the men in her house.

Frank had told her the guns were collected as insurance and protection, that they never intended to use them unless the rule of law broke down. Of course she hadn't believed him. She was certain they were planning something that would jeopardize everything. When word of the Painesdale murders reached their home, her first thought was of the guns downstairs. She had raced to the cellar, expecting to find them gone, proof of her suspicions. But they were as they had been, looking as innocent as a child falsely accused.

Nelma picked over the potatoes half-heartedly; her thoughts wandered. Since the shootings, they had found themselves on the defensive, no longer pushing forward their agenda, but instead, holding on fearfully, lest they completely lose their direction. There were evictions too. She feared they would be next. Rent hadn't been paid since the summer, and she worried that Edward would put up no argument.

Nelma picked up one of the rifles and placed its stock against her shoulder. She aimed at the potato bins, imagining the landlord at her door. Nelma had never shot a gun, though she knew of women who had. The Finnish trapper woman, Keras Kilpela, had offered to teach her once, but her mother had no trust of an eccentric, old woman living in the woods.

Now she wished she knew how to use one. She placed the gun back down, resting the barrel against the others.

She should ask Edward to teach her how to shoot a gun. If he refused, she could ask Frank. She became anxious at the mere thought of Frank, and wondered how much longer she could endure the closeness of him without being able to touch him, kiss him, and discover if he truly shared her feelings. She was certain he did.

When the men returned home, she was feeding the children a potato stew, though it should rightly be called potato soup. There was no meat and the stock was from the fatty remains of the Thanksgiving ham, discovered in the back of the icebox. She sent the children off to play and set the table for the three of them to eat. She pulled a fresh loaf of rye bread from the oven and thought about the bark bread that the old Finns used to bake in times of hardship. It was too late in the year to prepare now—she needed the bark of a young sapling taken in the spring. The thought of milling pine bark during next spring's thaw focused her anger on all the injustice they were fighting against. She had a vision of herself fighting as a soldier, and a soldier needed a gun.

Nelma joined the men at the table, and composed the words in her head before she spoke. "Edward, I want to learn how to shoot. No use having all them rifles downstairs if I don't know how to use them."

Edward and Frank both looked at her in surprise. Frank raised a single eyebrow, Edward just looked away.

"I'm not thinking that I'll be wanting to use them," she answered what she imagined they might be thinking. "It's just that the two of you are gone much of the day."

"Don't know why your mama never taught you how to handle a gun," Edward said. "I'll teach you one of these days."

"Tomorrow," Nelma said, crossing her arms across her chest. "No use putting it off. Them folks are just a moose hair from turning into a bunch of vigilantes. If I can stand here with a gun in my hands, they'll think twice before trying to throw us out of our home."

Frank looked like he was trying hard not to smile, but she could see the corners of his mouth crinkle.

"What do ya think, Frank?" Edward asked. "What do ya think of my wife walking around with a rifle in her hands?"

"I think maybe we should have the women leading the strike," he said.

"A union man can't go hiking around in the daytime with a rifle slung across his back," Edward said. "Especially now. It'll have to wait."

Excuses. *This was how Edward would face a threat*, Nelma thought. Edward offered her nothing anymore. No romance, no money, and no protection.

"Tonight then," Nelma said. "Under cover of darkness. We can ski into the woods—it shouldn't take long. Should it?"

LATER THAT NIGHT, with the children in bed and the neighbor girl over to sit, Edward and Nelma bundled up for a ski into the cold December night. The moon was just a few days from full, reflecting the white expanse of snow covering the ground at least three feet down. The icy air scraped her exposed cheeks, but it brought with it a stab of joy, not pain. She recalled slipping into the night with Edward years ago, leaving her mother's house in their wake, ahead of them a night of touching and groping that made her blush even now.

They skied until there was a hill and a valley between them and the houses, and set up a target in a wide expanse logged clear of trees. The snow was too deep stand in, so she unlatched her boots from the bindings and stepped crossways on her skis. Edward showed her how to load and hold a rifle, how to scope the target in the moonlight, and what to expect when she squeezed the trigger. Several times they went over the drill without ever firing a shot. He wrapped his arms around her and adjusted her grip, shoulders, and hips. Later, she would close her eyes and imagine it was Frank that touched her with such intimate familiarity. But now she focused on the task at hand, not noticing Edward's arousal with every touch he made.

Nelma felt a powerful connection with the first shot she fired. It was exhilarating, emancipating and magic. Her heart surged when she hit the target on her third try. The tin can exploded with a sound as exciting as her first fireworks. As she tried to reload, Edward was unable to keep his hands off her. He pressed her awkwardly against a tree and undid his trousers, pushed down her bloomers.

"No, Edward, no!" she said. "Not here. Not now."

"Don't make me stop," he whispered. "I know you want it."

With each thrust, bark etched the back of her head with scratches, and snow toppled off the branches and dusted her shoulders and face. The lesson was over, she thought wryly. Edward managed to tarnish every good moment together. She couldn't think of a single endearing time, these past few years, that hadn't ended with her disgust. She wished he would just disappear. Vanish into the night like so many yellow-bellied miners who had left the district. Leave so that someone else might take his place. Someone better behaved. Someone who talked of leaving the Keweenaw for other union battles, though in truth, she suspected Frank was leaving because he couldn't have her.

THE NEXT MORNING, Nelma woke in the darkness, as usual. Outside her window, the pre-dawn sky cast an odd glow, bringing to mind the curvature of the earth and the vastness of the planet. The futility of her life with Edward haunted this space. Her children's arms were skinny as twigs and their stomachs were always hungry. Her face had grown prematurely old, like her mother's. Sallow cheeks and dark circles under her eyes. She brushed her hair and went downstairs.

A half-pound of raw coffee beans waited on the kitchen counter. Nelma smiled as she remembered how Frank had presented them yesterday, as if they were nothing special, as if they were a common commodity. They had been getting by with mostly chicory in the morning. Nelma missed the aroma from roasting, especially in the cold of the winter, when there were no fresh breezes to flavor the air from outside. The morning sun, unfiltered by clouds or snow, started to brighten the kitchen through the window. She could imagine it was spring or even summer if she didn't look down at the drifts of snow pressed against the walls of the house. As the coffee roasted, she could feel the warmth of summer and the smell of new growth.

She thought about her outing with Edward last night, and wondered if all men were like that. She expected Frank would favor a bed for that sort of thing. As she stirred the coffee beans, she could imagine their powerful draw on him. Bringing him down the stairs, into the kitchen, placing his arms around her waist and embracing her. She didn't notice when he actually did enter the room and startled when he put his hand on her shoulder.

"That fine smell would cause an honest man to leave his wife," he said. "When will it be ready?"

"You'll have to make do with yesterday's brew—it'll be a while," Nelma smiled, cautiously acknowledging his flirt; unsure where Edward was at the moment.

"Hopefully not too much time," Frank said. "I can't be leaving the copper country without a cup."

"Not that long," Nelma said, with a deflated sigh. How soon would Frank be leaving? He managed a mention of his departure in almost every daily conversation. So consistent was this mention that she suspected he did it consciously. She could imagine him calculating when to bring up the subject each day. Perhaps at breakfast one day, walking to the union hall another.

Frank laughed, poured himself a cup from the stove. "I'm sure you'll be seeing me again. I'll come back for the victory party."

Nelma shook her head. "Have you picked a date yet?"

"After Christmas. I'll need to be back in Denver by the new year."

"Are you tired of us, Frank? I mean are you tired of our struggle?"

"I'll never tire of you, Nelma."

Nelma looked away, afraid to see how much of his words were in jest, and how much were sincere. "I better go rouse the children for breakfast."

It will be good when he leaves, she told herself. She would be able to put aside her fantasies, and focus on her family and what was left of the strike. So many had returned to work, many falling victim to the company's threat's and pressure. Others were driven to abandon the union by the onset of Christmas, now only two weeks away.

At the last union meeting, there was talk of a holiday party for the children, and rumors of this party had spread faster than the winds of an air blast. Now there was no backing down, no one could look a child in the face and tell them there would be no Christmas this year. None could afford it, yet everyone knew that it must be, they just didn't know how.

Edward came down the stairs after the children had been fed, the last one to rise. He had completely abandoned his early morning routine, his habitual waking before dawn was a thing of the past. Edward and the rest of the union men no longer dared to parade since the sheriff's overzealous crusade had been reborn. Midnight raids refilled the jails after weeks of relative calm. Stories of trumped up charges were traded at the union hall. There was nothing for him to do in the mornings, no reason to get up.

"How was that rifle lesson last night?" Frank asked. "I bet your lady is one heck of a shooter."

"She is indeed," Edward said, chuckling himself.

Nelma clenched her fist at the mention of last night. She wondered, not for the first time, how the lesson might have gone had Frank been there. She was certain she would be treated as a partner, and not as chattel.

After the breakfast dishes were washed and put away, the children were dressed and shuttled over to Ellen's house. She looked forward to work in the commissary today. In her own house she felt confined and limited, the same way she had felt as a child in her mother's home. She needed to break free, and yet understood that she had already played out that option. She was married with two children. Her future was cast.

When Nelma arrived at the commissary, Estelle was sitting behind the counter, paging through a catalog. She looked bored.

"How's your Mother?" Nelma asked, as she always asked. It was a morning ritual between them. Estelle would complain about her home life, and Nelma would reminisce about her own, about how it wasn't as bad or as stifling as she had once thought.

"She's been trying to keep daddy away from Otto's still," Estelle said. "He's wanders over there during the day, and then gets too drunk to find his way home. Or so he claims. I think it's not his lack of vision that's keeps him away, I think it's Mother."

Nelma suppressed her laughter, offering only a smile. She wanted to talk about something else today. "Did you ever learn how to shoot a gun?"

"That's a strange thing to ask – who you planning on shooting?"

"No one," Nelma said. "I'm just tired of waiting on these defeated men to do the right thing. I want to be able to defend myself. I want to get beyond this strike. I want to win and move on."

"I don't think nothing's moving anymore. We're just waiting for the last union man to give up."

"Don't you start," Nelma said. "We need a project to give us some hope."

This time it was Estelle's turn to hold back a snicker. "It'll take a lot more than a women's project for that."

Nelma ignored her comment. "We need to plan that Christmas party. We can do that. It'll raise everyone's spirits. I bet we could get some union money for small gifts."

"I could tear up this useless catalog and make paper streamers."

"We can have the party at the Tyomies building," Nelma said. "We already go there for union meetings."

"You should talk to Anne about reserving Italian Hall – it's newer and a lot bigger."

Nelma imagined the inside of Italian Hall decorated with streamers and lights. They could have a big Christmas tree up by the stage, maybe a second one under the balcony. She would bring her children up the gaily lit staircase, where they'd find candies and presents. Somehow they would make it happen, she was sure of it. Then they would find some new way to win the strike and turn the whole thing around.

DECEMBER 12, 1913

DURING THE LATE EVENING HOURS, when the miners had all gone home and only a few drunks remained, Russell had plenty of time for thinking. It was good to have a job again, though his new schedule did take some adjusting. Back at the boarding house, he took his breakfast hours after the others had left for work. Dinner was eaten here at Vairo's saloon, in the Italian Hall building, while he tended bar. Through the big picture windows, he watched the snow fall outside, sometimes thick like a fuzzy blanket, sometimes sparse like the occasional silver mixed with the copper rock underground.

The shootings had now faded in his memory into an unfortunate event, a terrible thing that he accepted and filed away in his mind with the other adverse moments in his life. He hadn't known the victims of the Painesdale shootings, and while he couldn't deny the tragic depth of the event, it didn't have the impact of a more personal tragedy, like when his favorite uncle Phil had fallen drunk off a barge into the cold waters of Lake Michigan, never to be seen again. The shootings were now firmly established in the past, a story he could share with others later, but they no longer weighed on him nor dissuaded him from staying.

Ollie had put in the word that got him this job, something to tide him over until his shoulder was better and he could get back to the mines. The money wasn't as good, but it was an easy job, compared to hauling rock two miles underground.

It was almost closing time, and Russell thought about Maria as he toweled the glasses dry before stacking them. In his head, he had composed many letters to her over the past week, but tonight he vowed to actually put one in the mail. As with the shootings, time had smoothed over the implications of Maria's last letter. He was sure he had over-reacted. A family funeral was a respectable reason for postponing a wedding. In the absence of the actual letter, which he had torn up in a rash of drunken self-pity, it was easy to imagine the pained thoughtfulness of her words. Of course the wedding would have to be postponed, but the wedding would still occur.

Once the glasses had all been cleaned and put away, Russell took a bar pen, used to draw hash marks against the accounts of some of the regulars, and began the letter. "My Dearest Maria," he wrote, and proceeded to bring her up to date on most of the happenings, leaving out the shootings, and unashamedly scattering words of love liberally throughout the text.

Upstairs there was a meeting; he could hear the shifting of chairs and the movement of feet across the ceiling. It was a society hall of some sort, but the union had been up there lately, spouting their rhetoric and licking their wounds. Russell tucked the letter in his inside coat pocket, locked up and hurried to the station before the streetcars shut down for the night. He glanced back at the building, still lit up and loud with activity. He wished he had something within his power, within himself to snuff the life out of the union. Shut it down and let folks who wanted to work, work in peace. Maria's letter, close to his heart, gave him a sense of righteousness. The cutting wind against his face sharpened the edges between right and wrong. He hurried to the station and caught the last streetcar moments before it left.

Russell nodded off on the ride, sleeping until the conductor shook him awake at his stop. From there it was a half-mile walk home, past the turnoff to Shute's Saloon. He missed the camaraderie of his fellow miners, especially the trammers. Underground, there was no better insurance on your life than a good partner, and none better to share a beer with at the end of the week. He felt he had neglected his old partner, Oscar, and thought he'd better stop by Shute's next weekend, to catch up.

The lights there were already turned down, and the street looked strangely vacant, like the abandoned mining locations further north. It made him wonder what the future held for this mining town, and if it were possible for a community of this size to whither away and die. Dark thoughts on a dark night, he decided, and best not to dwell on them.

Up ahead was another fellow out late. Russell picked up his pace to catch up, thinking perhaps it was a neighbor, or someone he might know. Strange how he hadn't seen him earlier; he must have come up the hill. He was a small man, judging from his silhouette, and seemed oddly proportioned like a litter runt that only grows in his arms and legs. The man passed under a streetlamp, and Russell could see the edges of his coat were quite worn. There was a curious patch towards the back bottom of the man's coat, and as he got closer, he noticed it was some kind of campaign button. Russell decided to catch a glimpse of the button before he hailed the man's attention. At the next streetlamp, he realized what it was.

"You!" Russell shouted. "You're one of those union troublemakers."

The man slowly turned around. Russell had several inches on him and the man looked up with a blank expression. Russell stood his ground, ready for the fight, but the man just shook his head and walked on.

"Take that button off your behind or I'll take it off for you," Russell shouted, determined not to have the encounter end without some sort of resolution. He reached for the man's coat, but was caught off guard by the little man's surprising log-like limb. Russell stumbled, regained his balance, and launched his fist at the man's nose. He put his whole body into the punch and felt his aim and timing gave him the best advantage. Before his fist found its target, though, something came up at his chin from underneath. The union man undercut his punch and struck Russell's jaw, causing tiny starbursts to explode all around him. His vision narrowed, as he paused to regain his senses, the man hit him again, this time on his shoulder, the bum shoulder that had been slowly healing for the last several weeks. Russell cried out in pain and fell into the snow bank along the road. The cold felt good against his injury, and he turned so that the side of his face was also enveloped in the snow. The union man walked away, laughing and patting his rear, where the "Citizens' Alliance" button had been placed in jest.

THE PAIN IN RUSSELL'S shoulder woke him before the sun slipped through the window, before the noises of the other tenants going to work, and before Mrs. Huhta rapped on his door. He shuffled to take a look in his small shaving mirror and saw his jaw was swollen and shaded in colors of purple and black. It could probably benefit from some ice. He tested his shoulder by rotating his right arm, producing a sharp and immediate pain. He considered lifting something, to further assess the damage, but decided he'd rather not find out just now. He collapsed back on the bed and rested a while longer before starting down the stairs for breakfast.

Mrs. Huhta raised her eyebrows when she first sighted him. "Have a bit of trouble last night, did you?"

"One of those union men did a number on my face," Russell replied. "Rather unfriendly of him, don't you think?"

"Let me get you an ice wrap, we'll wet some cloth and leave it outside to freeze. Wouldn't take more than a few minutes. Tell me what happened – should we call the sheriff?"

"It was dark, I don't think I would recognize the man. I had just closed up at Vairo's and was walking home from the station."

"So why did he start up a fight?" Mrs. Huhta asked. "Do you suppose he recognized you from the mines? Maybe he was on the picket line at your old location."

"Yea," Russell lied. "That must have been it."

"You ever see him again, you call the sheriff right away. They're not putting up with this violence anymore. You call the sheriff if you think you can identify him."

"Yes ma'am, I'll do just that."

As Mrs. Huhta prepared the ice wrap, Russell helped himself to a cup of coffee and thought about what had happened. Maybe the man had recognized him from the mines. Maybe he did have it in for Russell before he opened his mouth. With a self-serving intention, Russell adjusted the memory of what happened the night before. The whole thing seemed more palatable if he was a blameless victim. Maybe he had said a few things, but what was that thug doing with the button on his bum? Why did that striker start swinging at him—Russell was just talking, nothing threatening in that. The more he thought about it, the more it seemed to him an unprovoked assault.

Later that day at the bar, Russell embellished his story with every telling. In a way, the fight had become his rite of passage into the community. He felt accepted now, no longer an outsider, no longer an injured miner; he was a bartender. A service to the community. The saloons here were different than in Chicago; they seemed more reputable. No temperance movement to mar a man's enjoyment of a bottle of beer with friends. Russell dried glasses and looked around for any customers in need of a refill.

Outside, the twilight had passed into night, and the miners were filing in, almost as if they had lined up beyond the door. Russell was surprised to see his old tramming partner, Oscar, walk up to the bar.

"Good to see you," Russell said. "What'll it be—pint of Bosch?"

"Yea, that'll be good," Oscar said. "It's been a while. How you been? Ollie told me you'd been working up here. Told me you got into a bit of a scuffle last night."

"Word travels fast. Course that old bunch lives for this type of talk." Russell opened a bottle for his friend, not bothering to offer a glass as Oscar had never used one before.

"So tell me who it was."

"I swear I don't know; it was dark. That underhanded punch of his really rattled me. I might recognize the fist, though." Russell said with a grin. "It was a big son of a bitch."

"You know the sheriff's been deputizing citizens, anyone with a Citizens' Alliance button. You oughta get yourself one. They've been raiding the union halls, trying to stop any trouble before it begins. You might run across your guy."

"Nah. I'm not out for revenge or anything."

"Hell you're not," Oscar said. "I know you. You've probably been thinking about it all day."

Russell laughed, told him how good it was to see him, and asked about the other miners he'd worked with. After Oscar left, Russell realized how much he missed that crew. The smell of the rock, the rhythmic labor of filling up the tramcars. They were long days, but the pay was good. Damn good. His new bartender self-image wilted, and once again he found himself wanting his old job back. If not for that striker he'd probably be feeling better by now, he told himself.

Russsell never worked on Fridays. Fridays were a return to the old routine, dinner with the boarders, and afterwards, a drink or two at Shute's with the old pinochle gang. Tonight something was different, though. Ollie was standing, at the far end of the bar, embellishing some story with hands that danced through the air. Ollie wasn't usually this animated. Something was happening.

"Sheriff wants as many men as we can get," Ollie was saying. "Doesn't want any chances. He's got a special train waiting to take us to South Range at eleven o'clock tonight. If you ain't been deputized yet, show up a little early. That's all I got to say."

"You got a dangerous card game to attend to tonight, Ollie?" Russell joked. "What's this all about?"

"No joking tonight," Ollie said. "Those union people are planning some sort of major riot in South Range tomorrow. They got guns, munitions, and who knows what else. Sheriff's aiming to stop them with a show of force."

"Sound's like an old-fashioned posse to me."

"That's exactly what it is," Ollie said, grinning. "Let me show you what I'm bringing to the party." He pushed back the side of his coat to reveal a heavy looking revolver. "You should come."

Russell weighed the offer against his original plans. "I don't know, Ollie. South Range is a long way from here. Seems like they should have enough people there can take care of themselves."

"We don't need no more Painesdale shootings, my friend. You need to come."

Russell remembered the night he had heard of the shootings. It stirred an unpleasant fear across all his senses. It brought into question his commitment to this place. If this was home, then this was what he needed to do. He followed Ollie as they hiked down to the train station, knocking on doors along the way, spreading the news.

There were at least one hundred deputies waiting at the station when they arrived. One hundred and one, including himself. This was the first time Russell had been on a train since he had arrived in Houghton County months ago. Back then, there had been deputies too, but they were on the outside, guarding his midnight arrival against any trouble. He had been oblivious to the whole situation. This was different. This time he was one of the deputies, and he was no longer a stranger.

The train stirred up whorls of snow as it left the station and plowed through snowdrifts along the way. Ollie took the aisle seat next to him, talking with men all around them; he never seemed to be without friends. Russell figured if he stayed here long enough, he'd know everyone too. He liked the idea of living in a place surrounded by people he knew. Not too big of a place, but not too small either.

They were slowing down, approaching town. Russell could see the station lights up ahead. Ollie and most of the pinochle crew stood by the door, ready for action. Russell remained seated, and made sure he was one of the last off the car after it had stopped. The sheriff was up front giving an overview of the plan, but Russell only caught bits of the speech, most of it lost by the wind and scattered haphazardly into the void of the night.

They walked toward the union hall, and split up when they reached a fork in the road. The plan was to meet at the building, search it, and look for anything suspicious. Russell doubted anyone would be out this late, but when they reached the squat two-story structure, it was well lit. The union hall was upstairs. He heard some shouting, and braced himself for the sound of gunfire, but the confrontation seemed to stop as suddenly as it had started. The sheriff led a dozen handcuffed strikers through the crowd and back to the train.

Russell's pulse raced. He told himself that this was the only conflict they would witness, despite his feeling that there would be more. He felt like a coward hanging to the back of the crowd, but had no desire to move up front. Some of the deputies were already outside the union hall, the sound of their footfalls thundering through the dense cold air. Then silence. After a time, word was passed from one man to another that there were strikers barricaded inside and they were to wait until the sheriff returned. Some grumbled and wanted to break down the door. Others worried that the sheriff would avoid direct confrontation and bemoaned a long cold night ahead. Russell breathed a sigh of relief, a steamy cloud of condensation leaving his mouth. Nothing was to happen, and he felt he was the only one there to be pleased.

Cigarettes were smoked, a flask of whiskey was passed around, and some of the men stalked the union hall like restless hungry animals. A full moon cast the proceedings in an eerie spotlight. By two or three in the morning, Ollie had had enough.

"I'm heading up," Ollie said. "We're locked out here in the cold while they're sitting pretty in their heated union hall with the sights of their guns probably aimed right at us. Someone has to force their hand. Who's with me?"

Russell knew Ollie was looking straight at him, but kept his eyes downcast. He swept glances at the legs of those standing around him and then returned to his own boots. They were good boots, he thought, keeping his feet moderately warm on this frigid December night. Boots worth keeping wherever he might travel. Boots worth keeping if he ever decided to leave.

Ollie got several volunteers from the crowd. "All right, then," Ollie said. "Let's go. You with us, Russell?"

Russell nodded with great reluctance, and hung to the back as they made their way to the building. There was an outside door leading to a staircase, at the top was the union hall. The sheriff still hadn't returned from the train and no one barred their entry nor their ascent to the top. The union hall door was locked, though. Ollie knocked and waited, while the others filled the steps behind him.

"We're here representing the sheriff of Houghton County. We have a warrant to search the premises. Open up."

A woman pulled the door halfway and looked to be assessing their number. Dark circles around her eyes betrayed her fatigue. "Why don't you come back at a decent hour? We've children sleeping here." Another striker approached from behind her and slammed the door shut.

Ollie rapped on the door again, and waited. No one spoke. No one moved. Russell wondered if he could slip out of the building without being noticed. He was at the base of the stairs and if he slowly opened the outside door, perhaps no one would know. Everyone's eyes were focused above. This was the time to leave, before any trouble.

As Russell cautiously grasped the metal doorknob, a rifle blast ripped through the silence, splintered the union hall door, and catapulted Ollie down the stairs. The deputies fell like dominoes lined up for a child's game, until they all lay at the base of the stairs. Everyone was down except for Russell, who pulled back his hand as if he had received an electric shock and stood frozen in uncertainty.

The crowd outside rushed the door, revolvers ready, and faces intent on revenge. Ollie was the one who talked them down, advising caution, and describing the strange glimpse he had seen of the scene inside the union hall. It was filled with rifles and sleeping children, who had no doubt been awakened by now.

There were several interpretations on what had occurred. Some thought the whole incident must have been a mistake, why else had there been one solitary shot through the door. Others thought it was surely a trap, and trained their sights on the door expectantly. Russell was more concerned with his friend Ollie, whose left sleeve was dripping with blood. Outside, a deputy fired a warning shot, up into the air. It echoed against the windowpanes, the sound traveling up to the union hall. The door slowly opened and three unarmed men raised their hands defensively, and waited to be arrested. The stalemate was over and the strikers offered no further resistance.

Ollie had received only a minor flesh wound, which was bandaged up by the local doctor as Russell and the others searched the union hall. The women were questioned and released with the children. Their sleepy, innocent expressions, and excited whispers belied a misguided adventure. The gravity of the danger they had been in completely escaped their notice. The men were arrested and handcuffed. Inside, there were red flags, red jackets, and red brochures on the tables. Rifles and shotguns piled on the floor.

It seemed to Russell that his worst suspicions had been proven here tonight. This wasn't an innocent meeting of families; this was some sort of socialist rebellion. They were out for blood, probably out for his blood, and it set loose a hatefulness that had been growing in the shadows of his fear for weeks. It was a satisfying, consuming emotion. Clear and simple and pure. He walked back to the station in the company of his friends, nourishing a secret self-image of a vigilante.

DECEMBER 16, 1913

PATCHES OF BROWN, FROZEN GROUND were expanding and overtaking the usual snow cover. Hannah could not remember any prior December without several feet of snow underfoot and more on the way. This was supposed to be a time of long, dark nights and short, frigid days. Today didn't quite have the personality of spring, but was more like the precursor to spring, when the weather would occasionally tease with temperatures in the thirties and the sun would slowly melt away the months of accumulated snowfall. Then a patch of grass or dirt would be exposed and celebrated as much as the first appearance of crocuses downstate. The strange weather gave Hannah a sense of hope that had been absent in the many months since the strike had begun.

She foraged through her wardrobe looking for an outfit suitable for wearing to college. Some seemed too frivolous, others too formal. She wanted clothing that was scholarly and serious, not something she'd wear to the theater or to synagogue. Her first class wasn't until afternoon, and Hannah couldn't bear to wait. Finally, she selected a plain wool skirt and blouse, reasoning that it seemed to fit the bill as long as she left the matching jacket at home.

Mother called from downstairs, "Hannah hurry up! I still need you at the store this morning."

"Coming," Hannah called back, as she took one last look at herself in the mirror.

Mother was in the kitchen, going over the store's finances, next to a satchel of papers for Hannah to take to the store. She also had some final advice for Hannah's visit to campus, which Hannah had already heard, so she checked her hair in the reflection off the window. It was Mother's arrangement that she audit this class at the Michigan College of Mines, just a few miles across the portage, where one of their neighbors was teaching Business Correspondence and Technical Writing. Even though it was mid-semester, they were starting a new topic in the class, and the instructor thought it would be useful for Hannah to attend.

"Now when you go, you'll sit in the back of the class," Mother said. "Be respectful of those who are paying for their schooling and be sure to thank Professor Stevenson for being so accommodating."

"Yes, of course."

Mother continued for several more minutes while Hannah imagined herself in class, modestly answering the questions correctly, heads turning to take notice of her, and the professor nodding to acknowledge her grasp of his lesson plan.

"...and remember you're just as smart as those boys in the class."

Hannah gave Mother a hug and turned to get on her coat and outerwear.

At the store, Father and her brother Sam were maneuvering a large white pine into place in front of the picture window.

"Just in time to decorate," Father said.

"We're a little late this year, aren't we?" Hannah asked.

"We've been pre-occupied with other things," Sam said.

Hannah noticed a hostile look between her father and brother, and realized she shouldn't have said anything. Sam never did approve of a Jewish family putting up a Christmas tree, but Father always insisted. It was more of an American tradition, he had said. It was also good for business, but this year, it probably would make no difference. The family income was barely a third of what it had been a year ago. Even with many of the striking miners returning to work, it seemed no one had enough money to spend on holiday presents.

The box of decorations was still downstairs in storage, and Hannah went to retrieve them. She always enjoyed placing the hand-blown balls of glass, the tinsel and little figurines on the branches of the tree. Once, when she was a child, she and Nelma had tramped around behind the school and come back with a basket of rose hips, which Mother strung on a string and Father wrapped around the tree like bright red lights.

Thinking of Nelma soured her mood. The strike, the divided city, the shootings: how could Nelma still be involved? It wasn't just the union that couldn't see no prospect for winning, it was Nelma too that was equally blind. She had pushed their friendship aside and refused to back down. Hannah wondered if they had anything left in common.

Hannah returned upstairs with a box full of decorations. She pulled out small figurines, dreidels, and glass globes, which were her favorites, and tried to hang them evenly spaced across the tree. She came across a pretty blue one, with silver-colored ribbons embossed diagonally across the perimeter. This had been a gift from Nelma, a graduation gift when she finished high school, just last spring. It had seemed on odd present, given when the winter snows had just receded, and Hannah had stashed it away with the other ornaments and forgotten about it. Now she wanted to return it. Leave it in a box on Nelma's doorstep without explanation. Or perhaps she would toss it to her casually, watching her grab for the fragile orb, and then turn away.

Sam called from the next room, asking about the papers she had brought, his voice breaking her reverie and causing her to startle. The glass ornament fell from her hand and shattered. Tiny shards of glass spread across the wood floor. She cursed silently to herself. This wasn't what she had wanted. It was such a pretty gift. She probably would have kept it. Hung it on the tree facing the window, where Nelma might have seen it, had she walked by. *Damn.* Now there was this mess to clean up. She went into the closet for a broom.

The rest of the morning passed painfully slow. Hannah spent half her time posing in front of the bathroom mirror, and the other half listening to the ticking of the store's cuckoo clocks. The hour and minute hands teased her with their miniscule movement, and once Hannah was certain they had stopped all together.

Finally it was noon and Mother brought sandwiches for lunch. Hannah ate as quickly as possible, and set off for campus. She took the streetcar into Houghton, which went as far as College Avenue. The tall buildings on either side of the street funneled the wind straight down the middle, making walking difficult. Hers was the second building on the right. She had never been on a college campus before, even this one, nearly in her own city. There was a difference immediately felt, though difficult to identify. Later, she would decide it was the people, all young and male, that made her feel decidedly out of place.

The inside of her classroom smelled of stagnant air and old books. Three young men gathered near the window, and one raised his eyebrow at her arrival. His direct gaze unnerved her, and she hastened to take a seat in the back and look through her notebook, which was blank on every page, though she doubted he could see this. Earlier she had been disappointed that her first university experience would be at the local miner's college rather than downstate. Now she was thankful there would be a familiar home to go back to at the end of the day.

The professor entered the classroom a few minutes later and the rest of the class found their seats. He cast an air of authority that she had never seen during the summer, when he worked a small flower garden in back of his house. Some would talk about his peculiar hobby as unbecoming of a college professor, but Hannah found it endearing. He had once told her that he kept the garden in memory of his late wife. Every spring, he would bring the garden back to life.

Today he was at the blackboard, wordlessly sketching out today's lesson plan, which deconstructed a letter of inquiry and several options of response. He then turned, introduced himself, and took attendance. After taking attendance, he called "Hannah Weinstein", with a slight nod of acknowledgement in her direction, as if she too, were on the official classroom list. Hannah smiled with embarrassment, but was still gratified that he would make such an effort.

The lecture proceeded with a pace and tone that took Hannah by surprise. The professor's conversational tone lacked the condescending voice she often had heard in grade school, but it also challenged her attention and comprehension. She would have to review her notes this evening to try and make sense of it all. The hour passed quickly, and soon Hannah was packing up her papers and walking back home. One of the students from her class approached her outside the building.

"Excuse me, miss. My name's Thomas. Thomas Smether. You were in the Business Correspondence class?"

Hannah introduced herself. His hair was disheveled, and his breath reeked of tobacco. She couldn't imagine why he had approached her.

"I've been here since the fall, don't think I've seen you before," he said. "I hope you don't mind me being so forward. It's a bit unusual to see a woman at a mining college, that's all."

"I live in Hancock," Hannah said. "I'm taking a few classes before transferring downstate next year. I'll be going to the University of Michigan."

"That's a nice place, especially for women. My cousin studied there a few years ago and met her husband. Good man. They have two children now. I'm sorry, I'm talking too much, aren't I?"

"No, no, not at all," Hannah felt obligated to say. She wondered what he was trying to say and if he was making fun of a women going to college. "This was my first class today. It was a bit awkward—I'm glad you introduced yourself. Now I'll have a familiar face in the classroom."

"So will you be taking General Studies downstate? Or did you have a career in mind?"

"I'm not quite sure yet," Hannah said. The question caught her off guard. She had been so anxious to get away, to go to the university, to have great adventures, and yet she still hadn't decided where to focus her studies. Mother thought teaching would be the most practical, while Father wanted her to focus on business and domestic skills. She sometimes imagined herself as a lawyer or doctor, but was hesitant to voice such a dream. "Where are you from?"

"Do you know where Ishpeming is? Not too far by train. I like it here better. Terrible business, this strike, though."

"I think it should be ending soon. Many have gone back to work."

"Those people should just go back to where they came from. They can't even speak English, let alone understand how things work around here. Don't you think?"

"Well, this is their home. They just need to understand how wrong they've been."

"I don't know. They're trying to take over the country, throw out our democratic system. It's ridiculous. Can you imagine these uneducated foreigners in charge? They'd ruin everything. I'm sorry. I'm talking too much again."

"No, not really," Hannah lied. "But I should be going. I'll see you tomorrow."

Hannah walked past the streetcar stop and continued into town. She wanted to keep moving, away from campus, away from others who might favor her for conversation. Thomas' opinions angered her, though she couldn't find much fault in what he had said about the strikers. He was an odd sort, and she wondered if the university downstate had more men like him. She hoped not. She wondered what Nelma might have said to Thomas, had they met. How was it that she could so value Nelma's friendship and at the same time disagree with almost everything she believed? Tired of walking, she caught the streetcar in downtown Houghton.

As the streetcar crossed the bridge, Hannah recalled a long-ago trip with Mother that had run late into the Sabbath hour. They had taken this very same route but stepped down on the Houghton side of the bridge, and walked the last quarter mile to the synagogue on foot. Among other activities, riding in a car was not condoned on the Sabbath. Hannah wondered if her life was filled with an above average number of hypocrisies.

The house was empty when she returned home. Except for the parlor, the house was dark and cold. Hannah shoveled some coal into the furnace and left her papers upstairs in her room. There was some dough rising above the kitchen stove, and Hannah guessed that Mother had run out to buy something needed for dinner. She rolled up her sleeves and lifted the cover off the dough. It looked ready, and she divided it into two bread pans and placed them in the oven.

Hungry for a snack, Hannah searched the pantry for something simple to eat. There was an old bag of peanuts and a small box of crackers that looked to be good candidates. She chose the peanuts. On the top shelf was the family's collection of menorahs, waiting for Hanukkah, which would be starting in less than a week. She took them down and placed them on the kitchen counter.

The family menorah was an ornate silver piece with a decorative stamp for each of the twelve tribes of Israel. Mother had asked her to polish it, but she had forgotten. The other two were homemade concoctions of Hannah and Sam, made when they were children. They had started out as simple tin menorahs, but had been decorated with paint, scraps of copper, and other strange knick-knacks that Hannah could no longer identify. She was surprised Mother hadn't thrown them away years ago.

They had constructed the menorahs in the basement of the store, with several other families from their congregation. Old Mrs. Blumson, not yet a widow, had read them the story of the brave Maccabees fighting against Greek imperialism. The Maccabees were greatly outnumbered, but in the end they had prevailed. Hannah wondered who would represent the underdog Maccabees in today's conflict, but quickly discarded the analogy as both foolish and unsettling.

She heard the front door open and Mother's voice carried through the hallway.

"Please do come in," Mother was saying to someone. "Hannah would want to see you before you go."

Hannah recognized Aaron's voice as he replied.

"I didn't have much notice, unfortunately," Aaron said. "I'll be leaving on tomorrow's train. I guess the paper doesn't think the strike is newsworthy anymore."

"It does seem to be winding down," Mother said, as she entered the kitchen. "Hannah, Aaron has come to say goodbye."

"I heard," Hannah said, avoiding Aaron's eyes, feeling her heart race and afraid he would know. "Where are they sending you now?"

"Back to New York," he said. "It's nice to be going home, though there's a lot I'll miss."

"I need to run this package over to the neighbor's," Mother said. "Hannah, can you put the rest of these groceries away?"

Hannah's scalp tingled; she didn't want to be alone with him, didn't want to be tricked by his charms when she was resolved to turn him away.

"Your mother is such a mensch," Aaron said after Mother had left. "So nice of her to leave us alone for a few minutes."

Hannah turned to put the groceries in the pantry, determined to stay in control, and wishing desperately that Mother would come back soon.

Aaron followed her into the small space and cautiously placed one hand on her shoulder. Hannah tried to suppress a shiver that passed through her body at his touch. She thought about the articles he had written and how she felt used for insight into the Citizens' Alliance, but also about the way he made her feel special. No one else had ever had that effect on her. Her eyes dampened at the thought of his leaving, and these threatening tears drove her to anger.

"Don't," Hannah said, pulling away.

Aaron placed his other hand on her waist, and turned her around to face him. "Please, Hannah, You know how much I care for you. I don't want to leave. I wish you could come with me. I wish you could visit. You know New York is a fine place for college. Perhaps you'd consider someplace other than Michigan?"

Hannah hesitated. It sounded so appealing. It was exactly what she hoped he would say weeks ago. She tried to imagine a future where Father would let her run off to New York, where they might be engaged and see each other away from the eyes of her family.

"What are you saying?" Hannah asked. "Why are you telling me this now?"

"Because now I have to leave. Now I know how much I'll miss you."

"But why now? Every time I brought this up before, you changed the subject. As if I wasn't good enough once you returned to New York. As if it was foolish of me to even consider."

"I never said that."

Hannah looked into his eyes and tried to gauge his sincerity. His plaintive look only further angered her. "So what exactly are you suggesting? Would you be willing to talk to Father about your intentions, or are you just promoting the good universities of New York?"

"I was just hoping you'd be closer to me."

There was always a distinct break between what Hannah wished she could do and what she actually did. She was limited by the expectations of her family and of society. It was a limitation that she never questioned until now, when the air cracked with the sound of her hand slapping the side of Aaron's face. He let his calling card fall from his hand and it fluttered down to the floor.

"I'm sorry," he said, and he turned to go.

Hannah ran upstairs and watched from her bedroom window as he walked away. She knew that she had done the right thing, and yet already she missed him. She tried to imagine how things might have been different, and why it was he seemed unable to match his feelings with actions that would matter to her. He had returned to his world and left her behind, staring at the far horizon, and wondering when it would be her turn to go.

DECEMBER 23, 1913

AN HOUR BEFORE MIDNIGHT, the clouds scattered and a bloody aurora borealis painted the sky. In Nelma's experience, the northern lights were a common occurrence. She had seen the heavens colored in blue, green and sometimes hues of purple, but never before had she seen red. It seemed to be a living, breathing presence above. She found herself staring, questioning, and wondering what, if anything, it could mean.

In her darkest moments, she knew the strike was doomed. The strike, the union, the dawn of socialism in America, and sometimes even her own future seemed damned. But it was hard to keep believing in the death of nearly everything she held dear, so these thoughts tended not to last.

She stood in front of Italian Hall, looking up at its wide expanse of windows facing the street, nearly forty feet across. Downstairs housed Vairo's Saloon and the Atlantic & Pacific Tea Company, but the entire upstairs was a meeting hall spanning seventy-eight feet from front to back. The *Societa Mutua Beneficenza Italiana* was proud of their new building, and yesterday had given Nelma and her friends a tour. There was an outside entrance and stairwell that led directly to the room above, and a large stage at the rear of the building. A kitchen behind the stage provided a convenient space to prepare for tomorrow's Christmas Eve party. Hundreds were expected, and Nelma had spent the last few hours decorating the hall.

They had worked hard to assure that no child would be without a sense of joy and a gift to take home. Nelma had decorated the three Christmas trees with tinsel and paper streamers. Estelle had placed puffs of cotton along the boughs, as if they were snow. Dozens of women had pitched in. Over one hundred folding chairs were arranged in tidy rows in front of the stage, as if awkward early arrivals to a party. Candy had been stashed in the kitchen and the Santa suit had been discretely tucked away behind the stage curtain, ready for old Mr. Belafonte, who wouldn't be needing a fake beard.

Nelma's exhaustion had been held off by her constant movement all day. She had been up at dawn and worked most of the afternoon at the union commissary, and most of the evening preparing for the party. Now that she stood still, examining the night sky, her fatigue slipped through and quickly overtook her. She forgot what it was she was thinking and hurried home to bed.

The next morning, the sun rose over a cloudless horizon, and for a while the kitchen belonged just to Nelma and her daughter Lila. Frank was the next one awake, helping himself to coffee, sitting in his usual chair, settling into his usual patter on weather or union politics or far away events read from the paper. Nothing suggestive in his chatter, really, just a certain familiarity in his words. An assumption of mutual interest, that resonated within her more than any talk she ever shared with her husband.

Still, the house had grown small with Frank's company. When he left, Lila could move back into the children's room. Toivo was old enough to move there as well. She and Edward would have the bedroom all to themselves, for the first time in years. Nelma wondered what they would speak about when they didn't have Frank to carry the conversation. She couldn't remember much talk at all before Frank's arrival.

Edward was the last to wake, walking down the stairs with a jubilant Toivo grinning in his arms. Their son had been up for at least half an hour, she had heard him babbling upstairs, but with his good spirits, she hadn't found the need to retrieve him. Neither did she want to abandon Frank's company and charms, knowing how soon he would be leaving. Nelma turned back to the stove at Edward's arrival.

"G'morning," Nelma said. "Frank says you picked up some fish yesterday out at Kauppi's ice hole."

"It's hanging in the icehouse," Edward said. "Enough there for a couple meals, at least."

"Could you get the fish for dinner tonight? I'll prepare something for it before we leave for the party."

"You'll be taking both the children?"

"I think even Toivo would enjoy it. You might too. Johan will be there with his family. So will Elmer."

Edward nodded slightly, traded Toivo for a cup of coffee. After several minutes, he said, "I might."

NELMA SPENT THE morning baking bread, chopping potatoes, and entertaining the children. She marveled how a whole morning could go by with so little to account for at the end. Her daughter, Lila, had never been to any sizeable party, and was preoccupied with the clock, looking to see when both hands would meet at the top. Toivo didn't know what all the excitement was about, and tried valiantly, with his limited scope of words, to solicit an explanation that he could understand. Frank was off on some business, and Edward had yet to return from the icehouse with the fish. Probably drinking at Otto's still again, she guessed. Probably wouldn't be seeing him at the party today. At quarter to twelve, Nelma soaked the potatoes in a pot of cold water and allspice, dressed the children and headed out the door.

There was a circle of deputies eyeing them suspiciously as they approached Italian Hall, but Nelma was accustomed to this sort of intimidation. Even a Christmas party was threatening to them. Both children jumped out in anxious anticipation, and Nelma propped their sled against a line of others parked outside the building. The front door latch was a bit stiff in the cold winter air, but it opened after a bit of jockeying, and Lila raced up the stairs ahead of her mother and brother. Nelma realized that she had never been to such a large affair herself, and despite her involvement, or perhaps because of it, found her heart fluttering with an odd anticipation.

One of the women from the auxiliary was checking everyone for union cards before they entered the main room. There was a line, and the Christmas caroling had already begun. Nelma was surrounded by children in dresses and suits and high-topped shoes. Lila adjusted her hair, which was pulled back with a blue-satin ribbon. Toivo stared in amazement from his vantage point on Nelma's hip. Finally they were in and saw some seats near the stage.

"Mama, when is Santa Claus coming?" Lila whispered.

"Shhh," Nelma said. "He'll be here soon enough."

Nelma looked around for her friends in the sea of faces. There were so many men, women and children, so many people she didn't know. She spied Ellen with an empty spot beside her. Nelma pointed it out to Lila and Toivo before walking over.

"It's strange, all these little ones in one place," Ellen said. "I don't remember ever having a party like this when we were young."

"It's a children's zoo!" Nelma said.

"What?" Ellen shouted over the myriad voices. "I'm sorry, what did you say?"

"I said it's like a children's zoo," Nelma shouted back. There were Croatian dancers on stage now, and their foreign songs mingled with all the other chatter to create a strange collage of sound that would crescendo, ebb, vary, and crescendo once again.

At the end of the performance, Santa appeared, and the children tried to rush the stage, but there were enough parents in attendance to create order. Nelma found Lila a place in the long line that snaked the full length of the longest wall. Scanning the room, she was surprised to see Edward, who almost walked past them before Nelma caught his attention. "Can you keep an eye on Toivo?" Nelma said. "I need to go down to the kitchen to help pass out the candy. He's too young to stand in line with his sister."

"This place is packed fuller than the union hall at the start of the strike," Edward said. "As soon as Lila gets her gift, we should go home."

"I promised to help clean up. Can you take the children home when they're through?"

"Maybe," Edward said, breaking into a grin, revealing his mild stupor.

Nelma left for the kitchen, moderately annoyed. What a thing to say. She wondered if there was an ounce of responsibility left in him, a lick of common sense. Was there anything at all he had to offer her anymore?

There were two barrels of candy in the kitchen, and Nelma's job was to place a handful in the center of a paper napkin, tie it up with some string, and pass it up to the stage. Many had been done the night before, but not enough to satisfy the large turnout. The women checking union cards at the entrance estimated seven hundred guests had arrived, five hundred of whom were children. On the stage, the youngsters picked up their gifts from Santa, candy and perhaps a pair of knit mittens or a cap, before being funneled down the steps to the kitchen, and then back to the main room.

Nelma didn't see Lila approach until she was right by her side, mouth full of chocolate, asking if she could help scoop out the candy. They worked together for another half-an-hour, and Nelma looked aside whenever Lila would sneak an extra piece for herself. The sound of little feet had become a familiar rhythm, so commonplace that it escaped her notice until there was a discernable change.

The regular creaking of the stage, and then footfalls down the steps was transformed. It became erratic, wild and loud. There was shouting, but she couldn't make out the words. It brought to mind animals stampeding, though she couldn't imagine where she had come up with such an image. She became worried, without knowing the basis for her concern. Then there was a real stampede. Children and parents were racing down from the stage, into the kitchen. Someone said there was a fire. "Go! You must go." Everyone was screaming, pushing, crying. Chairs were knocked over. The candy was spilt on the floor. Nelma's skin tingled with fear and her heart pounded. Lila was pulled away in the crowd, out the fire escape in the rear of the kitchen. Nelma fought against the panic rising inside her. She had her own coat, but wanted to find her daughter's, which had been left behind on the main floor. Too many people streamed down from the stage. Yelling. "This way, this way! The front staircase is too crowded. This is the only way."

Outside the frigid air welcomed her. It was cold, but the cold felt safe. Familiar. This they could survive. Nelma found Lila waiting in the alley at the bottom of the fire escape. Her eyes were full of confusion. While others ran past them, she held her daughter, relishing the way Lila hugged with her whole body, and told her everything would be fine. She took her hand and they ran until they rounded the building and stood at the front. Here were firemen and deputies, all pushing them away. A man with a Citizens' Alliance button spoke to her, said right to her face, "Go back, go home. There is no fire."

Someone tried to take Lila away, but she held firmly to her hand. Where were Edward and Toivo? Where was the fire? Where was the smoke? Why were no people coming out the front entranceway? A man tried to hold her back, but she ducked under his arm. Another tried to stop her, and she hit him in the face, bloodied his nose. If these heartless bullies wanted a fight, she was prepared to serve them up in style. She didn't trust any of them. They were all her enemies. They were all holding her back, but she didn't know why until she saw them through the open doorway.

Piles of them. Twisted and contorted and wedged in the stairwell. Not people any longer, but bodies, piled nearly as high as the door. Children and babies, men and women. Hands and feet and faces all mixed together. Some were crying, but not many. Too many were silent. Too many had no words to say. How could this be? It made no sense. Nelma continued searching with her eyes, looking for her husband and son. Maybe they had found another way out, though she could think of none. Perhaps there was a window exit somewhere, somehow. The firemen worked to disentangle the bodies and pull them out, one by one. Little bodies, mostly. Limp little bodies all dressed in their Christmas best.

She saw them now, at least she saw her Toivo. Held aloft in the air by a familiar arm, as if Edward was wading underwater and only his arm was above the surface. He was buried in there, amongst his neighbors and friends, and yet there was Toivo. Alive.

"That's my son," Nelma shouted, reaching out with her one free arm, the other still gripping Lila's hand. "That's my Toivo." It felt like a dream and a nightmare at the same time. She had to hold him, touch him, inhale his baby breath, and then she would know it was real.

"He'd best be going to the hospital with the rest, ma'am," the fireman said. "They'll be wanting to have a look at him."

"Give me my son. I don't want none of you laying a hand on him. I'm not giving you a chance to finish whatever it is you've done to the others. Give me my son now."

"Ma'am..." The fireman started to say something, but must have thought the better of it. He placed Toivo in her arms, her son's face red from crying, his eyes glazed and afraid, but somehow he was otherwise unscathed.

She watched as they pulled Edward's pale-faced, contorted body from the stairwell; watched as they put him in the back of a morgue wagon. She tried to pretend he had too much to drink and just needed a ride home. Next to children who might be sleeping, having stayed too late at the party. "No," she wailed. "No, no, no!"

With Toivo on her hip and Lila in tow, she raced home, as if chased by demons, but inside found no refuge. The house was cold; she threw some logs into the woodstove. Toivo had fallen asleep, and she laid him in his bed, lingering to stare. Lila stayed by her side as Nelma restlessly paced the house. It was late before she realized they hadn't had any dinner, and opened the icebox to find Edward's fish, cleaned and filleted, stacked neatly in a pile. This is what broke her. Everything shattered. Everything emptied out. She sent Lila up to check on her brother, and told her to stay there until she was called back down. When Nelma was certain her daughter was out of sight, she fell to the floor and sobbed without restraint, without inhibition, and without comprehension.

DECEMBER 24, 1913

NELMA WASN'T SURE HOW LONG she'd been crying when Frank came home. She stood up, a bit unsteady, without any effort to compose herself. "Frank, what happened? Tell me what happened; I don't understand."

Frank looked pale, uncertain and angry. He left his walking cane by the door and with a lopsided gate walked over, took her in his arms and held her closer than he'd ever done before. She could smell his aftershave; feel the rough stubble on his cheek against hers, his warm breath tickling her neck. For a moment she forgot everything, her children upstairs, her dead husband, the countless bodies, and she felt safe. She hugged him and found her strength again. Slowly, she let him go.

"It was those copper boss thugs, somehow behind it all," Frank said. "Some people are saying they saw a man, a tall man wearing a Citizens' Alliance button yell 'fire' three times and then disappear. It's cold-blooded murder, is what it is."

"It's awful. I close my eyes and I see them all piled up like that. Why couldn't they get out? Those bastards must have held the door shut. They were trying to push me away, didn't want me to see what they'd done."

"Lila and Toivo?" Frank asked. She could see a fear in his eyes.

"They're upstairs. But Edward..."

"I know."

"I need to feed the children. I was about to cook something. Are you hungry?"

"No. I can't think of food."

"Well, the children need to eat."

Nelma took the fish from the icebox, and the knife from the drawer. She turned the knife in her hand, examined it as it reflected the light, and wiped away a water spot from the blade. She welcomed the clarity of the job at hand, a simple task where she could lose herself. The fish needed to be cubed. Small and consistent cubes of fish to be thrown in with the potatoes that had been soaking much of the day. A little cardamom would have been nice. She started to think about what to plant in next summer's garden, but stopped herself. The future had been chopped off and discarded today. Nothing could be imagined after today. It would all be different now.

Frank went upstairs to fetch the children. Toivo was awake and Lila had been playing with him. No one was hungry, though. They all picked at their food, as if it were a foreign thing to eat; as if they had forgotten why and how and what to eat, and no one was around to teach them. When they finished with their dinner, the children were put to bed.

Frank went to his room; Nelma sat on the couch downstairs. She took some children's clothing she had been mending and spread it out on her lap. She knew she should do something, try to keep her mind occupied, but she found it difficult to start. Edward's image kept invading her thoughts. She looked him over in her mind, remembering how frustrated he made her feel sometimes. There was such a distance between the Edward she had married and the one who had died. The former was who she missed most, not the latter, she realized.

She studied the plaid pattern in the boy pants, tugged on the waist. It would still be big for Toivo, but suspenders would keep it up. She just had to sew on the missing buttons. She kept a jar of spare buttons in the pantry. Instead of getting up to fetch them, she tried to remember which ones would work the best. There was a bright blue one that Toivo would probably really like, though there weren't any others to match.

Frank's footfalls paced overhead.

She thought maybe she might try to sew four buttons of different color, for a bit of variety. She thought there was an interesting striped one in the jar as well.

Frank was coming down the stairs now.

What else was there? She knew she had at least a dozen buttons in that jar, but couldn't remember what they looked like.

Frank stood at the doorway of the sitting room. Nelma could see him out of the corner of her eye, but she ignored him. There was a strange space between them, an opening that had not been there before. A naked presence, a broken chain. She should probably go and get that damn jar, but then she would have to face Frank, so she just fidgeted with the fabric and waited.

Frank sat down next to her, and gently brushed his hand across her cheek, through her hair. She turned and looked at him; she had never looked so closely before. She thought of the miles he had traveled, the sights he had seen, the places he had known. She thought of the train ticket he had purchased for tomorrow, the window he would look through, and his last view of the city.

Then they were kissing, embracing, exploring each other with hands and lips. He took her upstairs and removed her blouse slowly, cautiously undoing the buttons and tugging at the sleeves. Layers were removed with the attention usually given to an object of exceptional fragility and worth. Nelma had never been undressed like this before, and wanted to savor every moment. She could relive this day every day for the rest of her life and never tire of its glacier pace.

They were both undressed now, in the guest room, his room, and lying on his bed. For months now, she had dreamed of this, and now here he was, inside her and outside her. When they were done, she held onto him and didn't let go until after she fell asleep. In her dreams there was no Edward, no death, no marriage, no shame. In her dreams there was only Frank and herself, but when she woke the next morning, she was alone.

DECEMBER 25, 1913

RUSSELL SAT ON ONE OF THE BARSTOOLS at Vairo's, debating between a shot of whiskey and a bottle of beer for breakfast. He was on the customer side of the bar, but didn't care. He was alone. The saloon was closed, but he had known where a key was hidden by the back door. He hummed a Christmas tune he remembered from his childhood and tried hard not to think about the night before. His memory was fairly patchy, owing to the alcohol, so it wasn't that difficult to forget. He decided on the whiskey, got up and poured two fingers into a bar glass. He drank it down fast and poured himself another. Good stuff, he chuckled to himself. Too bad no one else was around to enjoy it.

After two slugs of whiskey, Russell forgot his resolution not to think about last night. Bunch of damn fools, they were. Jamming themselves so tight in the stairwell that they couldn't get out. Who'd have thought they'd do that? He had been tending bar, and the union families were filing up the stairs and stomping around his ceiling. Not too many people in the saloon then, but still, they didn't need to listen to that ruckus. Don't know why everyone was feeling so sorry for them. No Christmas presents for their children? It wasn't as if there was anyone but themselves to blame.

Yesterday afternoon there had been only himself and a couple customers, both of them crazier than loons. A blind old miner and a divorced lumberjack. He started drinking along with them. Hell, it was Christmas eve, and he still hadn't heard a word from his fiancée since she had postponed the wedding. He suspected she had no intention of ever writing back.

Both his customers were pretty good at holding their liquor, better than he was. They were three men, united in their loneliness on Christmas eve.

There was a moment, somewhere in the late afternoon when they were all laughing harder than jackals. Someone had said the funniest damn thing, and Russell could scarcely contain himself. Then things got a bit silly. The blind man took on Russell and the lumberjack at a game of darts, and was dangerously close to winning the match. The lumberjack started throwing darts at the ceiling, yelling at the strikers to quiet down upstairs.

Russell wished he could remember what happened next, but it was so obscured by the alcohol, that he wasn't sure if he'd ever remember it straight. Had he talked to those fellows about running upstairs and yelling fire, or had he merely thought about it? Was that idea planted in his head before or after the stampede of children down the stairs? Was that something he might have actually done? No. Not possible. Not something to consider. They were just a bunch of damn fools, they were. Damn fools that dug their own graves.

Firemen had arrived within minutes of the stampede, having heard claims of a fire at Italian Hall. Deputies and men walking down the street had come to help. By the time Russell realized what was happening, men, women and children were already piled several feet deep. Some of the firemen had climbed up the back fire escape and tried to keep people inside. But the erstwhile rescuers were pushed past, as the panicked strikers flung themselves on top of the heap, trying to crawl their way out. Hours later, when all seventy-three bodies had been moved to the town hall, when all the injured had been taken to the hospital, all that remained was the desperate scratches the dying children had left on the stairwell walls.

Russell put the whiskey bottle away and left his washed glass drying behind the bar. He had just wanted to see this place one more time before he left. He wasn't sure when the idea had arrived, but now it seemed as if it had been in his thinking for months. Time to pack up and leave; head back to Chicago and get a job in a factory. Maybe give the west coast another try.

He buttoned his coat, turned off the lights, and walked out into the cold. A Christmas service was just letting its parishioners onto the street, and there was a union man waiting on the corner, shouting at any who would listen.

"We all know who's to blame," he said. "It's each and everyone of you with a Citizens' Alliance button on your lapel. Everyone of you that spoke of undesirable citizens is now trying to help bury our dead. We'll take care of our own, thank you. You take care of yours."

"What kind of nonsense you throwing at these people?" Russell said. "It's Christmas. Let them be."

"And where might your conscious be on this calamity?" The man said. "If we didn't have your sympathy before this tragedy, we sure as hell don't want it now."

"I never said nothin' about sympathy," Russell muttered, as he lumbered past the union man, past the church, and away.

A team of horses approached from the edge of town, kicking up the snow and drowning out all other noise with the clatter of their hooves. Russell stopped, curious, to wait them out. The driver acknowledged him with a subtle nod. The open carriage behind him had several child-sized caskets, heading for the morgue. Russell watched them go, down the street and around the corner. He stood still, listening, even after they could no longer be heard.

He was surprised at a wave of melancholy that caught him off guard. He forgot where he was going, for a moment, before mocking himself at letting a bunch of empty caskets wear him down like a woman. Time to move on.

There were some ladies in front of the general store collecting money for the stricken families. They huddled around a red Salvation Army bucket, talking in hushed tones. Russell crossed to the other side of the street.

The boarding house was still empty when he got back home. Everyone was still at church. Upstairs, he stuffed his knapsack with clothes and the few things he had accumulated during his stay. He wore his new boots and threw his old shoes in with the clothes. He saved some of the trinkets off the nightstand, an odd-shaped native copper rock, a silver dollar he had won from the sailor, Jack, in a bet, and a derby hat he had worn over the summer. He left behind most of his mining equipment, the lunch pail and sunshine lamp, but kept the brass pocket container that held carbide crystals for the lamp. It might be useful for something, he figured, and threw it in the knapsack.

He was preparing a note in the kitchen when Mrs. Huhta returned. She looked at the rent money on the counter, the pen in his hand, and nodded her head.

"It looks like you'll be leaving," she said. "It's a shame to see you go. You've been a good tenant."

"Sorry about this, Ma'am," Russell said. "Hope this doesn't leave you short."

"Can I make you something to take with you? You wouldn't be finding anyplace serving food on Christmas day."

"Thank you, I'd like that." Russell set his knapsack by the door, sat down at the table. "Did they have a nice service today?"

"It was a hard one to get through, everyone's in mourning. This is a loss for the whole community. It's too bad the union don't see it that way."

"Why? What are they saying?"

"They're telling those poor people to turn their back on the charity of their neighbors. We've raised nearly two thousand dollars, can you imagine? Two thousand dollars, with even more promised. We're getting donations from people all over the state, from the governor and the mining companies."

"I can't even begin to understand them, ma'am."

"All this for the bereaved families, and the union's saying no thanks. They can't take care of their own, anyone can see that. It's criminal for them to be saying such things."

Mrs. Huhta wrapped up the sandwich she had made and handed it to Russell. "You're always welcome here, if you ever come back. I just wish it was those union people was leaving instead."

Russell opted to walk down the hill to the train station, there was plenty of time and no need for the streetcar. The weather was calm; no winds were pushing or resisting his travel. He thought again about what he might have done last night, or not done, but it was all muddled up. He couldn't remember a thing. Just the before and the after. Nothing in between.

He decided he was a moral man, a good man, and no amount of alcohol could change that fact. He had nothing to be ashamed of, his conscience was clear. He thought about what Mrs. Huhta had said, about all that money coldly turned away. He wondered if these strikers wouldn't be so foolish if it weren't for those out of town union organizers. They were the ones that should bear the blame for all that had happened.

At the train station, he purchased his ticket for Chicago. He had several hours before the scheduled departure, so he left his knapsack behind and set out looking for a newspaper. He found a boy outside Weinstein's department store, with one last paper in his satchel. Russell gave the kid a dime and told him to keep the change. Folded the paper under his arm and walked back to the station.

There was another man waiting when he returned. A dark-haired man with a walking stick. He looked familiar, though Russell couldn't remember where he had seen him. Russell sat on the opposite side of the bench and began to read. Tragedy was all over the front page. Who had died. How they had died. Relief Committees. Money raised for the bereaved. Russell didn't want to read any more and wanted to put it all behind him. But there was one more headline, in an ugly bold type, which drew his eye. "Union Uses Children's Deaths To Benefit Strike," it read, just like Mrs. Huhta had said. Then he realized where he had seen the man, he was a union man, sent in from out west to stir things up. A stick in the hornet's nest.

Russell wanted to hurt this man, wanted him to feel the pain of the survivors, the shame for accusing good people of peddling in blood money. He wanted to give this man a farewell he would never forget. The paper was still in his lap, but he no longer saw the words. He was planning and thinking of who might be able to help. He asked if he could use the stationmaster's phone, claimed it was urgent.

RUSSELL WAS WAITING outside the station house when they arrived. Oscar, his old partner from the Number Seven shaft, came along with the boxer from Detroit and the quiet kid from Escanaba. He knew that they could be counted on, people he could trust. It takes something like this to help you figure out what was right in the world, and what should no longer be tolerated.

"Hey, mister," Russell called to the man inside. "I'd like to show you something."

The man looked up at Russell. "I'm not looking for any trouble, friend. I'm sure you don't want any either," he said.

"Mister, I don't think you understand." Russell nodded to his friends and they walked into the station. Oscar took his arms and pushed him outside, where the boxer bloodied his nose. Russell took his walking stick and tried to break it, but the wood was too hard, so he hit him sideways in the stomach instead. The man doubled over in pain, slipped and fell on the packed snow. Russell threw the man's walking stick over the tracks.

"This is how we say goodbye around here," the kid from Escanaba said. "Don't even think about coming back to find out how we say hello."

Russell noticed they had drawn a small crowd, though no one made any move to intervene. Some even shouted words of encouragement.

"I'll be your personal escort, sir," Russell said. "I'll be on that train keeping an eye on you. See these people here?" Russell motioned to the people around him, "They're just as happy as we are to see you go." He gave the man a hard kick in the behind as he was trying to get up, sending him sprawling on the ground again.

The train whistle sounded down the tracks, not too far. Russell let the man collect his carpetbag. He walked with a pronounced limp and held his stomach. He wiped some of the blood from his face, but didn't entirely clean it off.

"What the hell is the matter with you?" the man demanded, pulling himself onto the train platform. "Have you no sense of who I am? Have you no idea what the American Labor Movement stands for?"

"Good bye and good riddance," Russell said to the man, and then sensing an eager audience, he turned to the crowd. "On my word, I'll make sure he never comes back."

The onlookers started to applaud, and for a moment, Russell once again felt a part of this place, a sense of attachment, a feeling of home. He questioned why he was leaving and wondered if he would regret it. Was there an honorable way to change his mind and stay after such a grand exit?

"You're a good man," Oscar said, slapping his shoulder. We'll miss ya 'round here."

"Send along a letter," the boxer said. "Let us know where you end up. You never know, we might be following your lead."

Russell shook his friends' hands and knew that despite his reluctance, it was time for him to go. There was something gnawing at him, a need to move on, that was stronger than any other feelings he had. He took his seat by the window, two rows behind the union man, and saw the people outside had already turned their backs and started to disperse.

The train whistle sounded again and the engine slowly started to plow through the snowy tracks. Screeching as if its wheels had frozen in the few minutes it had been stopped. The rocking train lulled him into a half-sleep, aided by the fading alcohol in his system. He closed his eyes and leaned against the window.

He remembered music, Christmas music, and it made him smile. There were children, hundreds of children lined up to see Santa Claus, queued in a long room filled with Christmas trees. A child looked overcome from the excitement, and her mother was calling for water, water please, water. Most of the families were Finns, Russell noticed. He tried to remember the few Finnish words he had learned from Mrs. Huhta. "Palo," he called out, slurring his words, pointing at the woman, "Palo." Several people looked at him with alarm. Was his pronunciation wrong? They started to scream, and point at him. Russell was afraid, he had just wanted to take a look, a quick look at his noisy upstairs neighbors. He ran down, went back to the bar. Poured himself another drink and tried to remember. Palo, palo, palo. *It meant fire, not water. He didn't have a lick of sense when it came to languages.*

Russell woke with a start. It was late, dark outside. He thought of the summer rains, falling on his face, soaking his hair and dripping down his neck. His face was wet, his collar, his eyes. He would remain awake the rest of the night, unable to sleep.

DECEMBER 25, 1913

HANNAH WALKED PAST HOUSES SHE had been by dozens of times, and noticed details she had never seen before. She had thought they were all the same, having been constructed at the same time by the same builders for the miners. Each was a narrow two-story clapboard house, with one chimney in the back. But there were differences, if you looked closely. Some had trees in the front yard; others had small sheds in the back. The houses on the street corners were more worn and faded. The paths through the snow around some houses revealed evidence of children. The curtains inside were different on each and every one. Some were faded grey, while others had more festive colors. Nelma's house was the third on the left, past the corner, but Hannah was searching for as many distractions as possible to delay her arrival.

She wasn't reluctant, exactly. She had wanted to come last night, as soon as she heard of the tragedy, but Mother had counseled waiting until this morning. Hannah had scanned through the names in the newspaper, trying to keep her mind focused on Nelma's family name, and trying not to see anything else, not the ages of the children, nor the amount of newsprint dedicated to listing each and every one who had perished. When she found Nelma's husband, she stifled a cry, but continued to search, to check for their children, who were safely absent from the list.

She filled a picnic basket with as much food she thought she could carry: bread, canned meats, and a dozen potato latkes leftover from Hanukkah. Nelma had always liked the latkes whenever she came to visit. She had tried to learn how to make them, but claimed they never came out the same back at home. The basket weighed down on her arm and Hannah rested it against a fence post. She wondered again what she could say. Every practiced set of words she tried out sounded shallow or empty. Mother thought it best to stick to familiar topics, such as the children, and let Nelma talk about what had happened when she was ready. Mother had said this was a horrible tragedy. It was time to bring the community back together to heal after so many months of unrest.

Hannah stepped lightly across the crusty snow, conscious of the sound of her footfalls in the unnatural quiet of the day. She felt the eyes of the neighbors on her back as she walked the path to Nelma's house. She knocked on the door, but there was no answer. Hannah paused, uncertain if it would be ruder to continue knocking or just open the door.

She decided to announce herself through the closed door. When that didn't elicit any response, she had visions of her friend collapsed in despair, unable to answer, unable to tend to her children. Hannah now felt silly carrying this basket full of food, as if that could offer her friend any solace. She pushed open the door.

Nelma was waiting on the other side, with a shotgun braced against her shoulder, and the barrel aimed straight at Hannah's heart. "I saw you coming down the street, you didn't have to yell."

"Nelma?" Hannah said, but was unable to continue. An avalanche of cold fear had fallen on her. She could feel it crawl down her neck, her spine, and her arms until her fingers were numb. There must be a mistake, a misunderstanding. They would talk about it, like they had always been able, and the gun would be lowered. They would laugh about it. Hannah forced a smile and spoke her friend's name again.

"You're not welcome here," Nelma said. "Not you, not your charities and not your murderous Citizens' Alliance."

"I brought some food," Hannah said, staring into the dark abyss of the barrel. "I thought..."

"You thought what? That we could still be friends?"

"Nelma, I'm so sorry..."

"After you've gone and murdered our children? My husband?"

"No, we didn't, we wouldn't…"

"Did you think we would give up the strike? Go back to spending our paychecks in your store? Take your blood money to bury our dead?"

"I can't imagine how you must feel." Hannah's eyes were growing hot and wet. "You're my friend."

"You're no friend of mine," Nelma said. "Go. Tell your people I've got a house full of guns and none of you are welcome in my home. Get out of here."

Hannah felt the chill again, creeping into her heart, freezing her lungs, making it difficult to breathe. She stepped away from the door, afraid to turn her back, unable to avert her eyes. When she got to the end of the footpath, she lowered the basket to the ground. It was so heavy. Maybe Nelma would get it later. She left it at the edge of the yard and began to run.

There was an explosion. The sound thundered through her body and shook her bones. The basket was shattered, the food was flying and there was an acrid smell in the air. Nelma still stood in the doorway. She looked surprised, maybe sorry, and lowered the barrel of her gun to the ground. Hannah's chill was gone. It was replaced by the spray of hot steam bouncing off sauna rocks, melting her legs until she felt there was nothing left. Hannah looked down and saw red. It seemed she was entering a dark tunnel, and just before the light completely faded away, she realized that she was bleeding.

ONCE, WHEN THEY were in grade school, Hannah had a falling out with Nelma. Some of the other girls were teasing a large Bavarian boy and calling him names. Nelma had felt sorry for the boy and tried to intervene. The other girls turned on her, wondering if perhaps she had a crush on the boy, and made great fun of a fish-head dating a beer-belly and whatever would the children look like, and so forth.

Hannah had been one of those girls, not intending to hurt Nelma's feelings, but enjoying her inclusion with those who would more often than not treat her as someone not quite up to some unspecified girlish code. She was feeling popular and perhaps a bit superior, until Nelma ran away in tears. It took many weeks before they would bring their friendship back to where it had been. Many more before their friendship became an oasis of security, a partnership where they could discuss anything, anything at all, and trust that the other would be supportive. It was after this that she had given Nelma that necklace, with the silver pendant inscribed with *chai*, the Hebrew word for life.

It was late in the afternoon. Still Christmas Day, but it seemed as if weeks has passed by. Hannah lay prone in a hospital bed, drowsy with morphine, staring out the window. She thought about the arc of their friendship, trying to find the exact moment it began to come apart. At the start of the strike, it seemed that Nelma was swept up in a popular uprising, a party that Hannah had no prospect for inclusion. But they were still friends, they picnicked and chatted and found comfort in each other's company. At least that was what Hannah had thought at the time. Now she wondered if even then Nelma had turned on her, secretly deriding her place in society, defaming her honor at union meetings. The bonds of friendship broken by the ideals of strangers, by strong words and empty promises.

A squeaky door announced Mother's arrival. Hannah turned over in bed to see Mother's concerned face, and in her hands, the requested contraband, a thermos of coffee from home. Hannah propped the pillow against the wall and pushed herself up to sit.

"Mmm, that smells good," Hannah said. "Do you have something to pour it in?"

"The thermos comes with its own metal cup," Mother said. "Clever, eh?"

"Very. How's Ida doing? She looked pretty upset when she was here earlier."

"It's Sam you should be worried about. He's ready to burn down Nelma's house," Mother said. "And with her in it, no less."

Hannah tried and failed to force a smile. "We shouldn't waste any more time on that family, for good or for ill," she said.

"The sheriff's already been to see her. He's delaying the formal charges until after the funerals." She poured a cup of coffee and placed it on the small table next to Hannah's bed.

"What business had she with that gun at all? Putting it in my face, shooting up my gift basket. She could have killed me! I tried to understand. But there's no point in it any longer. We're different, them and us. There is no common ground."

"Don't get yourself agitated, dear. It's not healthy. You need to rest."

Hannah rubbed her hand along bandaged legs, which seemed to belong to someone else. Someone else whose thighs had been perforated with birdshot, and whose anklebone had been chipped apart like a piece of granite. *It should heal without incident,* the doctor had said. *Maybe slow down your foxtrot,* he added with a chuckle. At the time she had been too self-absorbed to recognize his joke.

"Did the doctor say anything to you?" Hannah asked. "About my legs? Will they look ugly? Will they really heal?"

"These are good doctors. I'm sure you'll be fine." Mother handed her the thermos cup. "You should drink this before it gets too cool."

The coffee smelled of home and familiar times. She wrapped her hands around the cup and took a sip. It was hot, but not burning. She turned back to the window, where she could see the portage and the hills beyond. There were children skating on the frozen waterway, perhaps a hockey game the way they moved back and forth on the ice.

Hannah wondered if she would be able to skate after she healed, and what else would be forever altered. That was the nature of change, she realized. It was a winding path that never looped back, never crossed the same point in time. The strike would eventually end, but the town would never be what it was. Injured memories would haunt relations between everyone. When someone came to the store to shop, they would always be on one side of the divide or the other. Against the strikers or with them. The victims of Italian Hall would cast a shadowy presence on their surviving families for the rest of their days. They would always be known for what they had lost.

"Why does she hate us?" Hannah asked. "I went there in sympathy and all she had was anger."

"Only she can answer that," Mother said. "Everyone reacts to sorrow in their own way. Remember when your grandfather died, grandmother was bitter with resentment. She hadn't wanted to be alone. She had wanted to be first."

"You never told me that. What a strange reaction."

Mother stood up and squeezed Hannah's arm. "I need to go home and start dinner. Is there anything else you'd like? Some books perhaps?"

"Maybe some of Ida's magazines?"

Mother promised to come back with something to read, perhaps send Ida over tonight. Hannah listened to her footsteps echo down the hall, until they became too faint to hear. The hospital ward was quiet as a tomb; her room was far away from the other patients, from those who had survived Italian Hall last night.

Hannah thought about Aaron and wondered what he might be doing now. He had told her how New Yorkers spare no extravagance, with rows of Christmas trees lining both sides of Broadway and all lit up with electric lights. It must be bright as daylight. She imagined herself walking hand in hand with Aaron down the boulevard, laughing at the novelty, and discussing where to eat. Just as easily, though, she remembered him prying for details on the Citizens' Alliance, subtly criticizing her participation, behaving as if only he held the moral high ground. It was infuriating.

Was there anyone who didn't have a hidden agenda, or an allegiance that would trump the one between friends? When Hannah was a child, Mother would tell stories filled with dybbuks and golems and other magical creatures. She remembered the story about the Golem of Silver Mountain, where a peddler was betrayed by his partner. Was Mother trying to teach her of the fickle nature of friends? Hannah drifted to sleep feeling bitter and alone.

When she awoke in the night, her legs were throbbing and on fire. She rang the bell by her bed and waited. All was quiet. She heard the wind howling outside the windows. Somewhere down the hall there was a leaky drip, drip, drip of water. No one was here. The nurse had abandoned her as easily as her friends. She wondered if she could walk and search for medicine herself, but as she swung her legs towards the side of the bed, a searing pain shot through her senses. She rang the bell again, and this time heard footsteps approach.

This nurse was different than the one who had previously given Hannah the injection, when she had first been admitted. Her hair was not pulled back as severely, and her expression was not as starched as the little white nurse's cap on her head. This one looked kinder.

"I expected you'd be calling for me," the nurse said. "You're overdue for your medicine, but I didn't want to wake you."

Hannah wished she hadn't fallen asleep. "My legs, they hurt," she said.

The nurse opened up a leather medicine case, its wide selection of bottles looking like exotic jars of spices. She pressed a syringe into the top of one of the small bottles, filled it and laid it on the tray next to the bed. "This should get you through the night," the nurse said, as she bound Hannah's arm above the elbow. Hannah looked away as the needle pricked her skin. It was a wondrous thing, how it took away the pain so quickly. Relaxing like a glass of wine, yet so much more powerful. Hannah leaned into the bed and stared into the black night. When she looked back, the nurse was gone and she was alone again.

Hannah wished the nurse had left behind the medicine case. It reminded her of a magazine Ida had given her once, with pictures of a foreign land, an open market filled with strange foods and animals. Hannah had dreamed of traveling to this place and others, sending home letters from distant countries, which would be received with great fanfare. She knew it was a fantasy, a pleasant daydream, but it bothered her that even a fanciful future had been taken away by this gunshot. Her capacity to imagine was diminished and everything was colored in black and gray. Even if she did move downstate to the university, it would surely not live up to her expectations. Hannah looked into the future and saw only disappointment.

Someone was coming. Hannah listened and tried to predict who it might be. The footsteps lacked the authoritative and fast pacing of the nurse, though neither did they match Mother's slow but equally steady rhythm. These belonged to a hesitant visitor, and Hannah imagined it must be Ida, bringing her something to read. The footsteps stopped and started. They seemed to fade away as if turning down a distant hall, but then grew loud again. The door had been left open and Hannah looked out expectantly.

It was Nelma. Her eyes were glassy and her face was lined with tears. Around her neck was the necklace Hannah had given her years ago. She stood there wordlessly and still as a statue for so long that Hannah felt certain it must be delirium. The drugs were causing waking dreams, just like the nurse said they might. Hannah leaned back into her pillow and closed her eyes. She tried to imagine how things were last summer, before the strike, before everything became strange and violent. It was a futile effort. Ever since the strike had begun, Hannah wanted nothing more than a return to the past. Acquiescence by the strikers. An acceptance that they couldn't possibly win. A selfish desire to have them brush aside their complaints so that she could get on with her life. Go downstate to the university. Define herself away from everyone she had ever known. Leave behind the problems of her closest friend.

Hannah opened her eyes and saw it was no illusion. Nelma was still there. She wondered what she wanted to do. There were two choices, and both carried a high risk of regret. She could send her away, in anger, in fear, in retribution. Back to her diminished union that had nothing left to declare other than complete failure. Sentence her to suffer in the hate she had inflicted so painfully on Hannah. No one would challenge such an action, not even Nelma. Hannah questioned whether she even knew this person in front of her anymore. What kind of desperation brought her to act as she had, and yet, wasn't there a certain courage to come here after what she had done; some regard of their friendship? Perhaps some assessment of life, as inscribed on the pendant she wore around her neck. Hannah tried to imagine how she would remember this day, years later, and invited Nelma in.

Made in the USA
Columbia, SC
15 June 2021